I0784675

William Le Queux

An Eye for an Eye

OK Publishing 2021

William Le Queux

An Eye for an Eye

Murder Mystery

Published by

MUSAICUM

Books

- Advanced Digital Solutions & High-Quality book Formatting -

musaicumbooks@okpublishing.info

2021 OK Publishing

ISBN 978-80-272-7539-7

Contents

Chapter One
The Mystery Man

"Hush! Think, if you were overheard!"

"Well, my dear fellow, I only assert what's true," I said.

"I really can't believe it," observed my companion, shaking his head doubtfully.

"But I'm absolutely satisfied," I answered. "The two affairs, mysterious as they are, are more closely connected than we imagine. I thought I had convinced you by my arguments. A revelation will be made some day, and it will be a startling one — depend upon it."

"You'll never convince me without absolute proof — never. The idea is far too hazy to be possible. Only a madman could dream such a thing."

"Then I suppose I'm a madman?" I laughed.

"No, old chap. I don't mean any insult, of course," my friend the journalist, a youngish, dark-haired man, hastened to assure me. "But the whole thing is really too extraordinary to believe."

We were seated together one June morning some years ago, in a train on the Underground Railway, and had been discussing a very remarkable occurrence which had been discovered a few days before — a discovery that was a secret between us. Scarcely, however, had he uttered his final denunciation of my theory when the train ran into the sulphurous ever-murky station of Blackfriars, for the electrification of the line was not then completed: and promising to continue our argument later, he bade me good-bye, sprang out, and hastened away in the crowd of silk-hatted City men on their way to their offices.

He was rather tall, aged about thirty, with a well-cut, clever face, a complexion unusually dark, a well-trimmed black moustache, and a smart gait which gave him something of a military bearing. Yet his cravat was habitually tied with carelessness, and he usually wore a light overcoat except through the month of August. His name was Richard Cleugh, one of the sharpest men in Fleet Street, being special reporter of London's most up-to-date evening paper, the *Comet*.

When alone, I sat back in the ill-lit railway carriage and, during my short journey to Cannon Street, reflected deeply.

The affair was, as he had said, absolutely bewildering.

Indeed, this chain of curious facts, this romance of love and devotion, of guile, intrigue, and of the cardinal sins which it is my intention to here record, proved one of the strangest that has ever occurred in our giant London. It was an absolute mystery. Readers of newspapers know well the many strange stories told in courts of justice, or unearthed by the untiring "liner" and the reporter who is a specialist in the discovery of crime. Yet when we walk the streets of our Metropolis, where the fevered crowd jostles in the mad race of life, there is more romance around us, and of a character far more extraordinary than any that has ever appeared in the public prints.

The secrets of London's ever-throbbing heart, and her hidden and inexplicable mysteries which never get into the papers, are legion.

This is one of them.

In order to understand the facts aright, it is necessary to here explain that I, Frank Urwin, am myself a member of that ubiquitous and much maligned profession, journalism, being engaged at the time of the opening of this narrative as special reporter of a highly respectable London daily newspaper — a journal which was so superior that it never allowed itself to make any sensational statement. Its conductors as studiously avoided sensationalism as they did libel, and although we were very often in possession of "startling facts," and "sensational statements" which would have sold the paper, and caused it to be quoted next morning up and down the country, yet we of the staff, forbidden to write anything so undignified, kept our information to ourselves, or, as was once rumoured, the office boy, a thrifty youth, went forth and calmly sold it to one of our more enterprising rivals. Hence, owing to the heaviness of its articles, which usually contained "chunks" of foreign quotations, and the paucity of its news, the paper was dubbed by its staff "the Magazine."

Before being appointed to this pseudo-newspaper, where, by the way, work was light and remuneration good, I had been for several years engaged upon one of those enterprising evening journals who print their "specials" on tinted paper, and by reason of my constant investigations I had become well-known to the police, and perhaps something of a specialist in the revealing of hidden facts and the unravelling of mysteries.

Dick Cleugh was my most intimate friend, for we shared chambers in Gray's Inn, a rather dingy and typical bachelor's abode, be it said; but it had the advantage of being in close proximity to Fleet Street, and situated as we were, flying all over London day after day, we could not afford to live out in the peculiarly journalistic suburb of Brixton. Our little flat contained a very sad and shabby sitting-room — in which stood a couple of writing-tables whereat we often worked, joining in, and re-echoing, each other's imprecations — a couple of bedrooms and a small box-room which, containing a gas-stove over which the diurnal chops were fried, was termed by the Inn authorities a kitchen. We, however, irreverently termed it "the sink." Old Mrs Joad, a worthy old soul who lived across in Fetter Lane, "did for" us, and was known as "the Hag," on account of her *passé* and extremely *bizarre* appearance. Her duties were not very onerous, consisting of preparing our morning tea, "doing up" the rooms, cooking the eternal chops or the everlasting steaks at six, when, our respective "special editions" having gone to press, we both returned hungry to our dens, and lastly in drinking our whisky. She preferred gin, but took whisky in order to put us to no inconvenience.

Cleugh was one of the queer figures in journalistic London. Essentially of the Bohemian type, easy-going and possessed of a quaint, dry humour, many were the stories told in Fleet Street of his utter disregard for the *convenances*. Shrewd, witty, clever, well-educated, he was no respecter of persons. If he went forth to make an inquiry for his journal, he hesitated at nothing. With the constant companionship of an extremely foul briar pipe, it was his habit to "interview" people and obtain "latest details" of the day's sensation without removing it from his lips, and it was well-known down at the Press Club, that dingy but interesting institution in Wine Office Court, that on one field-day at Aldershot he had actually chatted with the Commander-in-Chief, pipe in mouth, and afterwards put the conversation "on the wire" in the form of an interview. When having nothing to do he would clean that pipe for recreation, and such operation usually caused a rapid exit from the vicinity. Known to all in Fleet Street as "the Mystery Man," he was clever-looking and dignified, and could snuff out an uncommunicative secretary, or a pompous policeman, with his marvellous control of expressions, sarcastic without being abusive. He was undoubtedly "a smart man" — and to be smart in journalism nowadays requires a good deal more than ordinary intelligence. An ex-Jesus man, he had been a True Blue, been ploughed for the Army, studied medicine, and travelled pretty widely, until having been a brilliant failure he had drifted into journalism, like so many other men have drifted, commencing as an outside contributor, or "liner," and eventually, by dint of the swiftness and marvellous tact and ability with which he got at the bottom of the inquiries he made, he joined the regular staff of a popular evening sheet — which, by reason of having once tried the experiment of printing on scented paper, was known in press circles as "The Stinker" — and subsequently became chief of the reporting staff of the *Comet* — as smart a staff as could be found in London.

In common with many other men in Fleet Street, that never-sleeping world of tape and flimsy, Dick had one failing — he had a penchant for a particular brand of whisky sold at the *Cheese*, the ancient house of steak-pudding fame, but he was always moderate, for his great pride was that his sub-editors could place the greatest reliance in him, as indeed they could. Dick Cleugh was certainly smart, even though his hair was often unkempt and a bundle of copy-paper usually poked out of the side-pocket of his well-worn overcoat. Over and over again had he proved himself a very brilliant pressman and had startled London by the "latest details" he had elicited where the police had failed.

I had arrived at our chambers about six, after a heavy day. I had visited Barking and Wandsworth, and had made an inquiry at Hammersmith, three districts far afield from one another, therefore I felt fagged and hungry. The Hag was engaged in fizzling the usual daily steak in the gas fumes, filling the place with a decidedly appetising odour; nevertheless, between Dick and I there was an arrangement that neither should eat without the other, unless a telegram arrived announcing a protracted absence. Therefore I lit a cigarette, cast myself into the trifle rickety but very comfortable armchair, and waited by the open window. I was just a trifle melancholy that evening, for there had come back to me recollections of a love-bond long since severed, of a face which was once very dear to me. But I was a lonely bachelor now. All was of the past. Soon, however, as I sat thinking, I saw Cleugh hurrying across the square, his silk hat, a trifle rusty, tilted at the back of his head, and a few moments later he burst merrily into the room, saying —

"Sorry to keep you so long, old chap, but we brought out an extra to-night. There's a bit of a row down in Parliament." Then, calling to Mrs Joad, who was pottering in the "sink" beyond, he said, "Come along, mother. Look sharp with the horseflesh!"

We sat down and commenced our meal, while he, overflowing with spirits, told me how he had been out on an inquiry near to the *Welsh Harp*, spending a very pleasant afternoon there, and how he meant to "write it up" for the "mornings." The old instinct of the "liner" was still upon him, and on his littered table he always kept his agate stylus and oiled tissue, known as "flimsy," his "blacks" and his square of tin whereon to write. The sub-editors of the morning papers, the judges of next day's intelligence, could always rely on Dick Cleugh's "stuff," therefore they used it, and he profited at the rate of a penny farthing per line. He was, in brief, purveyor of sensations to the newspaper-reading public.

"I'm going to take Lil out to-night," my companion said between mouthfuls of steak, for he was ravenously hungry. "Smart girl, Lil."

"Yes," I answered. "She's really awfully nice. By Jove! old chap, I envy you."

The Mystery Man smiled contentedly with a piece of meat poised gracefully on his fork, then he began humming the latest love-song which the barrel-organs had made popular, beating time with his fork, at the same time placing his hand upon his heart in true operatic style.

This proceeding was, however, interrupted by the entrance of the Hag bearing a telegram for me. On opening it I found it contained only the one word "Come," signed by the initial "P."

I tossed it across to my companion without comment, and as I did so was surprised to notice a strange, puzzled look upon his dark face.

He glanced at it, then handing it back to me, exclaimed — "Wonder what's up at Kensington?"

"Something unusual, or Patterson wouldn't have wired," I said.

"You'll go, of course?"

"Yes. I'll just see what it looks like, and if there's anything in it I'll let you know."

"Well, old dawdler," he laughed, "if it's a good thing, leave a bit of the latest intelligence for me to pick up for my early edition to-morrow. To-night I can't disappoint Lily, you know. She's a good girl, and never worries."

"I'll tell you all about it when I come back; then you can write up something in readiness for to-morrow. If it's a mystery my people won't touch it, you know."

"Of course," he said. "Your staff is only paid to look pleasant."

The mysterious telegram had come from the police headquarters at Kensington, an early intimation that something unusual had occurred. In years of reporting in London I had become friendly with many police inspectors and detectives, and had long ago made arrangements with some of them whereby they would send me a wire by day, or a line by boy-messenger at night with information of the latest "sensation." The reason why all were signed with initials was because such intimation was contrary to the order of the Chief Commissioner.

I therefore left Dick sucking his foul briar, and, taking a motor-bus to Kensington, entered the police-station, which stands back hidden in a courtyard opposite St. Mary Abbot's Church. In the charge-room, with its bare, grey-painted walls, its steel-railed dock for prisoners, its loud-ticking clock, and its desk, whereon the oblong charge-book lay open, I found my old friend Inspector Patterson in earnest conversation with two men of the working class, who spoke with a strong Cockney accent and addressed him familiarly as "guv'nor." They were evidently policemen's noses, or, in criminal parlance, "narks."

"Good evening, Mr Urwin," the inspector exclaimed, putting forth his big hand. He was a tall, fair-moustached, easy-going fellow, an excellent officer, tender-hearted where the deserving poor was concerned, but harsh and unbending towards the habitual offender. From constable, as I had first known him in the T or Hammersmith Division, he had been moved to St. Luke's, to Paddington, to Leman Street and to Bow Street, until, owing to the marks which various magistrates had made upon his charge sheets, he had now at last risen to the rank of first-class inspector.

He was discreet in his every action, therefore he did not refer to the telegram he had sent me lest any of the men should overhear, but when we had chatted for a few moments he whispered

—

"Go over to the bar at High Street Railway Station and wait there for me. I want to see you very particularly."

I nodded. Then, after some further conversation, I left him and wandered across to the refreshment room he had indicated.

Chapter Two
The Penny in Paper

About twenty minutes elapsed before Patterson rejoined me, but expressing a fear that we might be overheard there, we went forth together and strolled along High Street, until, coming to a quiet turning which, I think, led past the workhouse, we strolled along it, and there he commenced his explanation.

"The fact is," he said in a nervous, hushed voice, "there's been a most extraordinary occurrence here to-night. The mystery is the strangest in all my experience, and I've made inquiries into one or two in my time, as you know."

"Tell me all about it," I said, my curiosity whetted.

"I wish I could, my dear fellow," he answered.

"I mean, tell me all the known facts."

"Nothing is known — save the discovery," he replied. "As soon as it became known I wired to you. When the papers get hold of it, it will make the greatest sensation ever known in London."

"Well, that's saying a good deal," I remarked. "Who made the discovery?"

"I did," he answered, adding quickly, "but don't mention me, or the superintendent may suspect me of giving you information. He already has a suspicion that I'm a bit too friendly with you gentlemen of the press. A contravention of the Commissioner's orders against giving information to the papers might get me carpeted up at the Yard, you know."

"And the discovery?" I asked impatiently. "What's its nature?"

"Most astounding," he replied, with a bewildered look. "I'm a police officer, Urwin," he added hoarsely, "and I'm not often unnerved. But to-night, by Jove! I'm upset — altogether upset. The whole affair is so devilish uncanny and unnatural."

"Tell me the story," I urged. "If it is so strange the evening papers will have a good time to-morrow."

"No, no," he cried in quick alarm. "You must publish nothing yet — nothing. You understand that I give you these facts only on condition that you promise not to publish any thing until I give you permission. You alone will know of it. We must preserve the utmost secrecy. Not a word must leak out yet. You understand in what an awkward position you would place me were you to publish anything of this affair."

"Of course. I promise you to keep the matter a strict secret," I answered. "There are many cases in which the publication of the details of a crime might defeat the efforts of the police, and this I supposed to be one of them."

"Well," he said, "I made the discovery in a most curious manner. Just before seven o'clock this evening, just as it was growing dark, I was returning to the station after visiting the 'fixed-point' at the corner of Earl's Court Road. You know the spot — just opposite Holland Park."

I nodded. I knew that particular street-corner where Earl's Court Road joined Kensington Road quite well.

"I had previously been my usual round through Campden Hill Road and Holland Walk, and was strolling back along the main Kensington Road, past that terrace of houses Upper Phillimore Place, when my attention was suddenly arrested by seeing on the steps leading from the pavement up to the front garden of one of the houses a small object moving. It was inside the gate, and in the dim half-light I bent to examine it. What do you think it was?"

"Don't know," I replied. "Don't ask riddles — describe facts."

"Well, it was the very last thing one would dream of finding on a London doorstep — a small, strangely-marked snake."

"A snake!" I echoed. "You didn't arrest it for being found without visible means of subsistence, I suppose?"

"No," he answered, controlling the smile which played about his lips. "But the thing's too serious for joking, as you'll recognise when I've told you all. Well, the squirming reptile, as soon as it saw me, coiled itself round, and with head erect and swelled, commenced hissing viciously.

I saw that there was considerable danger in a thing like that being at large, and surmising that it had escaped from the house, having been kept in captivity by somebody fond of such pets, I opened the gate, passed it, not, however, without it making a dart at me, and walking up to the door, rang the bell. The house was in total darkness, but daylight had only just faded, and in many of the houses in the same terrace the gas in the hall had not yet been lit. I rang and rang, but there was no response. In a large house of that character it seemed strange that no servant was about. Indeed, most of the houses there, large, roomy and old-fashioned, let furnished apartments, but this one seemed to be superior to its neighbours, inasmuch as it has a balcony on the first floor, and the small front garden is well-kept in comparison to the patches of bald, weedy grass with which the others are content. As I stood on the doorstep, trying to arouse the inmates, I watched the reptile squirming about the paved path, apparently enjoying its liberty immensely. I placed my ear attentively at the door, trying to detect some sound of movement, but failed, until suddenly I heard within the ringing of an electric bell, subdued by reason of the closed door. It was certain that, after all, some one was within."

"Was your summons answered?" I asked eagerly.

"No. I rang fully a dozen times, but nobody came. It occurred to me that within might be an invalid, and that, hearing my ring, he or she had rung the bell to the kitchen, but the servants were absent. There was an area door, so I descended, and tried that. The handle yielded. It was unlocked. Therefore I pushed it open and went in, though I was certainly not prepared for the discovery I afterwards made. As I entered, the electric bell commenced ringing again, but it was apparently above me, on the ground floor, and not in the kitchen where I stood. In the cooking-stove the fire was dying out, and there were other signs that servants had been about recently. Finding no one in the basement I ascended to the first floor, when there greeted my nostrils a most delicious fragrance, very similar to the incense which the Roman Catholics burn. The place smelt like the Brompton Oratory."

"Well, what did you do next?" I asked, excited at his extraordinary narrative.

"I searched the two big rooms — a dining-room and a back sitting-room — on the ground floor, but finding no one, I stood at the bottom of the stairs and shouted, thinking to discover the whereabouts of the invalid who had rung the bell. There was no answer. The place was dark, so I struck a match, ascended to the first floor and entered the front room, which proved to be a good-sized, well-furnished drawing-room, dimly lit by the street-lamp opposite shining through the windows. At the further end, suspended from the ceiling, a curious lamp was burning in red glass, just like those one sees in Roman Catholic churches, and on examining it I found it to be a little float in oil, so arranged that it would burn continuously for many days and nights without attention. It looked strange and weird, a red spot in the darkness at the end of the room; but what was stranger and more amazing was a discovery I made a moment later when, my eyes having grown used to the semi-obscurity of the room, I discerned two human forms, one that of a woman lying back in an armchair as if asleep, and the other a man, who had fallen close by and was lying outstretched upon the carpet. Even the faint light of the match I struck told me that both were dead, and so startled was I by this unexpected revelation that with scarcely a second glance round the weird place I hastened downstairs and left by the front door."

"You went on to the station at once, I suppose?"

"Yes," he answered; then after a pause he looked straight into my face, adding, "but to tell the truth, Urwin, you and I are the only persons who know of this affair. I haven't reported it."

"Haven't reported it?" I echoed. "Why not? Delay may prevent the mystery being unravelled."

"I know it's absurd and foolish," he faltered in an unsteady voice, "but the fact is, I entertain a deep-rooted superstition about snakes. My poor wife was always dreaming of snakes before she died, and strangely enough, whenever I have seen those reptiles in my dreams some bad luck, catastrophe or bereavement has always fallen upon me immediately afterwards."

"It isn't like you to speak thus, Patterson," I said, knowing him to be a fearless man who more than once had boldly faced a burglar's revolver.

"I really don't know what to do," he said. "It's nearly two hours ago since I entered the place. I was so upset when I came out that I went to the telegraph office and wired to you, in the hope that you might be able to suggest some plan of action."

"Report at once and let's thoroughly investigate it," I said promptly.

"No. I can't report it on account of that snake. If I did, I feel assured that some fatality would fall upon me."

"You're unnerved by what you've seen," I said. "It certainly was not a nice position to unexpectedly find oneself alone with the dead in a dark deserted house like that. In any case, however, the matter is a queer one and must be sifted."

"Yes," he said, "it appears to be a most remarkable affair."

"Well," I exclaimed, "if you are determined not to report it just at present I'm ready to go with you and search the place. The area door is still unlocked, you say?"

He hesitated, pale and agitated. The effect of this discovery upon him had been really remarkable.

"Yes, the door is still unlocked, of course," he said reflectively, "but personally I don't care about returning."

"Rubbish, my dear chap," I exclaimed. "I don't believe in superstitions. The finding of the snake was curious, no doubt, but this isn't the first time snakes have been found in the streets of London. Lots have been discovered about Covent Garden Market, having come over in baskets of fruit."

He was silent. Evidently his discovery had been a very unusual one. I know well the row of houses he had indicated, the most old-fashioned, perhaps, in the district, for they had formed a part of old Kensington over a century ago, and even now the great iron extinguishers ornamented some of the doorways, mute remembrancers of the days of sedan chairs and linkmen.

"Let's go and explore the place, and report afterwards," I urged, my appetite for adventure whetted by his strong disinclination to return. "I'll report it as a discovery of my own if you are disinclined to do so."

"Very well," he answered at last, "let's go. But before we enter I tell you that it is a very mysterious house. Recollect that strange ringing I heard."

"We'll look into all that later on," I said, surprised at his unusual agitation. There, facing one of the busiest thoroughfares of the West End, little harm surely could come to us. "Come along," I said, and thus persuaded, he quickened his footsteps. We passed along Abingdon Villas into Earl's Court Road, where, meeting a constable on duty, he borrowed his lamp; then turning into the Kensington Road we at length reached the house of mystery, which, as he had said, was a gloomy-looking place in total darkness.

We peered eagerly inside the gate, but could distinguish no sign of the reptile which had so strangely attracted my friend's attention in the first instance. It had no doubt withdrawn among the plants and shrubs in the little smoke-dried garden, and was watching us unseen. Without hesitation, in order not to attract the curiosity of any passer-by whose attention might be arrested by Patterson's uniform, we walked straight to the area door, and gaining the kitchen, at once lit the gas. As he had said, there was every sign that the place had been recently occupied, but with only a cursory examination of the basement we passed upstairs to the dining-room. Here we also lit the gas and saw that the table had been laid for three persons in a manner quite luxurious, with real silver, cut glass and tiny vases of fresh flowers arranged artistically. Beside each plate were blue glass finger-bowls filled with water which gave out a strong perfume of roses. The chairs had been placed, and the *hors d'oeuvres*, olives, anchovies and caviare were already on the table, showing that all preparations for dinner had been made. Yet strangely enough, in the kitchen the greater part of the meat and vegetables remained uncooked.

From this room we passed into the smaller one adjoining, lighting the gas as we went, but this seemed to have been used as a smoking-room, and contained nothing of note.

It was, however, in the drawing-room above where we made the most astounding discoveries. The apartment was spacious for the size of the house, upholstered in pale-blue with furniture of expensive character, and large growing palms placed on stands. In the centre was a great circular settee, and in the corners wide soft divans of pale-blue velvet with golden fringe. Comfort and luxury had been studied by whoever had furnished the place, for as we lit one of the side gas-brackets we saw that it was really a very artistic room, the floor covered with a real Turkey carpet of softest hues, while the few paintings on the walls were choice examples of well-known artists. At the end opposite the grate was suspended from the ceiling by three gilt chains the mysterious little red lamp, burning steadily without a flicker, and beneath it, fallen back in a large armchair, was a woman, whose face, although waxen white, was eminently beautiful. The paleness of death was upon her, yet her handsome head with its wealth of gold brown hair was pillowed upon the cushion of yellow silk, and upon the cold, slightly-parted lips there played a strange, bitter smile. She was young, twenty or so, dressed in an artistically-made gown of pale mauve, trimmed with lace. Her teeth were even and perfect; her cheeks round and well-moulded; her chin slightly protruding, and a piquant little nose; but that smile in death seemed revolting in its hideousness. Her eyes large, of a deep blue, once luminous as stars no doubt, but now dull and filmy, were wide open, as though gazing out upon us in an endeavour to speak and tell us the truth of the strange and tragic occurrence. I looked upon her bewildered, dumbfounded.

Not three yards away, stretched at her feet, was a man of about thirty-five, well-dressed in frock coat and light-coloured trousers, with collar and cravat of the latest mode, and wearing on his cold, stiff hand a ring set with a single diamond of unusual lustre. His face was towards the carpet, and while I held the lamp, Patterson bent and turned him over. We then saw that he was dark and good-looking, a gentleman evidently, although from the upward curl of his moustache and his smartness of attire he appeared to be something of a fop.

"It looks a good deal like murder and suicide," Patterson exclaimed, still bending over him. "I wonder who he is?"

"There's initials on his sleeve-links," I said, for I had detected an engraved cipher upon the plain gold buttons at his wrists.

"They're two 'K's' intertwined, surmounted by a crest," my companion said in a strange voice. "I wonder what's on him?" and he proceeded to search the breast-pocket of the dead man's coat. The contents, which we afterwards examined together, consisted only of two prospectuses of new companies, an amber cigar-tube mounted in gold, and the envelope of a letter addressed in a woman's hand to "George Grove, Poste Restante, Charing Cross," and bearing the Manchester post-mark of three days before. The letter had unfortunately been destroyed; only the envelope remained. But we both recollected that persons who have letters addressed to the Poste Restante do not usually give their correct names.

In one of the vest pockets were three ten-pound notes folded carelessly together, while in the trousers pockets was a quantity of loose silver. Beyond that there was nothing else upon him. Contrary to the effect of death upon his unfortunate companion, his face was slightly distorted, the tip of the tongue protruding, and both hands clenched, showing that he had endured a momentary spasm of agony as the last spark of life died out, while from the fact that a small tripod table with painted plate-glass top had been overturned and broken it seemed apparent that he had staggered and clutched wildly at the first object within his reach.

But on neither could we detect any wound, nor was there anything to show the cause of death. I examined the hand of the woman, a tiny, slim, cold hand, the contact of which thrilled me by its chilliness, and saw that her rings, set with emeralds, rubies and diamonds, were of the finest quality.

"She's beautiful," Patterson observed, gazing down upon her. "Perhaps she was his wife."

"Perhaps," I said. "Curious that they should have both died together in this manner."

"They were evidently sitting here chatting before dinner, when both were either murdered, or died suddenly before assistance could reach them. She died before he did."

"What makes you think that?" I asked quickly, my eyes wandering around the large, comfortable room, the atmosphere of which was heavy with fragrant odours.

"Because he placed that cushion beneath her head," answered the shrewd, observant police-officer. "He had kissed her, and she was in the act of smiling at his last act of love when her heart suddenly failed, and soul and body parted."

"And he died immediately afterwards, you think?"

"Yes, that's what I surmise. What's your opinion?"

"I can form no theory at present," I answered, bewildered. In the course of years spent in the investigation of crime for journalistic purposes I had had my wits sharpened, and rather prided myself upon the soundness of the theories I propounded in the articles I wrote. Patterson knew this, and probably for that reason had invoked my companionship in this curious affair.

Together we made a searching examination of the whole room, but there was absolutely nothing to show the motive, or even the mode, of the tragedy. The absence of servants was of course extremely suspicious, but neither of us attached much importance to that. A close examination of the scene was our present object, experience having taught that upon the scene of most crimes there remains some trace of the assassin. The old saying that "Murder will out" is truer than the majority of people believe, for even that night we had had a striking illustration in Patterson's attention being attracted by the snake in the gateway.

Beside the dead woman's chair was lying a handkerchief, a tiny square of lawn and lace, which I picked up. It emitted an odour very sweet and subtle, such as I had never before smelt.

Patterson sniffed it, but placed it down.

"Some new scent," he said. "Women are always going in for the latest inventions in perfumes."

"But this is an extraordinary one," I said, again smelling it. "Terribly strong, too," I added, for the odour had a strange, half-intoxicating effect upon me. The small red light steadily burning, the fragrance of the incense, the two dead forms lying there, still and cold, and the single gas-burner, hissing as it flared, combined to present a weird, lurid picture, each detail of which has ever since been indelibly photographed upon my memory.

The smile of death upon that woman's lips was horrible. That look of hers has ever since haunted me, for now that I know the truth and have realised all that had taken place in that room prior to the tragedy, that laugh of derision has a significance which renders its recollection bitter, gruesome, hideous.

I know not what prompted me at that moment, but bending again beside the prostrate man I placed my hand inside his vest, recollecting that sometimes tailors, adopting the French mode, made pockets there, and that therein many men carried articles of value in secrecy and safety.

As I did so, I felt that there was a pocket in the lining, that it was buttoned, and that there was something within. Quickly I unbuttoned it and drew forth a small packet wrapped in glazed writing-paper, dirty and worn through being carried for a long time. With care I opened it, and inside found an object which caused us both to give vent to an ejaculation of wonder.

It was simply a penny.

"His mascot, I suppose," remarked the inspector. "A lucky coin."

"But it has no hole through it," I observed.

"The hole is of no importance. The coin may have been given him for luck," replied my companion. "Lots of people believe in such things, especially betting men."

"He was evidently very careful of it," I said, at the same time searching and finding another pocket on the other side of the vest, and from this I took a neat little cloth-covered case, not much larger than those containing cigarette tubes, and found on opening it that it contained a small hypodermic syringe, complete with its needles and accessories.

"This shows that he was addicted to the morphia habit," I remarked. "An overdose, perhaps."

My friend, who had now recovered something of his coolness and self-possession, took the tiny instrument and examined it carefully beneath the gas-light.

"There's been no morphia in this lately," he said. "It's quite dry, and certainly hasn't been used to-day."

"Let's search the whole house," I suggested. "We may find something which will give us a clue as to who and what these people were. Funny that the servants don't come back, isn't it?"

"I don't expect they will," answered Patterson.

"Depend upon it that there's more mystery in this affair than we at present suspect."

"Why?"

"Look at these," he said, passing over to me the three banknotes found upon the dead man. "They are spurious!"

No second glance was needed to convince me that he spoke the truth. They were clever imitations of ten-pound notes, but the paper, the despair of the forger, was thick and entirely different to that of the genuine bank-note.

Again I glanced at that beautiful woman's face with its smile of mingled ecstatic pleasure and bitterness. Her sightless eyes seemed fixed upon me, following me as I moved.

I drew back horrified, shuddering. Her gaze was ghastly.

"It certainly is a most mysterious affair," I ejaculated again, glancing around the place. "You ought at once to report it."

"No," cried my companion quickly. "The discovery must be yours. You must report it, Mr Urwin."

"Why?"

"Because, as I've already told you, I fear to do so on account of the snake."

I smiled at his curious objection, but an instant later grew serious because of the sharp and sudden ringing of an electric bell somewhere on the ground floor. It was the bell my companion had heard when first knocking at the door.

We both listened for a few moments while the ringing continued, until with sudden resolve I dashed downstairs to ascertain where the bell was. Without difficulty I found it, for there in the hall, revealed by the gas-lamp we had lit, was a telephone instrument with its bell agitated violently.

Without a second's delay I placed the receiver to my ear and gave the usual signal —

"Hulloa! Hulloa?"

The whirr and clicking stopped, and a voice, squeaky as that of an elderly person, said petulantly —

"I've been ringing up for an hour or more. What's wrong that you haven't replied? You're at fifty-eight, aren't you?"

"Yes," I answered, recollecting that fifty-eight was the number of that house. "Nothing is wrong. Why? Can't you be patient?"

"I felt uneasy," answered the mysterious voice apologetically. "I thought there might possibly have been some hitch as you haven't rung up."

"No," I responded. "None."

"Then of course it's all over?" inquired the voice. I started at this strange query. This unknown inquirer was evidently in possession of the truth, and believed himself to be talking to an accomplice. He knew of the commission of the crime, therefore it occurred to me that by the exercise of due caution I might be able to discover his identity.

"Yes," I answered, breathless in excitement.

"Both?" asked the voice.

"Both," I responded.

"Good. Then I shall see you at the place we arranged — eh?"

"Of course," I answered. "But when? I've forgotten."

"Forgotten!" echoed the squeaky voice in a tone of undisguised disgust. "Take care, or you'll blunder yet. You're a confounded idiot. Why, to-morrow at midday."

"I know I'm a fool," I replied. "But in the excitement it's quite slipped my memory where you said I was to meet you."

Then, holding the receiver tremblingly to my ear, I listened with quick heart-beating for the response of that mysterious, far distant voice which squeaked so strangely, sounding thin and high-pitched, more like that of a woman than of a man.

"You're a confounded fool to waste time like this if you're still at fifty-eight," said the voice.

"You've said so before," I responded. "But where shall I meet you?"

The voice answered at last —

"I'll meet you beside the lake in St. James's Park, Buckingham Palace end, at twelve to-morrow. Remember that."

"Very well," I responded eagerly. "Anything more?"

"No," was the reply. "Be careful how you get out, and where you go. So long!"

Then, next instant, I knew by the sound that the connexion had been switched off.

"What's the matter?" asked Patterson, now beside me.

"Wait, and I'll tell you afterwards," I said, at the same time ringing up again.

In response I was answered by a feminine voice at the Exchange, who inquired what number I desired.

"Tell me, miss, who has just been speaking to me. Kindly oblige me, as it's most important."

There was silence for a few moments, then the female voice inquired — "Are you there?" to which I responded.

"You were on a moment ago with 14,982, the public call-office at Putney."

"How long was I on?"

"About ten minutes."

"Have I been on to the same place before this evening?" I asked.

"No. Several numbers have been ringing you up, but you haven't replied."

"Who were they?"

"Oh, I really can't tell you now. It's quite impossible. I remember that the call-office at Piccadilly Circus was one, and I think the one in the Minories."

"They were all call-offices — no private persons?"

"I'm unable to say. I've been on duty for the past four hours, and have connected up thousands of numbers."

"Then you can't tell me anything else?" I asked disappointedly.

"No. I'm sorry I can't," replied the girl.

I was about to place the receiver on its hook when a sudden thought occurred to me, and again I addressed her.

"This matter is a most urgent one," I said. "Can't you ask at the call-office for a description of the man who has just been speaking?"

"There's no one there. It is merely an instrument placed in a passage leading to some offices," was the reply.

I hung up the receiver, and turning to Patterson repeated the conversation.

"Extraordinary," he ejaculated, when I had concluded. "We must keep that appointment. The inquiry is plain proof that murder has been committed, and further, that more than one person is in the secret."

"But is it not strange that this person, whoever he is, should dare to telephone in that manner?"

"It certainly is a bold move," my companion answered, "but from his conversation it is evident that the assassin promised to telephone to him, and was either disturbed in his work and compelled to escape hurriedly, or else forgot it altogether. Again, it's plain that to avoid detection the unknown man went from one call-office to another, always ringing up to this house, and never obtaining a response until you answered."

"His inquiry was certainly a guarded one."

"And your answers were smart, too," he laughed. "You were careful not to commit yourself."

"Do you think he'll keep the appointment?" I asked eagerly.

"That remains to be seen," answered my friend, glancing at the bull's-eye to see if it were burning well. "If he's not a blunderer he won't."

"Well, let's hope he does," I said. "You would arrest him, of course?"

"I don't know," he answered doubtfully. "We might learn more by keeping observation upon him for a day or two."

"Well," I said, "we haven't yet searched the place thoroughly. Let's see what is above."

My companion followed me upstairs rather reluctantly, I thought, passing the room where the mysterious tragedy had occurred and ascending to the floor above. There were four bedrooms, each well-furnished, but finding that they contained nothing of a suspicious character we continued to the top floor, where there were several smaller low-ceilinged rooms opening from a narrow passage. Two of them were evidently the sleeping apartments of the servants, the third was filled with lumber, but the fourth, which overlooked the back premises, long and narrow, was fitted as a kind of workshop or laboratory. A curious smell greeted our nostrils as we opened the door — a smell very much like the perfume on the dead woman's handkerchief.

We found a gas-jet and lit it, afterwards gazing round the place with some surprise. Upon shelves around the walls were various bottles containing liquids; on the table stood two curious-looking globes of bright steel, riveted like those of a steam-boiler, and connected by a long tubular coil rolled into three consecutive spirals which ended with a kind of nozzle. From the fact that an electric battery and a lathe also stood in the room we at once came to the conclusion that the master of that house had been engaged in some scientific investigations.

From place to place we went, searching every corner for any written document or letter, until at last I found, crumpled and cast into the empty grate, an old envelope on which I read the address: "Professor Douglas Dawson."

"At any rate we've got the name of the occupant of this place," I said, handing my find to the police-officer.

"Dawson?" he repeated, "Dawson? I fancy I've heard that name in connexion with scientific discovery."

"I don't know," I said. "If he's a well-known man we shall soon find out all about him at the Royal Institution."

I was standing near the fireplace with the envelope still in my hand when, of a sudden, I was startled by a strange scuttling noise near my feet.

"Good heavens!" gasped Patterson, his eyes riveted on the spot. "Look there! Look at that glass case! There are snakes in it!"

I sprang away, and looking in the direction he indicated saw that a glass case, standing on the ground, contained two great snakes with beautiful markings of yellow and black. Even as I looked they were coiled, with their flat heads erect and their bead-like eyes shining like tiny stars in the shadow, their bodies half-hidden in a blanket.

"Nice kind of pets, to keep in a house," observed Patterson. "That's one of them that's escaped into the garden, I expect."

"I quite agree," I said, "this place is decidedly the reverse of cheerful. Hadn't we better report at once? There's been a mysterious tragedy here, and immediate efforts should be made to trace the assassin."

"But, my dear fellow, how do you know they've been murdered?" he argued. "There's no marks of violence whatever."

"Not as far as we've been able to discover. A doctor can tell us more after the post-mortem," I responded.

There were many very strange features connected with this remarkable discovery. My friend's reluctance to commence an investigation, his firm resolve not to report the discovery, the mysterious voice at the telephone, the fact that some experimental scientist had his laboratory in that house, and the revelation of the unaccountable tragedy itself, were all so extraordinary that I stood utterly bewildered.

Absolutely nothing remained to show who were the pair lying dead, and no explanation seemed possible of that strange red light burning there so steadily, and unflickering. By the appearance of the glass, and the dust in the oil, the tiny lamp must have burned on incessantly for a very long time.

Strange it was that there, within a few yards of one of London's great arteries of traffic, that charming woman and her companion should have been cut off swiftly and suddenly, without a hand being stretched forth to save them.

In company we went downstairs, leaving the light in the laboratory still burning, and re-entered the drawing-room to take a final glance around. As I approached the prostrate body of the man I felt something beneath my foot, and glancing down saw that some coppers had evidently fallen from his pocket and were lying strewn about the carpet. Then, having remained a few minutes longer, we both went out by the door we had entered, locking it and taking the key.

"We must report it, Patterson," I said. "It certainly has some queer and very extraordinary features."

"Yes," he responded; adding slowly, "did you notice anything strange up in that top room where the chemicals and things were?"

"Yes, a good deal," I answered. "It isn't every one who keeps snakes as pets."

"I don't mean that," he answered. "But did you notice on the table a glassful of liquid, like water?"

"Yes."

"Well, that stuff was bubbling and boiling without any heat beneath."

"Perhaps the man who experiments there is a conjurer," I suggested, smiling at his surprise at seeing liquid boil when exposed to air. Police-officers know little of any other science save that of self-defence.

"Now," he said seriously, as we strode forward together in the direction of Kensington Church, "you must go to the station and report the discovery as if made by you — you understand. Remember, the snake attracted your attention, you entered, found the man and woman lying dead, lit the gas, searched the house, then left to get assistance, and met me."

"That's all very well," I answered. "But you forget that you borrowed that lamp from one of your own men, and that I called on you first."

"Ah!" he gasped; turning slightly pale. "I never thought of that!"

"Why don't you report it yourself?" I urged.

"For superstitious reasons," he laughed nervously.

"Hang superstition!" I cried. Adding: "Of course, I'll report it if you like, but it would be far better for you to do so and risk this mysterious bad luck that you fear."

He was silent for a moment, thinking deeply, then answered in a strange, hard voice, —

"Perhaps you're right, Urwin. I — I'm a confounded fool to be afraid," and with an effort quite apparent he braced himself up and we entered the police-station. Ascending the stairs we were soon closeted with Octavius Boyd, inspector of the Criminal Investigation Department attached to that Division, a middle-aged, dark-bearded, pleasant-faced man in plain-clothes, who, as soon as he heard our story, was immediately ready to accompany us, while five minutes later the clicking of the telegraph told that news of our discovery was being transmitted to headquarters at New Scotland Yard.

Patterson took down the *London Directory*, and turning it up at Upper Phillimore Place, found that the occupier of the house in question was Andrew Callender. He made inquiries in the section-house of the men off duty as to what was known of that house, but only one constable made a statement, and it was to the effect that he had, when on duty in Kensington Road, seen a youngish lady with fair hair, whose description tallied with that of the dead woman, come out and go across to the shops on the opposite side of the road.

"Do you know anything of the servants?" inquired Patterson.

"Well, sir," the man answered, "one was a man, and the other a woman."

"How do you know?"

"Because the servant of the house next door told me so. The woman was the cook, and the man did the housework. She said that the house was a most mysterious one."

"Is she there now?" my friend asked.

"No, sir. She was discharged a fortnight ago. Dishonest, I think."

"And you don't know where she is?"

Boyd had by this time called one of his plain-clothes men, who had obtained lamps, turning the dark slides over the flame, the station-sergeant had carefully ruled a line and written something in that remarkable register kept in every London police-station, wherein is recorded every event which transpires in the district, from a tragedy to the return of the sub-divisional inspector from his rounds, or the grooming of the horses. Then, after a short conversation with one of the second-class inspectors, we all four, accompanied by a sergeant, started for Upper Phillimore Place.

In order not to attract attention we separated. Patterson walking with me to the opposite side of the road, while the detectives walked together, and the sergeant alone. Little did the passers-by suspect when they saw Patterson and me strolling leisurely along that we were on our way to investigate what afterwards proved to be one of the strangest and most remarkable mysteries that had ever puzzled the Metropolitan Police.

Chapter Four
The Three Cards

On reaching the house, Boyd, an expert officer who had spent years in the investigation of crime, ascended with his subordinate to the drawing-room, while we remained on the ground floor to complete our search, the sergeant being stationed inside the hall.

Our further investigations were not very fruitful. The fact that dinner was laid for three indicated that a third person had been present, or was expected. The room did not differ from any other, except that it was perhaps better furnished than one would have expected in such a house, for although in a first-class and rather expensive neighbourhood the row of houses had declined in popularity of late years, and was now inhabited mostly by the lodging-house fraternity.

In moving about the room, however, my coat caught the plate laid for the person who was to occupy the head of the table, and it was nearly swept off. I saved it, however, but beneath was revealed a plain white card which, until that moment, had been concealed. Patterson caught sight of it at the same moment, and taking it in my hand I examined it, finding that it was a plain visiting card of lady's size, one side being blank, and other bearing a roughly-drawn circle in ink.

There was nothing else.

"That's certainly curious," my companion remarked, looking over my shoulder.

"Yes," I said, lifting a second plate to see what was there concealed, and finding another card, in all appearances similar, plain, but bearing across its reverse a single straight line drawn with a pen.

"By Jove!" observed Patterson, lifting the other plate, and finding a third card, "this is certainly very strange."

He turned the card over, but it was blank on both sides.

"I wonder what game is this, or whether these have any connexion with the crime?" I exclaimed, holding all three of the cards in my hand, turning them over and examining them carefully beneath the light. "By the ink they have the appearance of having been prepared long ago. See!" I added, holding one of them towards him, "the corners of this one are slightly turned up and soiled. It has been carried in some one's pocket, and is not a fresh card."

Again Patterson took it and examined it. It was the one with the line drawn across it. The others were quite clean, as if just taken fresh from a packet.

"There's some mystery about these," he said reflectively, as though speaking to himself. "If we could but solve it we should likewise solve the problem of the crime, depend upon it."

"No doubt," I assented. "Each of them have some meaning, occult but extraordinary. They were turned face downwards so that the accidental removal of the plate would not reveal the device upon them."

"The devices are simple enough, but undoubtedly they have some hidden meaning," my friend said.

"They were evidently concealed there, and the three persons, unsuspecting, were to discover them when the first plates were removed," I suggested.

He placed them together on the table, saying —

"Better let Boyd see them when he comes down. The affair grows more queer and complicated as we proceed."

"Don't you recollect," I said suddenly, "in the dead man's pocket was a card exactly similar, but quite blank. You threw it into the fireplace."

"Ah! of course," he answered quickly. "That fact shows that he had something to do with these mysterious symbols. I wonder what is their real meaning."

"I wonder," I said. "As you say, the mystery grows each moment more and more inexplicable. Curious, too, that the snake in the garden path should have directed your attention to it."

"No," he said quickly, his face in an instant pale and serious, "don't mention that, there's a good fellow. I'm trying not to think of it; for when I recollect all that it means to me I'm unnerved."

"Bah!" I laughed. "Surely there's nothing to fear. It only shows that however careful the assassin is to cover his crime it must be unearthed sooner or later. The finger of Fate always points to the crime of murder, however well it may be concealed."

"True," he sighed, his brows knit in serious thought. "But the finger of Fate has in this case shown me an omen of evil."

"You're a fool, Patterson," I said bluntly. "You have here every chance to distinguish yourself as a shrewd officer, yet you calmly stand by talking of omens and all that rot."

"Yes," he answered. "I know I'm an idiot, Mr Urwin, but I can't help it. That's the worst of it."

"Well," I suggested, "while Boyd is upstairs, why not make inquiries of the next-door neighbours regarding those who occupied this place?"

He at once acted on my suggestion, and together we went out and rang the bell of the house adjoining on the right. My friend's curious apathy in this matter surprised me, for usually he was a quick, active fellow, who prosecuted his inquiries methodically, and worked up evidence in a manner that had more than once called forth the commendation of the judge at the Old Bailey. That night, however, he was plainly upset — nervous, trembling and agitated, in a manner quite unusual to him.

Boyd, the keen-eyed, quick-witted detective inspector, had noticed this when at the police-station, but Patterson had only replied —

"I'm a bit unwell, that's all."

Our summons at the house next door was answered by the occupier's wife, a rather stout, white-haired, gaily-capped old lady named Luff.

The appearance of Patterson in uniform surprised her, but when she had asked us in, and we were seated, he said —

"There is no occasion to be alarmed, madam. I have merely called to make an inquiry of you. It is in your power to render us assistance in a rather confidential matter regarding the occupiers of the house next door — your neighbours on the left. What do you know of them?"

"Nothing," she answered. "They came about six months ago, a young lady and a very old gentleman, with a single maid-servant. They speak to no one, and, as far as I have observed, have very few friends. I have often remarked to my son, who is a civil engineer, and now away making the railway in China, that they are a mysterious couple. What is wrong with them?"

"Oh, it's simply a private matter," my companion answered carelessly, not wishing to alarm the neighbourhood by news of our discovery.

"What is the old gentleman like? Can you describe him?" I inquired. No doubt she took me for a detective, but at that moment this thought did not occur to me.

"He is sixty, I should think, old and decrepit, with white hair, and always walks with a stick."

"And the lady was his daughter?" suggested the inspector.

"I suppose her to be his daughter," she answered. "The old man's name is Dawson, I believe — at least one day a messenger-boy brought a note here by mistake, addressed to Professor Dawson. The daughter is a very good pianist, and plays every morning regularly."

"They are well off, as far as you can judge?" Patterson inquired with his assumed careless air.

"No, I don't think they are, because my maid heard at Boucher's — the grocer's across the way — that they owed a large bill which they couldn't settle. Again, people who have a house of that sort do not have coal by the hundredweight taken down into the kitchen as they do."

Patterson nodded. No more sure sign of a light purse is there than the purchase of coal by the half-sack. Yet the interior of that house, with its well-laid dinner-table, certainly did not betray any sign of poverty. Indeed, I had noticed in the cellar a dusty stock of choice wines, hocks, ports, and champagnes of expensive brands.

"You don't know the young lady's name, then?" asked my friend, after a slight pause.

"If she's really his daughter it would, I suppose, be Dawson," she replied with a smile. "But I'm not certain, remember, as to either of their names."

"Perhaps your servants may know something about them. Servants generally gossip and pick up information about one's neighbours, you know."

"You are right," answered the affable old lady, "they gossip far too much. Unfortunately, however, both my servants are out at this moment."

We chatted on, but it was evident from her conversation that her servants knew little beyond what she did. One statement she made was somewhat curious. She alleged that a few nights before she was awakened about two o'clock in the morning by hearing the loud shrill screams of a woman who seemed to be in the room next hers in the adjoining house. She could hear a man's voice talking low and gruffly, and three or four times were the screams repeated, as if the woman were in excruciating pain.

"What visitors came to the house?" Patterson asked at length.

"Very few. A youngish gentleman came sometimes. He called the other morning just as I was going out."

"Who admitted him?"

"The young lady herself."

Many more questions Patterson put to the old lady, but elicited no noteworthy fact, except that two large, heavy trunks had been sent away by Parcels Delivery a couple of days before. Therefore, thanking Mrs Luff, who, of course, was extremely curious to know why the police were taking such an active interest in her neighbour, we left and made inquiries of the people in the adjoining house on the opposite hand.

It was a lodging-house and the owner, a rather surly old widow, was not at all communicative. What she told us amounted practically to what we had already learnt. She, too, had long ago set the old man and his daughter down as mysterious persons, and her two servants had never been able to find out anything regarding them.

So after nearly half an hour's absence we returned to the house of mystery, watched, of course, by the persons in the houses on either side. None suspected a tragedy, but all remained at their windows expecting to see somebody arrested.

In the dining-room we found Doctor Knowles, the police divisional surgeon, who had been sent for by the police. He had already examined the bodies and was on the point of returning home.

"Well, doctor, what's your opinion?" asked Patterson.

"I can form none until after the post-mortem," answered the prim, youngish, dark-moustached man in silk hat and frock coat, a typical Kensington practitioner, who was known to be a great favourite with his lady patients.

"Are there no marks of violence?"

"None," he responded. "Although there seems no doubt that there has been foul play, yet the means used to encompass their death remains an entire mystery. That laboratory, too, is a very remarkable feature."

"Why?" I asked.

"Because the occupant of that place has made a discovery for which scientists have for years striven in vain," the doctor replied.

"What is it?"

"You noticed those strange globes with the coil of tubing," he said. "Well, from what I've found, it seems that the experimenter has invented a means for the liquefaction of hydrogen in large quantities."

"Is that anything very remarkable?" I asked, in my ignorance of recent science.

"Remarkable!" he echoed. "I should rather say it was. The discovery will create the greatest interest in the scientific world. Other gases have all been handled as true liquids in measurable quantities, while until now hydrogen has only been seen in clouds or droplets, and never collected into a liquid mass. Upstairs, however, there is actually a glass bowl of liquid hydrogen.

The experimenter, whoever he is, has determined at last the exact temperature at which it will liquefy, and thus a field for quite new researches, as also for new generalisations, has been thrown wide open."

"But why is the discovery so very important?" I asked, still puzzled at the doctor's unusual enthusiasm.

"Briefly, because by it physicists and chemists can henceforward obtain temperatures lying within thirty-five degrees from the so-called absolute zero of temperature — minus 459 degrees Fahrenheit. A possibility is thus given to study physical bodies in the vicinity of that point, which represents, so to say, the death of matter — that is, absence of the molecular vibrations which we describe as heat."

This explanation, technical though it was, interested me. I knew Doctor Lees Knowles to be a rising man, and when reporting lectures at the Royal Institution had often noticed him among the audiences. There was no doubt that he was highly excited over the discovery, for, like myself, he had seen the liquid hydrogen boiling without any visible heat. In the papers there had been lots about Professor Dewar's experiments in the liquefaction of oxygen, fluorine and the newly-discovered helium, and I remembered how all his efforts to bring hydrogen to a liquid state had failed. Now, however, the mysterious occupier of that house had succeeded, and every known gas could now be liquefied.

"But the murder," observed Patterson, his thoughts reverting to the crime, for to him the most wonderful scientific discovery was as naught. "Can you form absolutely no opinion as to how it was accomplished?"

The doctor shook his head.

"There is nothing whatever to account for their sudden death, as far as I can observe," he answered. "To the woman, however, death must have come instantly, while the man must have fallen and expired a few seconds later. There seem many mysterious features in the affair."

"The discoverer of this latest scientific fact is undoubtedly the old man who is absent, the father of the dead girl. From him we may learn something to lead us to form conclusions," I suggested.

"An old man!" echoed Dr Knowles. "Tell me about him."

Briefly Patterson related all that had been told us by the neighbours, and when he had finished the doctor exclaimed —

"Then I can tell you one thing which is proved undoubtedly. The old man seen to go in and out was in reality a young one, for while looking over the laboratory I came across a white wig and a make-up box, such as is used by actors. Go upstairs and you'll find a complete disguise there — broadcloth coat, pepper-and-salt trousers baggy at the knees, old-fashioned white vest, and collars of antique pattern."

"Surely that can't be true!" Patterson exclaimed in amazement.

"It certainly is," the doctor asserted. "Depend upon it that the man lying upstairs dead was the man who has been making these successful experiments, and who for some unknown reason desired to conceal his identity. Recollect that they had few friends, if any, and that their man-servant was a most discreet foreigner, who never gossiped."

"Then you think that to the world they assumed the position of father and daughter, while in reality they were husband and wife?" I said.

"Most likely," responded the doctor. "A man to make experiments on an elaborate scale as he has must necessarily have been absorbed in them. Indeed, that apparatus must have taken a year to prepare, and no doubt he has been making constant trials for months. He probably intended to give forth his discovery to the world as a great surprise, but has been prevented from doing so by some extraordinary combination of circumstances which has resulted in his death."

At that instant we heard a voice in the hall — a quick, sharp voice extremely familiar to me, but nevertheless it caused me to start. Next instant, however, there entered the room the well-known figure of Dick Cleugh.

"Hulloa, old fellow!" he exclaimed, greeting me and taking me aside. "I thought I'd run down and see what's in this. Funny affair it seems, doesn't it?"

"Yes," I answered. "A most remarkable mystery. But why have you come out here?"

"Soon after you left I went to find Lily, but she's gone into the country. So having nothing else to do I came down to see what had occurred. I knew, of course, from Patterson's telegram, that it was something unusual."

"Have you been upstairs?"

"Yes, I've been worrying around this last half-hour, while you and Patterson have been making inquiries next door. I've been having a look about with the Doctor. It seems that there's some wonderful apparatus in the laboratory — a discovery for liquefying hydrogen. Has he told you about it?"

"Yes," I responded. "What's your theory?"

"By Jove! old fellow," he said smiling, "the whole affair is so devilish uncanny, with those snakes upstairs, water boiling without any heat beneath it, and one thing and another, that I'm utterly at a loss how to account for it all."

"You think they've been murdered?"

"Of course," answered the astute Cleugh. "But the doctor can't discover how. There is not a scratch upon them. The discovery of those flash notes on the man looks as though he were a bit of a swell swindler, doesn't it?"

"Yes," I said. Then taking him across to the dining-table I explained how we had discovered the three cards concealed beneath the plates.

He took the cards in his hand, turning them over, and examining them carefully.

"Strange," he ejaculated. "This adds still another phase to the affair. It is really a most sensational discovery, and will work up well for to-morrow."

"No, Mr Cleugh," put in Patterson quickly, overhearing his remark, "I beg of you to publish nothing whatever about it until I give you permission. In this we are bound to preserve secrecy for the present in order that our inquiries may not be thwarted. Even the neighbours will remain in ignorance of the real nature of things, so carefully do I intend to guard against any public sensation. Whatever information I can give you I will do so willingly, in order that you can prepare your account of it, but remember that not a word must be published until I give you permission."

"Quite right," observed the doctor. "In such a matter as this any sensation in the Press might frustrate all your efforts to arrive at the truth."

"Very well," answered Dick, a trifle disappointedly. "Of course you'll give nothing to anybody else. I want to be first in the field with it."

"Of that I give you my word. Not a soul will know of this discovery outside the persons in this house at the present moment. Come, let's go upstairs and speak to Boyd," and while the doctor wished us good evening and left, my two friends accompanied me upstairs, where in the drawing-room the detectives were continuing their searching investigation.

"The woman is decidedly good-looking, isn't she?" observed Cleugh as we entered.

Instinctively I turned towards the chair in which the body was still reclining, but next instant, with a loud cry of dismay, which at the same moment was echoed by Patterson, I stood aghast, rigid, immovable.

The sight which met our eyes was utterly bewildering.

The woman we had discovered there, so lovely in form and feature, had a wealth of auburn hair, and eyes of a deep intense blue, while, amazing though it was, this woman before us was quite ten years older, dark-complexioned, with hair which in that light seemed blue-black, and half-closed eyes as dark as jet.

"Good Heavens!" I gasped. "Look! Why, that is not the woman we found when we first entered this place — but another. Where is the fair girl?"

"There's no fair girl," answered the detective Boyd, as all started back in surprise at my astounding assertion. "This is the woman we found, you must be mistaken."

"No," Patterson declared in the low, hoarse voice of one filled with fear. "There is no mistake. When we first entered there was another woman here, younger, prettier, with light hair and blue eyes. This is the most unaccountable, most amazing and most inexplicable of all our discoveries."

Chapter Five
The Second Woman

The statement that the woman found by Patterson on his first entry there, and seen by me afterwards, had disappeared, was at first discredited by our companions. It seemed too astounding to be the truth, nevertheless there was now reclining in the same armchair a woman who certainly bore no resemblance whatever to the beautiful, fair-haired girl with eyes of such deep, pure blue — those eyes that had stared at me so horribly in the ghastly rigidity of death. I recollected that smile upon her lips, half of sarcasm, half of pleasure; that strange expression which had held me entranced yet horrified.

She had disappeared, and here in her place was a dark-complexioned woman, older, nevertheless handsome — a woman in whose refined face was an air of romance and tragedy, and upon whose hand was the marriage bond. She, too, was dead. The doctor had examined her and pronounced life extinct.

"How could this have occurred?" I exclaimed, turning to Patterson as soon as I had recovered from the shock of the astounding discovery.

"It's simply amazing!" he declared. "I'm utterly at a loss to account for it. The woman we found here was most distinctly another person."

"Then there has been a triple tragedy," observed Boyd. "The body of the first woman must have been conveyed away during the time you were absent at the police-station."

"But why?" I asked. "What on earth could be the motive?"

"Impossible to tell," Patterson answered. "Perhaps the body is hidden somewhere in the house."

"No," Boyd replied. "We've made a complete search everywhere. It has undoubtedly been taken away. This fact, in itself, shows first, that there is more than one person implicated in the crime, and secondly, that they were absolutely fearless; while further, the incident of the telephone is in itself sufficient proof that they had taken the utmost precautions against detection."

"Are you quite certain that every cupboard and wardrobe has been looked into?" I asked doubtfully.

"Quite. From garret to cellar we've thoroughly overhauled the place. There are a couple of large trunks in one of the bedrooms, but we examined the contents of both. They contain books."

"But loose boards, or places of that sort?" I suggested.

"When we search a place," responded the Scotland Yard inspector with a smile, "we're always on the look-out for places of concealment. I've superintended the investigation myself, and I vouch that nothing is concealed within this house."

"Do you think that the assassin was actually in the house when we first entered?"

"That's more than likely," he answered with a pensive air. "Evidently the instant you'd gone the body of the fair-haired girl was somehow spirited away."

"Where?"

"Ah, that's what we must find out. Perhaps a taxi-driver will be able to throw a light upon the matter."

"This is certainly a first-class mystery," observed Dick, with journalistic instinct and a keen eye to those "special interviews" and "latest revelations" in which readers of his journal always revelled. "It will make no end of a stir. What a godsend, now that the gooseberry season is coming on."

A good murder mystery is always welcome to a certain class of London daily journals, but more especially in the season when Parliament is "up," the Courts are closed for the Vacation, and the well of sensations runs low. This season is termed, in journalistic parlance, "the gooseberry season," on account of the annual appearance of the big gooseberry, that mythical monster of our youth, the sea-serpent, and the starting of the usual silly correspondence upon "Why should we live?" or some equally interesting controversial subject.

We were all held in blank astonishment at this latest development of the extraordinary affair. It had so many remarkable phases that, even to Boyd, one of the shrewdest officers of the Criminal Investigation Department, it was bewildering.

To me, however, the disappearance of that dead woman with the fair, pure face was the strangest of all that tangle of astounding facts. That face had impressed me. Its every feature had been riveted indelibly upon my memory, for it was a face which, in life, I should have fallen down and worshipped as an idol, for there was about it a purity and charm which must have been highly attractive, a vivacity in those eyes which, even in death, had held me spell-bound.

"I don't see that we can do any more just now," Boyd remarked in a business-like tone to his subordinate.

"You've seen the three cards which were beneath the plates on the dining-table?" I asked.

"Yes," he responded. "There's some hidden meaning connected with them, but what it's impossible at present to guess. In order to prosecute our inquiries we must preserve secrecy. Nothing must be published yet. Indeed, Patterson, you'll apply to the Coroner at once to take steps to withhold the real state of affairs from the public. If the assassins find that no hue and cry is aroused we may have a far better chance of tracing them, for they may betray themselves."

"It's a pity," observed Dick, deeply disappointed. "A first-class sensation of this sort don't occur every day. Why, it's worth four columns if a line."

"Be patient," Patterson urged. "You shall have an opportunity of publishing it before long, and I'll see that you are a long way ahead of your contemporaries."

"Don't let the news agencies have a word. They always try and get in front of us," said Cleugh, whose particular antagonists were the Central News and the Press Association, which possess facilities for the collection of news and its transmission by wire to the various newspapers that form one of the most marvellous organisations in unknown London.

"Leave it to me," said the inspector. "As soon as it's wise to let the public know anything I'll give you permission to publish. The *Comet* shall be first in the field with it."

"Very well," answered Dick, satisfied with Patterson's answer. That officer had been prominent a few years before in the investigations relative to those mysterious assassinations of women in Whitechapel, and was very friendly with "the *Comet* man," as Cleugh was termed in the journal which he represented.

Many were the suggestions we put forth as to how the bodies of the victims could have thus been changed, but no theory we could advance seemed likely to have any foundation in fact.

The mystery was certainly one of the strangest that had ever puzzled the crime investigators of London. The cause of its discovery was a most remarkable incident, and at every turn as the investigation proceeded mystery seemed to follow upon mystery, until the whole affair presented so many curious features that a solution of the problem seemed utterly impossible.

I bent beside the body of the woman who, reclining in the armchair with one arm fallen by her side, presented the appearance of one asleep. Her presence there was a profound enigma. A thought, however, occurred to me at that moment. The dining-table below had been laid for three. Perhaps she was the third person.

For the greater part of an hour we remained in that house of grim shadows discussing the various phases of the astounding affair, until at last, about eleven, we all left, two constables in uniform being stationed within. So secretly had this search been carried out that the neighbours, though, perhaps, puzzled by Patterson's inquiries, entertained no suspicion of any tragic occurrence. In Kensington Road all the shops facing Upper Phillimore Place were closed save the tobacconist's and the frequent public-houses, the foot passengers were few, and at that hour the stream of taxis with homeward-bound theatre-goers had not yet commenced. Market garden carts from Hounslow or Feltham, piled high with vegetables, rumbled slowly past on their journey to Covent Garden, and a few empty motor-buses rattled along towards Hyde Park, but beyond all was quiet, for that great artery of Western London goes early to rest.

At the police-station we took leave of Patterson and Boyd, and entering a motor-bus at Kensington Church, arrived at our chambers shortly before midnight.

"There's something infernally uncanny in the whole business," said the Mystery-monger as we sat smoking, prior to turning in. It was our habit to smoke and gossip for half an hour before going to bed, no matter what the time. Our talk was generally of "shop" events in our world of journalism, the chatter of Fleet Street intermingled with reminiscences of the day's doings. Dick was sitting in the armchair reflectively sucking his eternal briar, while I sat at my table pondering over a letter I had found there on my return. It was from Mary Blain, for whom I had once long ago entertained a very strong affection, but who had since gone out of my life, leaving only a shadowy recollection of a midsummer madness, of clandestine meetings, of idle, careless days spent in company with a smart, eminently pretty, girl in blue serge skirt, cotton blouse and sailor hat. All was of the past. She had played me false. I was poor, and she had thrown me over for a man richer than myself. For nearly three years I had heard little of her; indeed, I confess that she had almost passed from my memory until that evening when I had sat awaiting Dick, and now on my return I opened that letter to discover it in her well-known, bold hand — the hand of an educated woman.

The letter, which had had some wanderings, as its envelope showed, and was dated from her father's house up the river, merely expressed a hope that I was in good health, and satisfaction at hearing news of me through a mutual friend. Such a letter struck me as rather strange. I could only account for it by the fact that she desired to resume our acquaintanceship, and that this was a woman's diplomatic way of opening negotiations. All women are born diplomatists, and woman's wit and powers of perception are far more acute than man's.

The letter brought back to me vividly the memory of that sweet, merry face beneath the sailor hat, the wealth of dark hair, the laughing eyes so dark and brilliant, the small white hands, and their wrists confined by their golden bangles. Yes, Mary Blain was uncommonly good-looking. Her face was one in ten thousand. But she was utterly heartless. I recollected how, when with her mother she had spent a summer at Eastbourne, what a sensation her remarkable beauty caused at Sunday parade on the Esplanade. She was lovely without consciousness of it, utterly ingenuous, and as ignorant of the world's wickedness as a child. The daughter of a wealthy City man who combined company-promoting with wine-importing, she had from childhood been nursed in the lap of luxury, and being the only child, was the idol of her parents. Their country house at Harwell, near Didcot, was in my father's parish, and from the time when her nurse used to bring her to the Rectory until that well-remembered evening when in the leafy by-lane I had for the last time turned my back upon her with a hasty word of denunciation, we had been closest friends. She had played me false. My hopes had been wrecked on Life's strange and trackless sea, and now whenever I thought of her it was only in bitterness. I have more than a suspicion that old Mr Blain did not approve of our close acquaintanceship, knowing that I was a mere journalist with an almost untaxable income; nevertheless, she had continued to meet me, and many were the happy hours we spent together wandering through that charming country that skirts the upper reaches of the Thames.

In order to see her I used frequently to run down from London to my home on Saturdays and remain till Mondays. With her mother she sat in her seat in front of the Rectory pew, and as she walked down the aisle her face would be illumined by a glad light of welcome. How restful were those Sundays after the wear and tear of London life! How peaceful the days in that sleepy little village hidden away in a leafy hollow three miles from the Great Western line! After we had parted, however, I did not go home for six months. Then, on inquiry, I found that the Blains had sold their place, presumably because they were in want of money, for it was said that they had taken a smaller house facing the Thames, near Laleham, that village a little beyond Shepperton, where in the churchyard lies Matthew Arnold. From all accounts old Blain had lost heavily in speculation and had been compelled to sell his carriages and horses, dispose of many of his pictures, and even part with some of the Louis Seize furniture at Shenley Court, where they had lived. This was, of course, indicative of a very severe reverse of fortune.

Since those hours of Mary's love and her subsequent falseness, my life had been a queer series of ups and downs, as it must ever be in journalistic London. Many dreary days of changeful care had come and gone since then.

I sat silent, thinking, with her letter still open in my hand.

"Why are you so confoundedly glum, old man?" Dick asked. "What's your screed about? Duns in the offing?"

"No. It's nothing," I answered evasively, smiling.

"Then don't look so down in the mouth," he urged. "Have a peg, and pull yourself together." He had been in India, and consequently termed a whisky-and-soda a "peg." The origin of that expression is a little abstruse, but is supposed to refer pointedly to the pegs in one's coffin.

I thrust the letter into my pocket, helped myself to a drink, and lit a cigarette.

"It's a really first-class sensation," Dick said, again referring to the curious affair. "Pity I can't publish something of it to-morrow. It's a good thing chucked away."

"Yes," I replied. "But Patterson has some object in imposing secrecy on us."

"Of course," he answered thoughtfully.

There was a pause. We both smoked on. Not a sound penetrated there save the solemn ticking of the clock and the distant strains of a piano in some man's rooms across the square.

"Do you know, Frank," my companion said after some reflection, and looking at me with a rather curious expression — "do you know that I have some strange misgivings?"

"Misgivings!" I echoed. "Of what?"

"Well," he said, "did anything strike you as strange in Patterson's manner?"

"To tell the truth," I answered, "something did. His attitude was unusual — quite unusual, to-night."

"He's a funny Johnnie. That story of the snake on the pavement — isn't it rather too strange to be believed?"

"At first sight it appears extraordinary, but remember that in the laboratory upstairs we found other snakes. The occupier of the house evidently went in for the reptiles as pets."

"I quite agree with you there," he said. "But there are certain circumstances in the case which have aroused my suspicion, old chap. Of all the curious cases I've ever investigated while I've been on the *Comet*, this is the most astounding from every point of view, and I, for one, shan't rest until we've fully solved the problem."

"In that you'll have my heartiest assistance," I said. "All the time I can spare away from the office I'll devote to helping you."

"Good," Dick exclaimed heartily, refilling his pipe. "Between us we ought to find out something, for you and I can get at the bottom of things as soon as most people."

"The two strangest features of this case," I pointed out, "are first the telephonic message, and secondly, the disappearance of the first woman we found."

"And those cards!"

"And that penny wrapped so carefully in paper!" I added. "Yes, there are fully a dozen extraordinary features connected with the affair. The whole business is an absolute puzzle."

"Tell me, old chap," Dick said, after a pause, "what causes you to suspect Patterson?"

"I don't suspect him," I answered quickly. "No. I merely think that he has not told the exact truth of the first discovery of the crime, that's all."

"Exactly my own opinion," responded Dick. "He's concealing some very important fact from us — for what purpose we can't yet tell. There's more in this than we surmise. Of that I feel absolutely confident."

"The snake story is a little too good," I said, rather surprised that his suspicions should have been aroused, for I had not related to him my conversation with Patterson and his very lame excuse for not making a report of the discovery at the police-station. What had aroused Dick's suspicions I was extremely puzzled to know. But he was a shrewd, clever fellow, whose greatest delight was the investigation of crime and the obtaining of those "revelations" which middle-class London so eagerly devours.

"A very happy invention of an ingenious mind, my dear fellow," exclaimed the Mystery-monger. "Depend upon it, Patterson, being already aware that there were snakes in that house, invented the story, knowing that when the place was searched it would appear quite circumstantial."

"Then you think that he's not in absolute ignorance of who lived there?" I exclaimed, surprised at my friend's startling theory.

Dick nodded.

"I shouldn't be surprised if it be proved that he knew all along who the dead man is."

"Why?"

"Well, I noticed that he never once looked at that man's face. It was he who covered it with a handkerchief, as though the sight of the white countenance appalled him."

"Come come," I said, "proceed. You'll say that he's the guilty one next."

"Ah! no, my dear fellow," he hastened to reassure me. "You quite misunderstand my meaning. I hold the theory that in life these people were friends of Patterson's, that's all."

"What makes you suspect such a thing?"

"Well, I watched our friend very closely this evening, and that's the conclusion I've arrived at."

"You really think that he is concealing facts which might throw light on the affair?" I exclaimed, much surprised.

"Yes," he answered, "I feel certain of it — absolutely certain."

Chapter Six
What I Saw in the Park

For a long time, sitting by the open window and looking out upon the starry night, we discussed the grim affair in all its details. The piano had stopped its tinkling, a dead silence had fallen upon the old-world square, one of the relics of bygone London, and the clock upon the hall had struck one o'clock with that solemnity which does not fail to impress even the most dissipated resident of Gray's. As a bachelor abode Gray's Inn is as comfortable and convenient a spot as there is in London, for there is always a quiet, restful air within; the grey, smoke-stained houses open on airy squares, and until a couple of years ago, quite a large colony of rooks made their home in the great old trees. It is an oasis of peace and repose in the very centre of that gigantic fevered city, where the whirl of daily life is unceasing, where in the east and south toiling millions struggle fiercely for their bread, while in the west is greater wealth and extravagance than in all the world besides.

"I think," said Dick at last, after he had put forth one or two theories, "that if we manage to get to the bottom of this affair we shall discover some very startling facts."

"That's absolutely certain," I answered. "The disappearance of the fair girl, and the substitution of the other, is in itself a fact absolutely unique in the annals of crime. Whoever effected that change must have been indeed a bold person."

"Didn't the people next door see any taxi drive up, or notice anything being brought up to the house?"

"No. That's the strangest part of it," I responded. "Nothing was seen of any cab or conveyance, although, of course, there must have been one."

"And that inquiry by telephone was a remarkable incident," Dick went on. "You say that the inquirer was popping about to various call-rooms ringing up his confederates. That shows that there were two or three in the secret. It hardly seems feasible that the man who rang up from the Minories was the same as the one with whom you spoke at Putney."

"No; but the arrangement to meet in St. James's Park to-morrow is extraordinary, to say the least."

"Ah, my dear fellow," observed my friend, with a smile, "I very much fear that that appointment won't be kept. Men such as they evidently are will hardly risk a meeting. On reflection, the individual, whoever he is, will see that he has given himself away, and his natural caution will prevent him from going near St. James's Park."

"Well, I only hope he does meet me," I observed.

"So do I. But to my mind such a circumstance is entirely out of the question. You see he went to call-boxes in order to avoid detection."

"The curious thing is, that if it were the same man who rang up each time he must have travelled from one place to another in an amazingly rapid manner."

"There might be two persons," he suggested.

"Of course there might," I answered. "But I think not. The girl at the exchange evidently recognised the voice of the persistent inquirer."

"I'm glad I came down — very glad," he said. "I went over to see Lily, but she's gone to Ipswich with her aunt, an old lady who feared to travel alone. It appears she wrote to me this morning, but the letter has missed the post, I suppose. It will come to-morrow morning."

"You had your journey to Peckham for nothing, then?"

"Yes," he answered. "She ought to have sent me a wire. Just like a woman."

I knew Lily Lowry, the pretty friend of Dick Cleugh, very well indeed. I did not know that he actually loved her. There was undoubtedly a mutual friendship between them, but nevertheless he often would go for a month and see nothing of her. The daughter of a struggling shopkeeper near the *Elephant and Castle*, she had been compelled to seek her own living, and was at present assistant at a large cheap draper's in Rye Lane, Peckham. Setting the *convenances* at naught, as became a London girl of the present decade, she had many times visited our dingy abode. I had always suspected that the love was on her side, for she was always giving him various little things — embroidered pouches, handkerchiefs and those semi-useful articles with which girls delight the men they love.

But Dick did not seem in the least concerned at not having seen her. He was annoyed that he had had a journey on the Chatham and Dover for nothing, and thought a great deed more of the mystery of Phillimore Place than of Lily's well-being. He was a pessimist in every sense of the word. Once he had told me the story of his first love, a strange tragedy of his life that had occurred in his days at Jesus. It was this, I always suspected, that had evoked from him the real ardent affection which a man should have for a woman who is to be his companion through life. Man loves but once, it is true, but the love of youth is in the generality of cases a mere heart-beating caused by a fantasy begotten of inexperience. The woman we love at sixteen — too often some kind-hearted housewife, whose soft speech we mistake for affection — we flout when we are twenty. The woman who was angelic in our eyes when in our teens, is old, fat and ugly when, four years later, the glamour has fallen from our eyes and we begin to find a foothold in the world. Wisdom comes with the moustache.

So it was with Dick. He had lost the woman he had loved in his college days, yet, as far as I could judge, none other had ever taken her place in his heart.

Two o'clock had struck ere we turned in, and both of us were up at seven, our usual hour, for evening papers, issued as they are at noon, are prepared early in the morning. We were always at our respective offices at half-past seven.

My first thought was of the meeting I had arranged in St. James's Park, and of my friend's misgivings regarding it. Full of anxiety, I worked on till eleven o'clock, when Boyd was shown into my room, greeting me merrily. His appearance was in no way that of a police-officer, for he wore a shabby suit of tweed, a soiled collar, and an old silk hat much frayed at the brim, presenting the appearance of the typical beery Fleet Street lounger.

"I've come to see you, Mr Urwin, regarding this meeting in the park," he said. "Do you intend going?"

"Of course," I answered, surprised that he should ask such a question. "Why?"

"Well, because I think it would be best to leave it entirely to us. You might be indiscreet and queer the whole thing."

"I don't think you'll find me guilty of any indiscretion," I said, somewhat piqued.

"I don't apprehend that," he said. "But on seeing you at the spot appointed, the mysterious person who made the inquiry last night will at once get away, for he will know that the secret is out. We must, as you know, act with greatest caution in this affair, so as not to arouse the slightest suspicion that the keeping of this appointment is in the hands of the police."

"Then what, in your opinion, is the best course to pursue?" I inquired.

"First, your friend Mr Cleugh must not go near the park. I've already written him a note to that effect. Secondly, you must act exactly as I direct. A single slip will mean that the individual will escape, and in this we must not court failure by any indiscreet move."

"And how do you intend that I should act?" I asked, sitting back in my writing-chair and looking at the shrewd detective who was known throughout London as one of the cleverest unravellers of crime, and who had been successful in so many cases wherein human life had been involved.

"Well," he said, hesitating, "truth to tell, I would rather that you didn't go to the park at all."
"Why?"

"Because you could not wait about in the vicinity of the spot indicated without betraying a sign that you were in expectation of some one," he answered. "Remember, you are not a detective."

"No," I answered, "I'm not a detective, but I've had a few years' training in investigations. I think I could disguise my anxiety sufficiently."

I was extremely anxious to keep the appointment, and his suggestion that I should not go caused me disappointment and annoyance.

"But if you were seen waiting about, the man we want would certainly not make his appearance. He'd scent danger at once. We've evidently got to deal with a very cunning scoundrel."

"I could conceal myself," I declared. "I promise you I will act with greatest discretion."

"Well," he said at length, after some further demur, "I suppose, then, you must have your own way. Personally, I don't think the man will be such a fool as to run his neck into a noose. There's been some clever work in connexion with this matter, and men capable of such ingenuity must be veritable artists in crime and not given to the committal of any indiscretion. The voice in the telephone was a squeaky one, I think you said?"

"Yes, weak and thin, like an old man's."

Boyd glanced at his watch — a gold hunter with an inscription. It had been given him by public subscription in Hampstead in recognition of his bravery in capturing two armed burglars in Fitzjohn's Avenue.

"It's time we went," he exclaimed; but as we rose Dick entered in hot haste. He had just received Boyd's note and had run round to my office.

"I've been out making an inquiry," he said, having greeted us and expressed disappointment at Boyd's decision. "I thought, in order to satisfy myself, and so that I could use the information later on, I would go round to Professor Braithwaite at the Royal Institution and ask his opinion of the scientific apparatus found in the laboratory. I went down to Patterson, got permission to remove it from the house, and took the whole affair in a cab to the Royal Institution."

"Well, what's the result?" I inquired breathlessly.

"The result?" he answered. "Why, the old Johnnie, when he saw the paraphernalia, stood dumbfounded, and when he put it together and commenced experimenting seemed speechless in amazement. The discovery, he declared, was among the greatest and most important of those made within the last twenty years. He sent messengers for a dozen other scientific men, who, when they saw the arrangement, examined it with great care and were equally amazed with old Braithwaite. All were extremely anxious as to the identity of the discoverer of this mode of liquefying almost the last of the refractory gases, but I, of course, held my tongue for a most excellent reason — I did not myself know. I merely explained that the apparatus had fallen into my hands accidentally and I wished to ascertain its use."

"Then quite a flutter has been caused among these dry-as-dust old fossils," I observed, laughing.

"A flutter!" Dick echoed. "Why, the whole of the scientific world will be in a state of highest excitement to-morrow when the truth becomes known. Old Braithwaite declared that the discoverer deserves an immediate knighthood."

"Let's be off," Boyd said. He took no interest in the discovery. Like myself, his only object was to solve the mystery.

"Then I'm not to go?" Dick said inquiringly.

"No," the detective replied. "I'm sorry, but a crowd of us will queer the thing. You shall have all the details later. Patterson has promised that you shall publish first news of the affair."

Dick was sorely disappointed, I saw it in his face; nevertheless, with a light laugh he wished us goodbye when we emerged into Fleet Street, and hurried away back to the offices of the *Comet*, while Boyd and myself jumped into a hansom outside St. Dunstan's Church, and drove along Pall Mall as far as St. James's Palace, where we alighted and entered the park. The detective explained his tactics during the drive. They were that we should separate immediately on entering the park, and that he should go alone to the spot indicated by the mysterious voice, while I idled in the vicinity. I was to act just as I pleased, but we were not to recognise one another either by look or sign.

I own, therefore, that it was with considerable trepidation that I left the detective on entering the Mall and wandered slowly along beneath the trees, while he crossed and entered the park himself. In that thoroughfare, which forms a short and pleasant cut for taxis going eastward from Victoria station, there was considerable traffic at that hour. The sky was blue, and the June sun shone warmly through the trees, giving the Londoner a foretaste of summer, and causing him to think of straw hats, flannels and holiday diversions. A bright day in a London park at once arouses thoughts of the country or the sea. With my face set towards the long, regular façade of Buckingham Palace — a grey picture with little artistic touches of red, the scarlet coats of the Guards — I wondered what would be the outcome of this attempt to obtain a clue. That thin squeaky voice sounded in my ear as distinctly at that moment as it had done on the previous night, a weird summons from one unknown.

At last, just as Big Ben, showing high across the trees, chimed and boomed forth the hour of noon, I entered one of the small gates of the park and strolled along the gravelled walk down to the edge of the ornamental water, where, for some minutes, I stood watching a group of children feeding the water-fowl.

Though trying to look unconcerned, my eyes were ever on the alert. I had expected to see Boyd, but there was no sign of him, therefore I strolled along, passing the end of the water, the exact spot indicated. There was no one there beyond half a dozen school children feeding the birds with portions of dinners brought with them from distant homes.

Undecided whether to halt there, I kept my attention fixed upon the children, then, fearing to annoy Boyd by remaining at that point, I strolled slowly along the shore in the direction of Birdcage Walk. The detective had certainly concealed himself successfully, for although I kept my eyes on the watch I could discover no sign of him.

The hour of the appointment had passed, but, not daring to turn back to look, I kept straight on, until, at some distance beyond, I came to a seat beside the path and there I rested, drawing a newspaper from my pocket and pretending to read. Unfortunately, from where I sat, at a point opposite the Wellington Barracks, I could obtain no view of the meeting-place, and although Big Ben struck the quarter I was compelled to remain there inactive, watching furtively the few passers-by.

With a diligence perhaps unworthy of a journalist I read and re-read my newspaper for nearly half an hour, and in the course of that time the people who went along did not number a dozen. Of none of these did I entertain any suspicion. They included a couple of soldiers, two or three old women, a lady with a small child, a couple of nurses with children, a park-keeper, and a bank clerk with his wallet chained to his belt.

Secreted somewhere in the vicinity, Boyd was watching, but where I knew not. His surmise had unfortunately proved correct, I reflected, as the half-hour chimed. The man, whoever he was, was no fool.

For five minutes longer I remained, when a sudden impatience seized me, and I folded my paper and rose.

As I did so there came round the bend of the path, from the direction of the spot the mysterious voice had indicated, a slim figure in deep mourning, evidently a lady. She walked with an even swinging gait, not as one who was idling there, but as though with some fixed purpose. On her approach I saw that she was attired entirely in black, wearing a dress of the latest mode, the wide skirt of which rustled as she walked; a large hat with swaying feathers which at that moment struck me as somewhat funereal, and a thick spotted veil. Her black silk sunshade she carried on her arm, and as she came nearer I could not help being struck by her neatness of figure, her small waist, wide hips and well-moulded bust.

I lingered at the seat to brush the dust from my coat, so that she might pass and allow me a glance of her face.

She went by with a loud frou-frou of silken underskirt, and at that same instant I turned my gaze upon her and looked into her face.

Next second I drew back, startled and aghast.

Her hair was fair, her eyes large and blue, her features familiar. Even that thick veil could not conceal her marvellous beauty.

I looked again, believing it to be some chimera of my disordered imagination.

No. There was no mistake. It was an astounding, inexplicable truth.

She was the woman I had discovered cold and dead in that house in Kensington on the previous night — the woman whose body had so strangely disappeared.

For a few moments I stood rooted to the spot. The discovery held me petrified.

Then, with sudden resolve, I moved forward and followed her.

Chapter Seven
Eva Glaslyn

I glanced behind me, but saw no sign of Boyd. Of a sudden it crossed my mind that he had not been present at our first discovery; therefore, expecting a man to keep the appointment, he had allowed her to pass the spot unnoticed.

The appearance of that neat figure before me, the figure of the woman over whose beauty I had mourned as dead, was in itself a most startling fact, adding still another feature to the already dark and inscrutable mystery. I wanted to have a word with Boyd and ask his advice, for I knew not how to act in such unexpected circumstances. One of the victims was actually keeping an appointment with an accomplice of the assassin, for there seemed no doubt that murder had been committed by some secret means.

When she passed me I noticed the queer, half-suspicious glance she cast at me with those large blue eyes of hers, a glance in which anxiety was mingled with terror and despair. Evidently she had sought some one whom she had not been able to find, and was disappointed in consequence. With the silhouette of her figure before me like some phantom which I was endeavouring to chase in vain, I strolled on at a respectable distance, endeavouring to look unconcerned. I saw what a strikingly smart figure hers was; how slim the waist, how wide and well-rounded the hips, and how through the bodice of her dress was shown the outline of those narrow French corsets, mere bands for the waist which only women with superb figures ever dare to wear. Her skirt of fine black cloth hung in folds unusually graceful, for London skirts are always more or less "bunchy," dragging behind and rising in front, unless made by the first-class houses in Regent Street or Bond Street. London dressmakers cannot cut a skirt well. But her gown was a model of simplicity and good fit, evidently the "creation" of some expensive ladies' tailor.

Her hair, in the full light of day, was not golden brown as I had believed it to be, but really auburn, and her black hat suited her admirably. From moment to moment I feared lest she should glance back and discover me following her, but fortunately she kept straight on at the same even pace, passing out of the park by Storey's Gate, and continuing along Great George Street until she entered the bustle of Parliament Street. Here, fearing she might escape me, I was compelled to approach nearer, at risk of being discovered, and even then was still utterly undecided how to act. My first impulse was, to walk up to her, introduce myself and tell her of the circumstances in which I had discovered her in that house, apparently lifeless. On reflection, however, I judged that by her presence in the park she was acquainted with the assassin or his associate, and that by keeping close watch upon her I might discover more than by at once exposing my hand. There seemed in her very appearance, in that deep mourning, something grim, weird, mysterious.

At the corner of Parliament Street, outside the steamy tea-rooms, she stood for a few moments gazing anxiously up and down, as if in search of an omnibus. A man approached her, crying the second edition of the *Comet*, a copy of which she purchased eagerly, folding it small and placing it within the folds of her sunshade.

Why had she done that? I wondered. Did she expect to find in that paper an exposure of the secret tragedy of the previous night?

I stood reading some excursion time-tables outside the railway booking-office on the opposite corner, watching her furtively. From her manner I could plainly see how nervous and excited she was.

After some hesitation she turned and walked along to King Street, where she entered the telegraph office and dispatched a telegram. She evidently knew that part of London, or she would not have known the whereabouts of that office hidden down the short side street. I waited in Parliament Street until her return, and unnoticed strode back behind her to the corner of Bridge Street, where she at length entered a taxi and drove off.

From the telegram I might, I thought, obtain some clue, but, alas! telegrams are secret, and I should be unable to get a glance at it. To apply at the office would be useless. The police might perhaps obtain permission to read it, but so many dispatches are daily handed in there that to trace any particular one is always a difficult matter.

I was divided in my impulses. Should I go back to King Street and make instant application regarding the telegram, so that it might be marked and easily traced afterwards, or should I follow the taxi which at that moment was crossing Westminster Bridge?

I decided upon the latter course, and jumping into another motor, pointed out the taxi I desired to follow.

Our drive was not a long one — only to Waterloo Station, the busy platform of the loop line. Here I could easily conceal myself in the crowd of persons every moment arriving and departing, and as I stood near the booking-office, I heard her ask for a first-class ticket to Fulwell, a rather pleasant and comparatively new suburban district between Twickenham and Hampton.

The Shepperton train was already in the station, therefore she at once took her seat, while I entered another compartment in the front of the train. I did this in order to be able to alight quickly, leave the station before her, and thus avoid recognition. The journey occupied about three-quarters of a hour, but at length we drew into the little rural station situated in a deep cutting, and ere the train stopped I sprang out, passed the barrier and leaped up the steps, escaping ere the gate was closed by the ticket inspector. By this quick movement I gained several minutes upon her, for the barrier was closed, and alighting passengers were not allowed to leave before the train had again moved off.

The high road from London opened right and left, one way leading back to Strawberry Hill, the other out to New Hampton. I felt certain that she would walk in the direction of the latter place, therefore I started off briskly until I came to a small wayside inn, which I entered, and going to the window of the bar-parlour called for refreshment, at the same time keeping a keen look-out for her passing.

Several persons who had come by train hurried by, and at first I believed she had taken the opposite direction. But at last she came, holding her skirts daintily and picking her way, for it had been raining and the path was muddy. She, however, was not alone.

By her side walked a young rather handsome man about twenty-five, who wore tennis flannels, and who had apparently met her at the station. She was laughing merrily as she passed, while he strode on with a light, airy footstep indicative of happiness.

"There's a lady just gone past," I exclaimed quickly, turning to the innkeeper's wife, who had just brought in my glass of beer. "I often see her about. Do you know who she is?"

With woman's curiosity she went to the door and looked out after her.

"Oh, that's Lady Glaslyn's daughter," she said.

"Lady Glaslyn's daughter!" I echoed in surprise.

"Yes, it's Miss Eva, and the young gent with her is Fred Langdale, the son of the great sugar-refiner up in London. They both live here, close by. Lady Glaslyn, a widow, is not at all well off, and lives along at The Hollies, the big white house with a garden in front on this side of the way, while the Langdales have a house further on the road to Hampton, overlooking Bushey Park."

"Oh, that's who they are!" I said quite unconcernedly, but secretly delighted with this information. "And who is this Lady Glaslyn? Has she lived here long?"

"Nearly a year now," the good woman answered. Then, confidentially, she added, "They are come-down swells, I fancy. That they've got no money is very evident, for the tradespeople can't get their bills paid at all. Why, only last week, Jim Horton, the gas company's man, was in here, and I heard him tell his labourers that he'd got orders to cut the gas off at The Hollies because the bill wasn't paid."

"Then they must be pretty hard up," I observed. "Many aristocratic families come down in the world."

The name of Glaslyn puzzled me. It sounded familiar.

"Who was her ladyship's husband? Do you know?"

"No, sir. I've heard several stories. One was how that he was a baronet who led an exploring party somewhere in South America, and died of fever, and another that he was a shady individual who was connected with companies in the City. But nobody here knows the truth, I think."

A glance at Debrett or Burke when I returned to my office would quickly settle that point, I reflected; therefore, having obtained all the information I could from her I wished her good-day, and left.

Along the Hampton Road I strolled in the direction the pair had taken, and in the distance saw the mysterious Eva take leave of her companion and enter a house, while he lifted his hat and walked on. I proceeded slowly, passing The Hollies on the opposite side of the way. It was a rather large place, decidedly old-fashioned, standing back in its own grounds and approached by a carriage drive, a three-storied redbrick house with those plain windows surrounded by white wooden beams of the early Georgian era. In the old-world garden, hidden by a high wall, grew a profusion of roses and wallflowers which diffused a sweet scent as I passed, and half the house seemed hidden by ivy and creepers. The small lawn in front, with its laurels and monkey-trees, were well kept, and the place seemed spick and span, and altogether comfortable.

As I passed I fancied I saw a black-robed figure standing at one of the ground-floor windows. What if she recognised me? I dared not to look around again, but kept on my way, walking through New Hampton, past the long wall of Bushey Park, until I came to Old Hampton town, whence, half an hour later, I took train back to Waterloo.

I had, at any rate, made one discovery, which was in itself absolutely bewildering. At first I had doubted that this sweet-faced, clear-eyed woman was actually identical with the dead form that lay back in her chair on the previous night. I believe that she only bore some striking resemblance, heightened, perhaps, by the agitated state of my mind. But all doubts on this point had been set at rest by one fact. The woman whose cold hand I had grasped had worn in her bodice a brooch of unusual pattern — a tiny enamelled playing-card, a five of diamonds quaintly set in gold — and this same ornament, striking on account of its originality of design, was at the throat of Eva Glaslyn, showing plainly against the dead black of her dress.

The mystery was certainly most remarkable. In wonder how Boyd had fared, or whether Patterson had been prosecuting inquiries in other directions, I went straight to Kensington from Waterloo, and found the inspector in his room over the police-station. It was a small apartment with drab-painted walls, plainly furnished as police-stations are. The table whereat he sat was littered with papers, mostly pale straw-colour, and on the mantelshelf stood an interesting collection of photographs of people "wanted," each bearing a number in red ink corresponding to the index book, wherein a short account of their crime was recorded.

"Why," he cried, as I entered, "wherever have you been? I've been hunting high and low for you."

"I've been down to Hampton," I laughed.

"To Hampton!" he echoed. "What on earth have you been doing down there?"

"Making inquiries," I answered, affecting an air of unconcern. "I've made a rather queer discovery."

"What is it?" he asked, as I took a seat before him.

"I've found the woman whom Patterson and I discovered dead last night, and the strangest part about it is that she's alive and quite well."

"My dear fellow, are you mad?" he asked, looking at me strangely. "People aren't in the habit of coming to life again, you know."

"I'm well aware of that," I responded. "Nevertheless, the fact remains that the woman seen by Patterson and by myself is actually alive. I met her in the park, and followed her home to New Hampton."

"Met her in the park!" he cried. "There was one woman I noticed, fair-haired, and dressed in black."

"The same," I answered. "Fortunately I recognised her and kept her under observation."

Then, in response to his demand, I related to him the whole circumstance in detail.

"And her name?" he inquired, when I had concluded.

"Eva Glaslyn, daughter of Lady Glaslyn."

"Glaslyn!" he ejaculated. "Good heavens! Surely it can't be the same!"

"Why the same?" I inquired.

"Oh, nothing!" he answered evasively, quickly seeking to allay my suspicions. "There was some mystery, or scandal, or something connected with that family once, if I recollect aright. I may, however, be mistaken in the name. At any rate, Mr Urwin, you've acted with tact and discretion, and discovered a most important fact."

"What have you been doing?" I asked.

"Well," he answered in hesitation, "the fact is, I've had a somewhat exciting experience."

"Did you, then, discover the man?" I inquired anxiously.

"I met a man, but whether he was the one who made the appointment by telephone I don't yet know," he said. "I waited until a quarter to one, concealed behind some bushes, and presently saw a grey-haired old gentleman, well-dressed in frock coat, and silk hat, strolling in my direction. He was quite a dandy with well-pressed trousers, varnished boots, gold-headed cane and single eyeglass. His air was that of a lawyer or doctor. As if in search of some one he lingered in the vicinity, subsequently sitting upon a seat at the very end of the lake, the exact spot which had been indicated."

"And what did you do?"

"I waited and watched. There was no one near, yet from his sharp glances in all directions I saw that he was in fear lest some one might approach whom he didn't wish to see. He appeared violently agitated, and at last, when he was entirely alone, he placed his hand into his inner pocket, took out something, and rising from the seat with a swift movement cast the object far away into the water."

"Something he wanted to get rid of. Suspicious, wasn't it?"

"Of course," said the detective. "After that you may rest assured that I didn't lose sight of him. When the object he had thrown away had fallen into the lake he turned, and after glancing up and down in fear that his action might have been observed, he returned to his seat, and waited until Big Ben struck again. Then he rose and left the park, strolling airily along the Buckingham Palace Road, peering a good deal under the bonnets of the pretty women who were looking in the windows of the shops. He entered the bar of Victoria Station, drank a whisky-and-soda, and then continuing along to Ebury Street passed twice or three times up and down in front of a house on the left-hand side. There were a number of people in that street at the time, but the instant he thought himself unobserved, he dived down the area of the house he kept passing and repassing. In a moment I noted that the number was twenty-two, and having done so placed a watch upon the house, well satisfied that I had taken the first step towards unravelling the mystery."

"Remarkable," I said, "I wonder what it was he threw away?"

"That's impossible to tell without dragging the lake, and to do that at present would excite suspicion. He evidently went there in order to meet the assassin, but as the latter did not keep the appointment, this unknown object, which might prove convicting if found upon him, he resolved to get rid of, and no better place could there be than at the bottom of the lake. There's lots of pieces of evidence there, you bet."

"Then there must be some mysterious connexion between the appearance of Eva Glaslyn at that spot and this man who got rid of some evidence of the crime," I observed.

"Most certainly," the detective said. "It almost seems as though she came there for the purpose of meeting him, but he being late she grew impatient and left before his arrival. At every step we take the enigma becomes more complicated, more extraordinary, more bewildering."

Chapter Eight
Some Remarkable Evidence

Three days went by, days full of wonder and anxiety.

Many were the discussions between Patterson, Dick and myself regarding the extraordinary development of the mystery which had now resolved itself into as complete a puzzle as ever occupied the attention of Scotland Yard. In Ebury Street and at Hampton most careful observation was being carried on night and day, but according to Boyd absolutely nothing suspicious could be discovered. Lady Glaslyn was, according to Debrett, widow of a Sir Henry Glaslyn, a Scotch baronet who had died several years before, leaving no heir to continue the title, and only one daughter, Eva.

In the meantime the bodies of the man and the woman had been removed to the mortuary secretly in the early hours of the morning in order not to arouse the suspicion of the neighbours, and a post-mortem had been held by two local doctors, with the result that it was found possible to hold the inquest on the afternoon of the third day. The Coroner held his inquiry in a small back room in the Kensington Town Hall, not far from the scene of the tragedy, and, in opening, made a short address to the jury, pointing out the necessity for preserving the utmost secrecy in the matter, and expressing a hope that no one present would defeat the ends of justice by giving any facts to the newspapers.

"Pardon me, sir," exclaimed the tradesman who had been elected foreman, "but I see two gentlemen of the Press present."

"Both have assisted us in our inquiries," Patterson briefly explained to the Coroner.

"Of course," the Coroner answered, "this is a public court, and therefore we cannot exclude any one. Yet I am confident the reporters will respect my wishes."

This we both promised to do, Cleugh, well-known to the Coroner, speaking first.

The Coroner, when the jury had returned from viewing the bodies, made a few further observations, pointing out to the jury that although the affair was one of the most mysterious and inexplicable that had ever come beneath his notice in the course of his twenty years' experience as a London coroner, yet they were there to try and decide the cause of death alone. They had no concern with any other facts except the cause of death, and he trusted they would give the matter their undivided attention.

Patterson was the first witness. In terse language he gave an account of his discovery and of his second visit to the house in my company. Then, when he had concluded, I was called and bore out his statement, relating how we had entered the laboratory and found the marvellous scientific apparatus, and how in the pocket of the dead man I had found a penny wrapped in paper. The cards with the strange devices which had been beneath the plates on the dining-table were handed round to the jury for their inspection, and then a statement which I made startled even the Coroner. It was how the body of the woman at present in the mortuary was not the same as the one we had at first discovered.

"Impossible!" exclaimed the Coroner, while the twelve jurymen stood aghast at my statement.

"That is quite true, sir," exclaimed Patterson, rising from his seat. "The lady we first discovered was younger, with fair hair."

"Then there must have been a triple tragedy," observed the Coroner, astounded. "This is most extraordinary."

I was about to explain how I had recognised in the girl I met in St. James's Park the identical woman whom we had discovered lifeless, but a sharp look from the inspector silenced me.

"We are making diligent inquiries," the officer went on, "and we have reason to believe that we shall be able to make a further statement later — at the adjourned inquiry."

The Coroner nodded, and turning to the jury, said —

"Of course, gentlemen, it would not be wise at this stage for the police to disclose any of the information in their possession. Their success in such matters as this mainly depends upon secrecy. I think we may now, perhaps, hear the medical evidence."

The jury stirred uneasily and settled themselves to listen intently as Dr Lees Knowles, the police divisional surgeon, stepped forward and was sworn.

"I was called by the police to the house," he said, "and found there two deceased persons, a man and a woman, in the drawing-room on the first floor. The attire of the man was rather disarranged, as the police had already searched him, but there were no signs whatever of a struggle."

"You made a cursory examination, of course," suggested the Coroner.

"Yes. Life had been extinct sometime, and *rigor mortis* had commenced. There was, however, no external sign of foul play."

"And the post-rnortem?"

The Court was silent in anxious anticipation of the doctor's response.

"Assisted by Doctor Lynes I made a post-mortem, but found absolutely nothing to account for death. There was no mark of violence on either of the bodies, and no physical defect or slightest trace of disease. Nevertheless, the position of the bodies when found makes it evident that both persons died with great suddenness, and without being able to obtain assistance."

"Was there nothing whatever to give any clue to the cause of death?" asked the Coroner, himself a medical man.

"Nothing," responded the surgeon. "One thing, however, struck us as peculiar. On the inside of the right forearm of both the man and the woman were identical tattoo marks. The device, nearly an inch in diameter, represented a serpent with its tail in its mouth, the ancient emblem of eternity. The mark on the man had evidently been traced several years ago, but that on the woman is comparatively fresh, and could not have completely healed over more than a month ago. It is as though the mark on the man has been copied upon the woman."

"And what do you think is the signification of this mark?" inquired the Coroner, looking up from the blue foolscap whereon he had been writing down the depositions.

"I'm utterly at a loss to know," the doctor answered. "Yet it is very curious that upon one of these cards we found beneath the plates there is a circle drawn, while it also seemed that snakes were kept in the house as pets. To my mind all three circumstances have some connecting significance."

The jury bent together and conversed in whispers. This theory of the doctor's seemed to possess a good deal of truth, even though the mystery was increased rather than diminished.

Many more questions were put to the doctor, after which his colleague, Dr Lynes, was called, and corroborated the police surgeon's evidence. He, too, was utterly unable to ascribe any fatal cause. The tattoo marks had puzzled him, but he suggested that the man and woman might be husband and wife, and that in a freak of caprice, to which women of some temperaments are subject, she had caused the device on her husband's arm to be copied upon her own. Opinions were, however, divided as to whether the pair were husband and wife. For my own part I did not regard his theory as a sound one.

"You did not overlook the contents of the stomach, of course?" the Coroner exclaimed.

"No, we sent them in sealed bottles to Dr Marston, the analyst of the Home Office."

"And have we his report?" inquired the Coroner.

"Dr Marston is here himself, sir. He has come to give evidence," Patterson answered from the back of the room, while at the same time an old grey-haired gentleman in gold-rimmed spectacles rose, and walking forward took the oath.

"You received from the previous witnesses two bottles?" suggested the Coroner. "Will you please tell us the result of your analysis?"

"I tested carefully with group reagents for every known poison, and also for ptomaine," he said, "but all the solvents — alcohol, benzol, naphtha, ammonia and so forth — failed. I tested for the alkaloids, such as strychnine, digitalin, and cantharidin, and used hydrochloric acid to find either silver, mercury or lead, and also ammonia in an endeavour to trace tin, cadmium or arsenic. To none of the known groups does the poison — if poison there be — belong. Therefore I have been utterly unable to arrive at any definite conclusion."

"Is there no direct trace of any poison?"

"None," was the answer. "Yet from the result of certain group reagents it would appear that death was due to the virulence of some azotic substance."

"You cannot, we take it, decide what that substance was?"

"Unfortunately, no," the renowned analyst answered, apparently annoyed at having to thus publicly acknowledge his failure. "The state of the stomach of either person was not such as might cause death. Indeed, there was only a secondary and most faint trace of the unknown substance to which I have referred."

"Then, to put it quite plainly," said the Coroner, "it is your opinion that they were poisoned?"

"I can scarcely go so far as that," the witness responded. "All I can say in evidence is that I found a slight trace of some deleterious substance which all tests refused to clearly reveal. Whether it were an actual poison which resulted in death I hesitate to say, as the result of my analysis is not sufficiently clear to warrant any direct allegation."

"Do you suggest that this substance, whatever it was, must have been baneful and injurious to the human system?"

"I think so. Even that, however, is not absolutely certain. As you know, certain poisons in infinitesimal quantities are exceedingly beneficial."

"Then we must take it that, presuming these two persons actually died of poison, it must have been by a poison unknown in toxicology?" observed the Coroner.

"Exactly," the analyst responded, standing with his hands behind his back and peering through his spectacles at the expectant jury.

The Coroner invited the jury to ask any questions of the analyst, but the twelve Kensington tradesmen feared to put any query to the man who had the science of poisoning thus at his fingers' ends, and whose analyses were always thorough and absolutely beyond dispute. He was the greatest authority on poisons, and they could think of nothing further to ask him. Therefore the Coroner politely invited him to sign his depositions.

After he had withdrawn, the Coroner, placing down his pen, sighed, leaned back in his chair with a puzzled expression, and once more addressed the twelve men who had been "summoned and warned" before him. They had heard the evidence, he said, and it was now for them to decide whether the two persons had died from natural causes, or whether they had met with foul play. In the circumstances he acknowledged that a decision was extremely difficult on account of the many mysterious side issues connected with the affair, yet he pointed out that if they were in real doubt whether to return a verdict of natural death or of wilful murder, there was still a third course, namely, to return an open verdict of "Found dead," and thus leave the matter in the hands of the police. He was ready, of course, to adjourn the inquiry, but from what he knew of the matter, together with the evidence which had just been given, it was his honest opinion that no object could be obtained in an adjournment, and further by closing the inquest at once they would prevent any inexpedient facts leaking out to the newspapers.

The jury retired to consult in an adjoining room, and in ten minutes returned, giving an open verdict of "Found dead." Thus ended the inquiry, and while the law had been complied with, public curiosity remained unaroused, and the police were enabled to work on in secret.

With Cleugh I lingered behind, chatting with Patterson and Boyd.

"We're keeping observation at Upper Phillimore Place," Boyd explained, in response to my inquiry. "Funny thing that nobody else calls there, and that the servants have never come back."

"Have you found the snake that was in the garden?" Cleugh asked of Patterson, with a significant glance at me.

"No," he responded, rather confused. "You see any search there might arouse suspicion. Therefore we are compelled to be content with watching for the return of any one to the house."

"But you haven't yet succeeded in establishing the identity of the pair," Dick observed.

"No. That's the queerest part of it," Boyd exclaimed. "The owner of the house, a builder who has an office in Church Street, close by, says that the place was taken furnished by a Mrs Blain, who gave her address at Harwell, near Didcot. She paid six months' rent in advance."

"Harwell!" echoed Cleugh, turning to me. "Isn't that your home, Urwin?"

"Yes," I gasped. The name of Blain caused me to stand immovable.

"Why," Dick exclaimed, noticing my agitation, "what's the matter, old fellow? Do you know the Blains?"

"Yes," I managed to reply. "They must be the Blains of Shenley Court. If so, they are friends of my family."

I had never told my companion of my bygone love affair, because it had been a thing of the past before we had gone into diggings together.

"Who are they?" inquired Boyd quickly. "Tell me all you know concerning them, as we are about to prosecute inquiries in their direction."

"First, tell me the statement of the house owner," I said.

"Well, he describes Mrs Blain as a middle-aged, rather pleasant lady, who came to his office about a year ago in response to an advertisement in the *Morning Post*. She appeared most anxious to have the house, and one fact which appears to strike the old fellow as peculiar is that she took it and paid a ten-pound note as deposit without ever seeing the interior of the premises. She told him that it was for some friends of hers from abroad, and that they not having arrived she would sign the agreement and accept all responsibility."

"Anything else?"

"Yes," the detective replied. "She was accompanied by a young lady, whom old Tritton, the landlord, took to be her daughter. Now, tell me what you know."

I paused, looking at him fixedly. The disclosure that Mrs Blain was the actual holder of that house of mystery was certainly startling. It was remarkable, too, that on the very night of the crime I should receive a letter from Mary, the woman who had so long lingered in my memory. Was that, I wondered, anything more than a mere coincidence?

"I don't know that I can tell you very much about the family," I answered, determined to put him off the scent and make inquiries myself. "They were much respected when at Shenley, where they kept up a fine country house, and entertained a great deal. They were parishioners of my father, therefore I went there very often."

"Do you know Mrs Blain well?"

"Quite well."

"And her daughter?" suggested Dick, much interested. "What's she like? Pretty?"

"Passable," I answered, with affected indifference.

"Then they are not a shady family at all?" suggested the detective.

"Not in the least. That is why the fact of Mrs Blain having taken the house is so surprising."

"It may have been sub-let," Cleugh observed. "Her friends from abroad may not have arrived after all, and she might have re-let it, a circumstance which seems most likely, as no one appears to have seen her enter the place."

"At any rate it's most extraordinary," I said. Then, turning to Boyd, I asked, "Why not leave the inquiry in that quarter to me? Knowing her, I can obtain information far more easily than you can."

"Yes," Cleugh urged. "It would be a better course — much better."

"Very well," answered the detective, not, however, without some hesitation. "But be careful not to disclose too much. Try and find out one fact only — the reason she took the house. Leave all the rest to us."

I promised, and after drinking together over in the refreshment bar at High Street Station we parted, and Cleugh and I took a bus back to our chambers.

He stopped in Holborn to buy some last editions of the papers, while I hurried on, for, being terribly hungry, I wished to give old Mrs Joad early intimation of our readiness for the diurnal steak.

With my latch-key I entered our chambers. The succulent scent of grilled meat greeted my nostrils, and I strode eagerly forward shouting for the Hag.

As I entered the sitting-room I started and drew back. A quick word of apology died from my lips, for out of our single armchair there arose a tall female dark, well-fitting dress, bowing with a grace that was charming.

I saw before me, half concealed beneath a thin black veil, a smiling face eminently pretty, a tiny mouth parted to show an even row of pearly teeth, a countenance that was handsome in every feature.

That pair of eyes peering forth at me held me motionless, dumb. I stood before my visitor, confused and speechless.

Chapter Nine
The Love of Long Ago

There are hours in our lives which are apparently without importance, but which, nevertheless, exercise an influence on our destiny.

Little wonder was it that at this instant I stood before my visitor voiceless in amazement, for in her erect, neat figure I recognised the broken idol of those long-past summer days — Mary Blain.

Of all persons she was the one I most desired at that moment to meet. Her letter to me, and her presence in my chambers that evening, were two facts that appeared pre-arranged with some ulterior motive rather than mere coincidence. Not an hour before Boyd had made a most puzzling statement regarding her mother, and here she was, confronting me with that smile I knew so well, as if anxious to make explanation.

"I believe I've startled you, Frank," she exclaimed, laughing, as she held out her gloved hand in greeting. "Is it so long since we met? Perhaps it is indiscreet of me to come here to your chambers, but I wanted to see you. Mother would be furious if she knew. Why didn't you answer my letter?"

"Forgive me," I said in excuse. "I've been busy. The life of a daily journalist leaves so very little time for correspondence," and I invited her to be re-seated in our only armchair.

She shrugged her shoulders, smiling dubiously.

"You men are always adepts at the art of excuse," she remarked.

She was pretty — yes, decidedly pretty. As I sat looking at her, there came back to me vivid recollections of a day that was dead, a day when we had exchanged vows of undying affection and had wandered in secret arm-in-arm along those quiet leafy lanes. She was a girl then, and I not much more than a stripling youth. But we had both grown older now, and other ideas had sprung up in our minds, other jealousies and other loves. Almost four whole years had passed since I had last seen her. She had grown a little more plump and matronly, and in her dark, luminous eyes was a look more serious than in her old hoydenish days at Harwell. How time flies! It did not seem four years since that autumn evening when we parted in the golden sunset. Yet how great had the change been in the fortunes of her purse-proud family, and even in my own life.

There was no love between us now. None. The days were long-past since a woman's touch and words would make me colour like a girl. Even this meeting when she pressed my hand and her eyelids fluttered, did not re-stir within me the chord of love so long untouched. I had heard of her only as a flirt and fortune-hunter, and had read in the newspapers a paragraph announcing her engagement to the elder son of a millionaire ironfounder of Wigan. Nevertheless, a month ago the papers contained a further paragraph stating that the marriage arranged "would not take place." Since we had parted she had evidently been through many love adventures. Still, she was nevertheless uncommonly good-looking, with a grace of manner that was perfect.

"I've often wondered, Frank, what had become of you," she said, leaning her elbow on the table, raising her veil and looking straight into my eyes. "We were such real good friends long ago that I've never failed to entertain pleasant recollections of our friendship. Once or twice I've heard of you through your people, and have now and then read your articles in the magazines. Somehow I've felt a keen desire for a long time past to see you and have a chat."

"I feel honoured," I answered, perhaps a trifle sarcastically, for mine was but a bitter recollection. "It is certainly pleasant to think that one is remembered after these years." Then, in order to add irony to my words, I added: "I've heard you are engaged."

"I was," she responded, glancing at me sharply. "But it is broken off."

"You found some one you liked better, I presume? It is always so."

"No, not at all," she hastened to assure me. "The fact is there was very little love on either side, and we parted quite amicably."

"As amicably as we did ourselves — eh?"

"No, Frank," she said with a sudden seriousness, dropping her eyes to the table. "Do not refer to that. With years has come wisdom. We were both foolish, were we not?"

"Perhaps I was when I believed your vow to be a true one," I responded a trifle bitterly, for I had thought the summer of my life over and at an end.

"Ah, no!" she cried. "I did not come here to reopen an incident that has been so long closed. You love another woman, no doubt."

"No," I answered. "I loved you once, until you forsook me. I have not loved since."

"But I was a mere girl then," she urged. "Ours was but a midsummer madness — that you'll surely admit."

I was silent. I had believed myself proof against all sentiment in this respect, for of late I had thought little, if at all, of my lost love. Yet alone with her at that moment all the bitter past flooded upon me, my wild passion and my shattered hopes, with a vividness that stirred up a great bitterness within me. Not that I loved her now. No. On the contrary, I hated her. She had played others false and treated them just as she had treated me.

"After madness there is always a reaction," I answered, recollecting how fondly I had once loved her, and how, since the day we parted, my life, even Bohemian as it must ever be in journalistic London, was nevertheless loveless and misanthropic, the life of one whose hopes were shattered and whose joy in living had been sapped. Shenley was but the tomb of those summer recollections. I never now visited the place.

"But all this is very foolish, Frank," she exclaimed with a calm philosophical air and a smile probably meant to be coquettish. "Why recollect the past?"

"When one has loved as I once did, it is difficult to rid oneself of the memory of its sweetness or its bitterness," I said. "Your visit here has brought it all back to me — all that I have striven so long and so strenuously to forget."

She sighed. For a single instant her dark eyes met mine, and then she avoided my gaze.

"I ventured here," she explained in a low, apologetic tone, "because I believed that our youthful passion had mutually died, and that I might renew your acquaintance not as lover but as friend. If, by coming here, I have pained you, or caused you any particularly unhappy recollections, forgive me, Frank — forgive me," and she stretched forth her hand and placed it upon my arm with a gesture of deep earnestness and regret.

"Certainly, I forgive you," I answered, annoyed with myself for having thus worn my heart on my sleeve. It was foolish, I knew. That idyllic love of ours was a mere dream of youth, like the other castles in the air we build when in our teens. It was unwise to have spoken as I had, for after all, truth to tell, I was at that moment secretly glad of my freedom. And why? Because the mysterious woman, whose beauty was perfect, yet whose very existence was an enigma, had awakened within my soul a new-born love.

Since that bright morning when she had first passed me in St. James's Park my thoughts had been constantly of her. Although I had not exchanged a single word with her I loved her, and all thought of this dark-eyed woman who had once played me false had passed from me.

Thus, angry with myself at having spoken as I had, I strove to remedy whatever impression my words had made by treating my visitor with a studied courtesy, at the same time seeking to discover the real motive of her call. I recollected the mystery, together with the fact that had been elicited regarding the tenancy of the house, and felt convinced that her visit was not without some strong incentive. She either came to me in order to learn something, or else with the object of satisfying herself upon some point remaining in doubt.

This thought flashing through my troubled brain placed me on the alert, and as we with mutual eagerness changed the topic of conversation, I sat gazing into her mobile countenance, filled with ecstatic wonder.

"As you know," she chattered on, quite frankly, in her rather high-pitched key, "before we left Shenley father had some very heavy losses in the City. At first we found a smaller house simply horrible, but now we are quite used to it, and personally I'm happier there, because we are right on the river and can have such jolly boating."

"But Riverdene is not such a very small place, surely?" I said. Dick, who knew the river well, had once told me that it was a fine house situated in one of the most picturesque reaches.

"No," she laughed, "not really so very small, I suppose. But why not come down and see for yourself? Mother often speaks of you, and you know you're always welcome."

Now, in ordinary circumstances I should have refused that invitation point-blank, but when I reflected that I was bound to make certain inquiries of Mrs Blain, I, with apparent reluctance, accepted.

"Mother will be most delighted to see you. We have tennis very often, and boating always. It's awfully jolly. Come down the day after to-morrow — in the afternoon. I shall tell mother that I met you in the street and asked you down. She must, of course, never know that I came here to see you," and she laughed at her little breach of the *convenances*.

"Of course not. I won't give you away," I said. Then suddenly recollecting, I added: "May I get you a cup of tea?"

"Oh, no, thanks, really," she answered. "I've been in Regent Street to do some shopping, and I had tea there. I was on my way home, but thought that, being alone, I'd venture to try and find you."

"I'm very glad we have met," I said enthusiastically, for, truth to tell, I saw in her opportune invitation a means by which I might get at the truth I sought. There was something extremely puzzling in this allegation that the calm-mannered, affable Mrs Blain, whom I had known so well, was the actual tenant of the mysterious house in Phillimore Place. Then, looking at her steadily, I added: "In future our relations shall be, as you suggest, those of friendship, and not of affection — if you really wish."

"Of course," she replied. "It is the only sensible solution of the situation. We are both perfectly free, and there is no reason whatever why we should not remain friends — is there?"

"None at all," I said. "Tell your mother that I shall be most delighted to pay you a visit. You have a boat, I suppose?"

"Oh, yes. And a punt, too. This season I've learned to punt quite well."

I smiled.

"Because that pastime shows off the feminine figure to greatest advantage," I observed. "Girls who punt generally wear pretty brown shoes, and their dresses just a trifle short, so that as they skip from end to end of the punt they are enabled to display a discreet *soupçon of lingerie* and open-work stocking — eh?"

"Ah, no," she protested, laughing. "You're too sarcastic. Punting is really very good fun."

"For ladies, no doubt," I said. "But men prefer sculling. They've no waists to show, nor pretty flannel frocks to exhibit to the river crowd."

"Ah, Frank, you always were a little harsh in your conclusions," she sighed. "I suppose it is because you sometimes write criticisms. Critics, I have always imagined, should be old and quarrelsome persons — you are not."

"No," I responded. "But old critics too often view things through their own philosophical spectacles. The younger school take a much broader view of life. I'm not, however, a critic," I added, "I'm only a journalist."

I could hear old Mrs Joad growling to herself because the steak was ready and she could not lay the cloth because of my visitor. Meanwhile, the room had become filled to suffocation with the fumes of frizzling meat, until a blue haze seemed to hang over everything. So used was I to this choking state of things that until that moment I never noticed it. Then I quickly rose and opened the window with a word of apology that the place "smelt stuffy."

She glanced around the shabby, smoke-mellowed room, and declared that it pleased her. Of course bachelors had to shift for themselves a good deal, she said, yet this place was not at all uncomfortable. I told her of my companion who shared the chambers with me, of his genius as a journalist, and how merrily we kept house together, at which she was much interested. All girls are more or less interested in bachelors' arrangements.

Our gossip drifted mostly into the bygones — of events at Harwell, and the movements of various mutual friends, when suddenly Dick Cleugh burst into the room crying —

"I say, old chap, there's another first-class horror! Oh! I beg your pardon," he said in apology, drawing back on noticing Mary. "I didn't know you had a visitor; forgive me."

"Let me introduce you," I said, laughing at his sudden confusion. "Mr Cleugh — Miss Blain."

The pair exchanged greetings, when Cleugh, with that merry good humour that never deserted him, said —

"Ladies never come to our den, you know, Miss Blain; therefore please forgive me for blaring like a bull. Our old woman who cleans out the kennels is as deaf as a post, therefore we have contracted a habit of shouting."

"What is the horror of which you spoke?" she asked, with a forced laugh, I was looking at her at that instant and noticed how unusually pale and agitated her face had suddenly become.

"Oh, only a startling discovery in to-night's special," he answered.

"A discovery!" she gasped, "Where?"

He glanced at the paper still in his hand, while she bent forward in her chair with an eagerness impossible of concealment. Her cheeks were pallid, her eyes dark, wild-looking and brilliant.

"The affair," he said, "seems to have taken place in Loampit Vale, Lewisham."

"Ah!" she ejaculated, quite involuntarily giving vent to a sigh of relief which Cleugh, quick and observant, did not fail to notice.

My friend threw the paper aside, sniffed at the odour of burnt meat, and suggested that the Hag was endeavouring to asphyxiate us.

"The Hag!" exclaimed Mary, surprised. "Who's the Hag!"

"Old Mrs Joad," responded Dick. "We call her that, first, because she's so ugly; and secondly, because when she's cooking for us she croons to herself like the Witch of Endor."

"She certainly is decidedly ugly with that cross-eye of hers. It struck me, too, that she had an ancient and witch-like aspect when she admitted me," she laughed.

Thus we chatted on until the bell on the Hall struck seven and she rose to go, first, however, inviting Dick to accompany me to Riverdene, an invitation which he gladly accepted. Then she bade him adieu and I accompanied her out into Holborn, where I placed her in a taxi for Waterloo.

On re-entering the room, Dick's first exclamation was —

"Did you notice how her face changed when I mentioned the horror?"

"Yes," I said.

"Her name's Blain, and I presume she's the daughter of Mrs Blain who is tenant of that house in Kensington?"

I nodded.

"An old flame of yours. I remember now that you once spoke of her."

"Quite true."

"Well, old fellow," he said, "it was quite apparent when I mentioned the tragedy that she feared the discovery had been made in Kensington. Depend upon it she can, if she likes, tell us a good deal."

"Yes," I answered thoughtfully, "I agree with you entirely, Dick. I believe she can."

Chapter Ten
On the Silent Highway

Whatever might have been Mary's object in thus renewing my acquaintance at the very moment when I was about to seek her, one thing alone was apparent — she feared the revelation of the tragic affair at Kensington. There are times when men and women, whatever mastery they may possess over their countenances, must involuntarily betray joy or fear in a manner unmistakable. Those sudden and entirely unintentional words of Dick's had, for the moment, frozen her heart. And yet it was incredible that she could have any connexion with this affair, so inexplicable that Superintendent Shaw, the chief of the Criminal Investigation Department at Scotland Yard, had himself visited the house, and, according to what Boyd had told me, had expressed himself utterly bewildered.

Next day passed uneventfully, but on the following afternoon we took train to Shepperton, where at the station we found Simpson, the chauffeur who had been at Shenley, awaiting us with a smart motor-car, in which we drove along the white winding road to Riverdene.

Dick's description of the place was certainly not in the least exaggerated when he had said that it was one of the most charming old places on the Thames. Approached from the highway by a long drive through a thick belt of elms and beeches, it stood, a long, old-fashioned house, covered with honeysuckle and roses, facing the river, with a broad, well-kept lawn sloping down to the water's edge. The gardens on either side were filled with bright flowers, the high leafy trees overshadowed the house and kept it delightfully cool, and the tent on the lawn and the several hammocks slung in the shadow testified to the ease and repose of those who lived there. Many riparian residences had I seen during my frequent picnics and Sunday excursions up and down the various reaches, but for picturesqueness, perfect quiet and rural beauty, none could compare with this. I had expected to find a mere cottage, or at most a villa, the humble retreat of a half-ruined man; yet on the contrary it was a fine house, furnished with an elegance that was surprising, with men-servants and every evidence of wealth. City men, I reflected, made money fast, and without doubt old Henry Blain had regained long ago all that he had lost.

How beautiful, how tranquil was that spot, how sweet-smelling that wealth of trailing roses which entirely hid one-half the house after the dust and stuffiness of Fleet Street, the incessant rattle of traffic, and the hoarse shouting of "the winners." Beyond the lawn, which we now crossed to greet our hostess and her daughter, the river ran cool and deep, with its surface unruffled, so that the high poplars on the opposite bank were reflected into it with all their detail and colour as in a mirror. It was a warm afternoon, and during our drive the sun had beat down upon us mercilessly, but here in the shadow all was delightfully cool and refreshing. The porch of the house facing the river was one mass of yellow roses, which spread their fragrance everywhere.

Mrs Blain was seated in a wicker chair with some needlework, while Mary was lying in a *chaise-longue* reading the latest novel from Mudie's, and our footsteps falling noiselessly upon the turf, neither noticed our approach until we stood before them.

"I'm so very pleased you've come, Frank," exclaimed the elder lady, starting forward enthusiastically as she put down her work, "and I'm delighted to meet your friend. I have heard of you both several times through your father. I wonder he doesn't exchange his living with some one. He seems so very unwell of late. I've always thought that Harwell doesn't suit him."

"He has tried on several occasions, but the offers he has had are in towns in the North of England, so he prefers Berkshire," I answered.

"Well," she said, inviting us both to be seated in comfortable wicker chairs standing near, "it is really very pleasant to see you again. Mary has spoken of you, and wondered how you were so many, many times."

"I'm sure," I said, "the pleasure is mutual."

Dick, after I had introduced him to Mrs Blain, had seated himself at Mary's side and was chatting to her, while I, leaning back in my chair, looked at this woman before me and remembered the object of my visit. There was certainly nothing in her face to arouse suspicion. She was perhaps fifty, with just a sign of grey hairs, dark-eyed, with a nose of that type one associates with employers of labour. A trifle inclined to *embonpoint*, she was a typical, well-preserved Englishwoman of motherly disposition, even though by birth she was of one of the first Shropshire families, and in the days of Shenley she had been quite a prominent figure in the May flutter of London. I had liked her exceedingly, for she had shown me many kindnesses. Indeed, she had distinctly favoured the match between Mary and myself, although her husband, a bustling, busy man, had scouted the idea. This Mary herself had told me long ago in those dreamy days of sweet confidences. The thought that she was in any way implicated in the mysterious affair under investigation seemed absolutely absurd, and I laughed within myself.

She was dressed, as she always had dressed after luncheon, in black satin duchesse, a quiet elegance which I think rather created an illusion that she was stout, and as she arranged her needlework aside in order to chat to me, she sighed as matronly ladies are wont to sigh during the drowsy after-luncheon hours.

From time to time I turned and laughed with Mary as she gaily sought my opinion on this and on that. She was dressed in dark blue serge trimmed with narrow white braid, her sailor hat cast aside lying on the grass, a smart river costume of a *chic* familiar to me in the fashion-plates of the ladies' papers. As she lay back, her head pillowed on the cushion, there was in her eyes that coquettish smile, and she laughed that ringing musical laugh as of old.

A boatful of merrymakers went by, looking across, and no doubt envying us our ease, for sculling out there in the blazing sun could scarcely be a pleasure. Judging from their appearance they were shop-assistants making the best of the Thursday early-closing movement — a movement which happily gives the slaves of suburban counters opportunity for healthful recreation. The boat was laden to overflowing, and prominent in the bows was the inevitable basket of provisions and the tin kettle for making tea.

"It's too hot, as yet, to go out," Mary said, watching them. "We'll go later."

"Very well," Dick answered. "I shall be delighted. I love the river, but since my Cambridge days I've unfortunately had but little opportunity for sculling."

"You newspaper men," observed Mrs Blain, addressing me, "must have very little leisure, I think. The newspapers are always full. Isn't it very difficult to fill the pages?"

"No," I answered. "That's a common error. To every newspaper in the kingdom there comes daily sufficient news of one sort or another to fill three sheets the same size. The duty of the journalist, if, of course, he is not a reporter or leader-writer, is to make a judicious selection as to what he shall publish and what he shall omit. It is this that wears out one's brains."

"But the reporters," she continued — "I mean those men who go and hunt up details of horrors, crimes and such things — are they well paid?"

That struck me as a strange question, and I think I must have glanced at her rather inquiringly.

"They are paid as well as most professions are paid nowadays," I answered. "Better, perhaps, than some."

"And their duty is to make inquiries and scrape up all kinds of details, just like detectives, I've heard it said. Is that so?"

"Exactly," I replied. "One of the cleverest men in that branch of journalism is our friend here, Mr Cleugh."

She looked at the man I indicated, and I thought her face went slightly paler. It may, however, only have been in my imagination.

"Is he really one of those?" she inquired in a low undertone.

"Yes," I responded. "In all Fleet Street, he's the shrewdest man in hunting out the truth. He is the *Comet* man, and may claim to have originated the reporter-investigation branch of journalism."

She was silent for a few moments. Lines appeared between her eyes. Then she took up her needlework, as if to divert her thoughts.

"And Mr Blain?" I asked at last, in want of some better topic. "How is he?"

"Oh, busy as usual. He's in Paris. He went a fortnight ago upon business connected with some company he is bringing out, and has not been able to get back yet. We shall join him for a week or two, only I so much dislike the Channel crossing. Besides, it is really very pleasant here just now."

"Delightful," I answered, looking round upon the peaceful scene. At the steps, opposite where we sat, was moored a motor-boat, together with Mary's punt, a light wood one with crimson cushions, while behind us was a well-kept tennis-court.

Tea was brought after we had gossiped nearly an hour, and while we were taking it a boat suddenly drew up at the landing-stage, being hailed by Mary, who jumped up enthusiastically to welcome its occupants. These were two young men of rather dandified air and a young girl of twenty, smartly dressed, but not at all good-looking, whom I afterwards learnt was sister to the elder of her companions. When the boat was at last moored, and the trio landed amid much shouting and merriment, I was introduced to them. The name of sister and brother was Moberly, a family who lived somewhere up beyond Bell Weir, and their companion was a guest at their house.

"We thought we'd just catch you at tea, Mrs Blain," cried Doris Moberly as she sprang ashore. "And we are so frightfully thirsty."

"Come along, then," said the elder lady. "Sit down, my dear. We have it all ready."

And so the three joined us, and the circle quickly became a very merry one.

"They kept us so long in the lock that I feared tea would be all over before we arrived," young Moberly said, with a rather affected drawl. He appeared to be one of those young sprigs of the city who travel first-class, read the *Times*, and ape the aristocrat.

"Yes," Doris went on, "there was a slight collision between a barge and a launch, resulting in lots of strong language, and that delayed us, otherwise we should have been here half an hour ago."

"Did you call on the Binsteads?" Mary asked. "You know their house-boat, the *Flame*? It's moored just at the bend, half-way between the Lock and Staines Bridge."

"We passed it, but the blinds were down. They were evidently taking a nap. So we didn't hail them," Doris responded.

Then the conversation drifted upon river topics, as it always drifts with those who spend the summer days idling about the upper reaches of the Thames — of punts, motor-launches, and sailing; of the prospects of regattas and the dresses at Sunbury Lock on the previous Sunday. They were all river enthusiasts, and river enthusiasm is a malady extremely contagious with those doomed to spend the dog-days gasping in a dusty office in stifled London.

After tea followed tennis as a natural sequence, and while Moberly and his sister played with Dick and the youth who had accompanied the Moberlys, Mary and I wandered away into the wood which skirted the grounds of Riverdene. She was bright and merry, quite her old self of Shenley days, save perhaps for a graver look which now and then came to her eyes. She showed me the extent of their grounds and led me down a narrow path in the dark shadow to the bank to show me a nest of kingfishers. The spot was so peaceful and rural that one could scarcely believe one's self but twenty miles from London. The kingfisher, startled by our presence, flashed by us like a living emerald in the sunlight; black-headed buntings flitted alongside among the reeds, and the shy sedge warbler poured out his chattering imitations, while here and there we caught sight of moor-hens down in the sedge.

She had, I found, developed a love for fishing, for she took me further down where the willows trailed into the stream, and pointed out the swirl over the gravel where trout were known to lie, showed me a bush-shaped depth where she had caught many a big perch, and a long swim where, she said, were excellent roach.

"And you are happier here than you were at Shenley?" I inquired, as we were strolling back together, both bareheaded, she with her hat swinging in her hand.

"Happy? Oh, yes," and she sighed, with her eyes cast upon the ground.

"That sigh of yours does not denote happiness," I remarked, glancing at her. "What troubles you?"

"Nothing," she declared, looking up at me with a forced smile.

"It is puzzling to me, Mary," I said seriously, "that in all this time you've not married. You were engaged, yet it was broken off. Why?"

At my demand she answered, with a firmness that surprised me, "I will never marry a man I don't love — never."

"Then it was at your father's suggestion — that proposed marriage of yours?"

"Of course, I hated him."

"Surely it was unwise to allow the announcement to get into the papers, wasn't it?"

"It was my father's doing, not mine," she responded. "When it was broken off I hastened to publish the contradiction."

"On reading the first announcement," I said, "I imagined that you had at length found a man whom you loved, and that you would marry and be happy. I am sure I regret that it is not so."

"Why?" she asked, regarding me with some surprise. "Do you wish to see me married, then?"

"Not to a man you cannot love," I hastened to assure her. I was trying to learn from her the reason of her sudden renewed friendship and confidence, yet she was careful not to refer to it. Her extreme care in this particular was, in itself, suspicious.

Her effort at coquetry when at my chambers two days before made it apparent that she was prepared to accept my love, if I so desired. Yet the remembrance of Eva Glaslyn was ever in my mind. This woman at my side had once played me false, and had caused a rent in my heart which was difficult to heal. She was pretty and charming, without doubt, yet she had never been frank, even in those long-past days at Shenley. Once again I told myself that the only woman I had looked upon with thoughts of real genuine affection was the mysterious Eva, whom once, with my own eyes, I had seen cold and dead. When I reflected upon the latter fact I became puzzled almost to the verge of madness.

Yet upon me, situated as I was, devolved the duty of solving the enigma.

Life, looked at philosophically, is a long succession of chances. It is a game of hazard played by the individual against the multiform forces to which we give the name of "circumstance," with cards whose real strength is always either more or less than their face value, and which are "packed" and "forced" with an astuteness which would baffle the wiliest sharper. There are times in the game when the cards held by the mortal player have no value at all, when what seem to us kings, queens, and aces change to mere blanks; there are other moments when ignoble twos and threes flush into trumps and enable us to triumphantly sweep the board. Briefly, life is a game of roulette wherein we always play *en plein*.

As, walking at her side, I looked into her handsome face there came upon me a feeling of mournful disappointment.

Had we met like this a week before and she had spoken so softly to me I should, I verily believe, have repeated my declaration of love. But the time had passed, and all had changed. My gaze had been lost in the immensity of a pair of wondrous azure eyes. I, who tired before my time, world-weary, despondent and cynical, was angry and contemptuous at the success of my companions, had actually awakened to a new desire for life.

So I allowed this woman I had once loved to chatter on, listening to her light gossip, and now and then putting a question to her with a view to learning something of her connexion with that house of mystery. Still she told me nothing — absolutely nothing. Without apparent intention she evaded any direct question I put to her, and seemed brimming over with good spirits and merriment.

"It has been quite like old times to have a stroll and a chat with you, Frank," she declared, as we emerged at last upon the lawn, where tennis was still in progress. The sun was now declining, the shadows lengthening, and a refreshing wind was already beginning to stir the tops of the elms.

"Yes," I laughed. "Of our long walks around Harwell I have many pleasant recollections. Do you remember how secretly we used to meet, fearing the anger of your people; how sometimes I used to wait hours for you, and how we used to imagine that our love would last always?"

"Oh, yes," she answered. "I recollect, too, how I used to send you notes down by one of the stable lads, and pay him with sweets."

I laughed again.

"All that has gone by," I said. "In those days of our experience we believed that our mutual liking was actual love. Even if we now smile at our recollections, they were, nevertheless, the happiest hours of all our lives. Love is never so fervent and devoted as in early youth."

"Ah!" she answered in a serious tone. "You are quite right. I have never since those days known what it is to really love."

I glanced at her sharply. Her eyes were cast upon the ground in sudden melancholy.

Was that speech of hers a veiled declaration that she loved me still! I held my breath for an instant, then looking straight before me, saw, standing a few yards away, in conversation with Mrs Blain, a female figure in a boating costume of cream flannel braided with coral pink.

"Look?" I exclaimed, glad to avoid responding. "You have another visitor, I think."

She glanced in the direction I indicated, then hastened forward to greet the new-comer.

The slim-waisted figure turned, and next second I recognised the strikingly handsome profile of Eva Glaslyn, the mysterious woman I secretly loved with such passionate ardour and affection.

"Come, Frank, let me introduce you," Mary cried, after enthusiastically kissing her friend.

I stepped forward, and as I did so, she turned and fixed on me her large, blue laughing eyes. Not a look, not an expression of her pure countenance was altered.

As I gazed into those eyes I saw that they were as dear as the purest crystal, and that I could look through them straight into her very soul. I bowed and grasped the tiny, refined hand she held forth to me — that soft hand which I had once before touched — when it was cold and lifeless.

Chapter Eleven
Beauty at the Helm

Together we stood on the lawn near the river-bank gossiping, and as I looked into Eva's flawless face, whereon the expression had now become softened, I longed to tell her the most sacred secret of my heart. Had she, I wondered, recognised in me the man she encountered in St. James's Park when on that mysterious errand of hers? What could have been the nature of that errand? Whom did she go there to meet?

One fact was at that moment to me more curious than all others, namely, her friendship with Mrs Blain, the woman who, according to the landlord, rented that house of mystery. By the exercise of care and discretion, I might, I told myself, learn something which would perhaps lead, if not to the solution of the enigma, then to some clue upon which the police might work. But to accomplish this I should be compelled to exercise the most extreme caution, for both mother and daughter were evidently acute to detect any attempt to gain their secret, while it seemed more than probable that Eva herself — if actually aware of the affair, which was, of course, not quite certain — had some motive in keeping all knowledge of it concealed.

Who, a hundred times I wondered, was the man who, after lingering opposite Buckingham Palace, had entered the house in Ebury Street? Without doubt Eva had gone to the park to meet him, but it seemed that, growing impatient, or fearful of recognition by others, she had left before his arrival.

True, the police had watched the house wherein the man disappeared, but up to the present he had not been seen again. Boyd had told me, when I had seen him that very morning, that he had left by some exit at the rear, and that his entry there was only to throw any watcher off the scent.

It was evident that the man, whoever he was, had very ingeniously got clear away.

Dick, who was playing tennis, at last came forward to be introduced to my divinity, and presently whispered to me his great admiration for her. I was about to tell him who she really was, but on reflection felt that I could act with greater discretion if the truth remained mine alone, together with the secret of my love for her. Therefore I held my peace, and he, in ignorance that she was the missing victim of that amazing tragedy, walked at her side along the water's edge, laughing merrily, and greatly enjoying her companionship.

Mrs Blain invited us all to dine, but the Moberlys were compelled to decline, they having a party of friends at home. Therefore, we saw them off amid many shouts, hand-wavings and peals of laughter, and when they had gone we sat again on the lawn, now brilliant in the golden blaze of sundown.

It still wanted an hour to dinner, therefore Mary suggested that we all four should go out on the water, a proposal accepted with mutual enthusiasm. As I was not an expert in punting, Mary and Dick pushed off in the punt, the former handling the long pole with a deftness acquired by constant practice, while, with Eva Glaslyn in the stern of a gig, I rolled up my sleeves and bent to the oars.

The sunset was one of those gorgeous combinations of crimson and gold which those who frequent the Thames know so well. Upstream the flood of crimson of the dying day caused the elms and willows to stand out black against the cloudless sky, while every ripple caused by the boat caught the sun-glow until the water seemed red as blood.

A great peace was there. Not a single boat was in sight, not a sound save the quiet lapping of the water against the bows and the slight dripping of the oars as I feathered them. We were rowing upstream, so that the return would be easier, while Dick and his companion had punted down towards Chertsey. For the first time I was now alone with her. She was lovely.

She had settled herself lazily among the cushions, lying back at her ease and enjoying to the full the calm of the sunset hour, remarking now and then upon the beauty of the scene and the charm of summer days upstream. Her countenance was animated and perfect in feature, distinctly more beautiful than it had been on that well-remembered night when I had found her lying back cold and lifeless. How strange it all was, I thought, that I should actually be rowing her there, when only a few days before I had beheld her stiff and dead. Alone, with no one to overhear, I would have put a direct inquiry to her regarding the past, but I feared that such question, if put prematurely, might prevent the elucidation of the secret. To get at the truth I must act diplomatically, and exercise the greatest caution.

I sat facing her, bending with the oars, while she chatted on in a voice that sounded as music to my ears.

"I love the river," she said. "Last year we had a house-boat up beyond Boulter's, and it was delightful. There is really great fun in being boxed up in so small a space, and one can also make one's place exceedingly artistic and comfortable at very small expense. We had a ripping time."

"It is curious," I remarked, "that most owners of house-boats go in for the same style of external decoration — rows of geraniums along the roof, and strings of Chinese lanterns — look at that one over there."

"Yes," she laughed, glancing in the direction I indicated. "I fear we were also sinners in that respect. It's so difficult to devise anything new." And she added, "Are you up the river much?"

"No," I responded, "not much, unfortunately. My profession keeps me in London, and I generally like to spend my three weeks' vacation on the Continent. I'm fond of getting a glance at other cities, and one travels so quickly that the thing is quite easy."

"There are always more girls than men up the river," she said. "I suppose it is because men are at business and girls have to kill time. We live down at Hampton, not far from the river. It's a quiet, dead-alive sort of place, and if it were not for boating and punting it would be horribly dull."

"And in winter?"

"Oh, in winter we are always on the Riviera. We go to Cannes each December and stay till the end of April. Mother declares she could not live through an English winter."

This statement did not coincide with what the innkeeper's wife had told me, namely, that the Glaslyns were much pressed for money.

"I spent one season in Nice a few years ago," I said. "It is certainly charming, and I hope to go there again."

"But is not our own Thames, with all its natural picturesqueness, quite as beautiful in its way?" she asked, looking around. "I love it. People who have been up the Rhine and the Rhone, the Moselle and the Loire, say that for picturesque scenery none of those great European rivers compare with ours."

"I believe that to be quite true," I answered. "Like yourself, I am extremely fond of boating and picnicking."

"We often have picnics," she said. "I'll get mother to invite you to the next — if you'll come."

"Certainly," I answered, much gratified. "I shall be only too delighted."

We were at that moment passing two fine house-boats moored near one another, one of which my companion explained belonged to a well-known City stockbroker, and the other to a barrister of repute at the Chancery Bar. Both were gay with the usual geraniums and creepers, having inviting-looking deck-chairs on the roof and canaries in gilded cages hanging at the windows.

"Shall we go up the backwater?" she suddenly suggested. "It is more beautiful there than the main stream. We might get some lilies."

"Of course," I answered, and with a pull to the left turned the boat into the narrower stream branching out at the left, a stream that wound among fertile meadows yellow with buttercups, and where long lines of willows trailed in the water.

I was hot after a pretty stiff pull; therefore, when we had gone some distance, I leaned on the oars, allowing the boat to drift on under the bank where the long rushes waved in the stream and the pure white of the water-lilies showed against the dark green of floating leaves. Heedless of the rudder-lines, Eva leaned over and gathered some, trailing her hand in the water.

"How quiet and pleasant it is here," she remarked, her calm, sweet, beautiful face showing what a great peace had come to her at that moment. It may not have been quite in keeping with the *convenances* that she should have gone out like this alone with me, a comparative stranger, yet girls of to-day think little of such things, and she was nothing if not modern in dress, speech and frankness of manner.

We were far from the haunts of men in that calm hour of the dying day. Indeed, already the crimson of the sun was fading into the rose of the afterglow, and the stillness precursory of nightfall was complete save for the rustle of some water-rat or otter among the sedge, or the swift flight of a night-bird across the bosom of the stream. The shadows were changing and the glow on the water was turning from one colour to another. The cattle had come down to the brink, and wading to their knees, whisked the flies away with their tails as they slowly chewed the cud.

"Yes," I agreed. "There is rest, perfect and complete, here. How different to London!"

"Ah, yes," she answered. "I hate London, and very seldom go there, except when necessity compels us to do shopping."

"Why do you hate it?" I asked, at once pricking up my ears. "Have you any especial reason for disliking it?"

"Well, no," she laughed. "I suppose it's the noise and bustle and hurry that I don't like. I'm essentially a lover of the country. Even theatres, concerts and such-like amusements have but little attraction for me. I know it sounds rather absurd that a girl should make such a declaration, but I assure you I speak the truth."

I did not doubt her. Any one with an open face like hers could not be guilty of lying. That statement was, in itself, an index to her character. She possessed a higher mind than most women, and was something of a philosopher. Truth to tell, this fact surprised me, for I had until then regarded her as of the usual type of the educated woman of to-day, a woman with a penchant for smartness in dress, freedom of language, and the entertainment of the modern music-hall in preference to opera.

I was gratified by my discovery. She was a woman with a soul beyond these things, with a sweet, lovable disposition — a woman far above all others. She was my idol. In those moments my love increased to a mad passion, and I longed to imprint a kiss upon those smiling lips, and to take her in my arms to tell her the secret that I dared not allow to pass my lips.

She leaned backwards on the cushions; her hands were tightly clasped behind her head; her sleeves fell back, showing her well-moulded arms; her sweet, childlike face was turned upward, with her blue eyes watching me through half-closed lids; her small mouth was but half shut; she smiled a little.

It entranced me to look upon her. For the first time the loveliness of a woman had made me blind and stupid.

I wanted to know more of the cause of her dislike of London, for I had scented suspicion in her words. Nevertheless, through all, she preserved a slight rigidity of manner, and I feared to put any further question at that moment.

Thus we rested in silence, dreaming in the darkening hour.

I sat facing her, glancing furtively at her countenance and wondering how she had become a victim in that inexplicable tragedy. By what means had she been spirited from that mysterious house and another victim placed there in her stead? All was an enigma, insoluble, inscrutable.

To be there with her, to exchange confidences as we had done, and to chat lightly upon river topics all gave me the greatest gratification. To have met her thus was an unexpected stroke of good fortune, and I was overjoyed by her spontaneous promise to invite me to one of their own river-parties.

Joy is the sunshine of the soul. At that restful hour I drank in the sweetness of her eyes, for I was in glamour-land, and my companion was truly enchanting.

We must have remained there fully half an hour, for when I suddenly looked at my watch and realised that we must in any case be late for dinner, the light in the wild red heavens had died away, the soft pale rose-pink had faded, and in the stillness of twilight there seemed a wide, profound mystery.

"We must be getting back," I said quickly, pulling the boat out into mid-stream with a long stroke.

"Yes. The Blains will wonder wherever we've been," she laughed. "Mary will accuse you of flirting with me."

"Would that be such a very grave accusation?" I asked, smiling.

"Ah, that I really don't know," she answered gaily. "You would be the accused."

"But neither of us are guilty, therefore we can return with absolutely clear consciences, can't we?"

"Certainly," she laughed. Then, after a brief pause, she asked, "Why did you not bring Mary out in preference to me?"

"Why do you ask?" I inquired in surprise.

"Well — it would be only natural, as you are engaged to her."

"Engaged to her?" I echoed. "I'm certainly not engaged to Mary Blain."

"Aren't you?" she exclaimed. "I always understood you were."

"Oh, no," I said. "We are old friends. We were boy and girl together, but that is all."

Her great blue eyes opened with a rather bewildered air, and she exclaimed —

"How strange that people should make such a mistake! I had long ago heard of you as Mary's future husband."

Then again we were silent, both pondering deeply. Had this remark of hers been mere guess-work? Was this carefully-concealed question but a masterstroke of woman's ingenuity to ascertain whether I loved Mary Blain? It seemed very likely to be so. But she was so frank in all that I could not believe it of her. No doubt she had heard some story of our long-past love, and it had been exaggerated into an engagement, as such stories are so often apt to be.

Soon we emerged from the backwater into the main stream, and with our bow set in the direction of Laleham I rowed down with the current without loss of time. The twilight had fast deepened into dusk; the high poplars and drooping willows along the bank had grown dark, though the broad surface of the stream, eddying here and there where a fish rose, was still of a blue steely hue, and far away upstream only a long streak of grey showed upon the horizon. The stars shone down in the first faint darkness of the early night. Presently I glanced behind me, and in the distance saw a yellow ray, which my companion, well versed in river geography, told me was a light in one of the windows of Riverdene.

It had grown quite chilly, and the meadows were wreathed in faint white mist, therefore I spurted forward, and soon brought the boat up to the steps.

I knew that the world now held nothing for me but Eva.

When we entered the dining-room, a fine apartment with the table laid with shining plate, decorated with flowers, and illuminated with red-shaded candles, we were greeted, as we expected, by a loud and rather boisterous welcome by Dick and Mary. We were, of course, full of apologies, being nearly half an hour late. But up-river dinner is a somewhat movable feast, so Mrs Blain quickly forgave us, and while I sat by Mary on her one hand, Dick seated himself at Eva's side.

Gaily we gossiped through a merry meal, washed down with a real Berncastel, and followed by old port, coffee, and curaçoa. Yet my mind was full of strange apprehensions. What possible connexion could these three women have with that crime which the police were withholding from the public? That they were all three aware that a tragedy had taken place seemed quite clear. Yet all remained silent.

I had detected in Mrs Blain's manner an anxiety and nervousness which I had never before noticed, yet I refrained from putting any further question to her, lest I might, by doing so, show my hand. She could not keep from her tone when she spoke to me a note of insincerity, which my ear did not fail to detect.

Our conversation over dessert turned upon dogs, the performances of Mary's pug having started the discussion, and quite inadvertently Dick, whose mind seemed always centred upon his work, for he was nothing if not an enthusiast, suddenly said —

"Dogs are now being used by the police to trace criminals. There is no better method when it can be accomplished, for a bloodhound will follow a trail anywhere with unfailing accuracy, even after some hours."

"Do they actually use them now?" asked Mrs Blain in a strained, faltering voice, her wine-glass poised in her hand.

"Yes," he responded. "They've been utilised with entire success in two or three cases this week, not only in London, but in the provinces also. They are unfailing, and will track the guilty one with an accuracy that's absolutely astounding."

Eva and Mary exchanged quick glances across the table, while Mrs Blain sipped her wine and stirred uneasily in her chair.

I noticed that the colour had died out from the faces of all three, and that in their blanched countenances was a look of mingled fear and suspicion.

My friend had led that conversation with remarkable tact to quite an unlooked-for result.

He lifted his eyes to mine for an instant and read my thoughts. My mind became filled with a presentiment of future ill.

Chapter Twelve
The Deformed Man's Statement

Youth is as short as joy, and happiness vanishes like all else. In the mad hurry of life, however, we heed not such things. We live only for to-day.

On our way back to Waterloo that night Dick earnestly discussed the situation.

"And what's your opinion now?" I inquired, as he sat opposite me in the corner of the railway carriage.

Dick smiled slightly. "Both mother and daughter are connected with the affair, and are in deadly fear," he replied decisively. "While in the punt with Mary Blain I had a long chat with her, and the conclusion I've formed is that she knows all about it. Besides, she was very anxious to know your recent movements — what you had been doing during the past week or so."

"I wonder whether she suspects?"

"No, I don't think so," he answered. "Neither mother nor daughter dream that we are in possession of the secret. You see no one has returned to the place since the fatal night, and, as nothing has appeared in the papers, they naturally conclude that the affair has not yet been discovered."

"They evidently devour almost every morning and evening paper as it arrives down there. Did you notice the heap of papers in the morning-room?" I asked.

"Of course. I kept my eyes well open while there," he replied. "Did it strike you that the plate used at dinner was of exactly the same pattern as that on the table at Phillimore Place, and further, that among a pile of novels in the drawing-room was a book which one would not expect to find in such a place — a work known mainly to toxicologists, for it deals wholly with the potency of poisons?"

"No," I said in surprise, "I didn't notice either of those things."

"But I did," he went on reflectively. "All these facts go to convince me."

"Of what?"

"That we are working in the right direction to obtain a key to the mystery," he responded. Then suddenly he added: "By the way, that girl Glaslyn is certainly very beautiful. I envied you, old fellow, when you took her for a row."

I smiled. I had determined not to reveal to him her identity as the woman whom I had first discovered lifeless, but his natural shrewdness was far greater than mine. He was a born investigator of crime, and had not Fate placed him in a newspaper office, he would, I believe, have become a renowned detective.

"Glaslyn? Eva Glaslyn?" he repeated, as if to himself. "Why, surely that's the name of the girl you met in St. James's Park and followed to Hampton — the woman whom you found dead on your first visit to the house with Patterson? Is that really so?" he cried, in sudden amazement.

I nodded, without replying.

"Then, Frank, old chap," he answered in the low, hoarse voice of one utterly staggered, "this affair has assumed such a devilishly complicated phase that I fear we shall never get at the truth. To approach any of those three women would only be to place them on their guard, and without their assistance we can't possibly act with success."

"Then what do you suggest?" I asked.

"Suggest? I can suggest nothing," he answered. "The complications on every side are too great — far too great."

"Only Eva Glaslyn can assist us," I observed. "Yes. She alone can most probably tell us the truth, but her friendship for the Blains is proof positive that her secret is a guilty one, even though she was so near being a victim."

"She was a victim," I declared. "When I saw her she was apparently lifeless, lying cold and still in the chair, with every appearance of one dead. But what causes you to think that her secret is a guilty one?" I asked hastily.

"The Blains undoubtedly are implicated in the matter, and she, their friend, is in possession of their secret," he argued. "As a victim, she would be prompted to expose them if she did not fear exposure herself. She's therefore held to enforced silence."

His argument was a very forcible one, and during the remainder of the journey to London I sat back calmly reflecting upon it. It was a theory which had not before occurred to me, but I hesitated to accept it, because I could not believe that upon this woman who held me beneath the spell of her marvellous beauty could there rest any such hideous shadow of guilt. I remembered those clear blue eyes, that fair open countenance, and that frank manner of speech, and refused to give credence to my friend's allegation.

Slowly passed the days. Summer heat increased and in London the silk-hatted world had already turned their thoughts towards the open fields and the sea-beach. The summer holidays were drawing near at hand. How much that brief vacation of a week or fortnight means to the toiling Londoner! and how much more to his ailing wife and puny family, doomed to live year after year in the smoke-halo of some black, grimy street into which the sun never seems to shine, or in some cheap, crowded suburb where the jerry-built houses stand in long, inartistic, parallel rows and the cheap streets swarm with unwashed, shouting offspring! I had arranged to take my holiday in winter and go down to the Riviera, a treat I had long since promised myself, therefore both Dick and I continued our work through those stifling days, obtaining from Boyd every now and then the results of his latest inquiries. These results, it must be said, were absolutely nil.

I had agreed with Dick to keep our suspicions entirely to ourselves, therefore we gave no information to Boyd, preferring to carry out our inquiries in our own method rather than seeking his aid. It was well, perhaps, that we did this, for the police too often blunder by displaying too great an energy. I was determined if possible to protect Eva.

At Riverdene, Dick and I were welcome guests and were often invited to Sunday river-parties, thus showing that any suspicions entertained of us in that quarter had been removed. Time after time I had met Eva, and we had on lots of occasions gone out on the river together, exploring over and over again that winding shaded backwater, and picking lilies and forget-me-nots at the spot where on that memorable evening we had first exchanged confidences.

I had received no invitation to The Hollies, but she had apologised, saying that the unusual heat had prostrated her mother, and that for the present they had been compelled to abandon their picnics. Many were the afternoons and evenings I idled away in a deck-chair on that well-kept lawn, or, accompanied by Mary, Eva, Cleugh and Fred Langdale, who, by the way, turned out to be an insufferable, over-dressed "bounder" who was continually dangling at Eva's skirts, we would go forth and pay visits to various house-boats up and down stream.

Langdale looked upon me with a certain amount of jealousy, I think, and, truth to tell, was not, as I had imagined, of the milk-and-water genus. Eva seemed to regard him as a necessary evil, and used him as a tame cat, a kind of body servant to fetch and carry for her. From her remarks to me, however, I had known full well from the first that there was not a shadow of affection on her side. She had explained how she simply tolerated him because companions were few at Hampton and he was a fairly good tennis player, while he, on his part, was unconsciously making an arrant ass of himself in the eyes of all by his efforts to cultivate a drawl that he deemed aristocratic, and to carefully caressing his moustache in an upward direction.

Dick Cleugh, thorough-going Bohemian that he was, cared but little, I believe, for those riparian gatherings. True, he played tennis, rowed, punted and ate the strawberries and cream with as great a zest as any of us; nevertheless, I knew that he accepted the invitation with but one object, and that he would far rather have strolled in one of the parks with Lily Lowry than row Mary Blain up and down the stream.

Lily often came to our chambers. She was about twenty-two, of a rather Southern type of beauty, with a good figure, a graceful gait, and a decidedly London *chic*. She spoke, however, with that nasal twang which stamps the true South Londoner, and her expressions were not absolutely devoid of the slang of the Newington Butts. Yet withal she was a quiet, pleasant girl.

Thus half the month of July went by practically without incident, until one blazing day at noon, when, I went forth into Fleet Street for lunch, I unexpectedly encountered Dick, hot and hurrying, his hat tilted back. He had left home very early that morning to work up some "startling discovery" that had been made out at Plaistow, and already hoarse-voiced men were crying the "Fourth *Comet*" with the "latest details" he had unearthed.

In reply to his question as to where I was going, I told him that after luncheon I had to go down to Walworth to make some trifling inquiry, whereupon he said —

"Then I wish you'd do a favour for me, old fellow."

"Of course," I answered promptly. "What is it?"

"Call at the Lowrys and tell Lily to meet me at Loughborough Junction at eight to-night, at the usual place. I want to take her to the Crystal Palace to see the fireworks. I was going to wire, but you'll pass her father's place. Will you give her the message?"

"Certainly," I answered. "But is she at home?"

"Yes. She's got her holidays. Tell her I'm very busy, or I'd have come down myself. Sorry to trouble you."

I promised him to deliver the message, and after eating a chop at the *Cock*, I walked along to the Gaiety and there took a blue motor-bus, which deposited me outside a small, very dingy shop, a few doors up the Walworth Road from the *Elephant and Castle*, which bore over the little, old-fashioned window the sign, "Morris Lowry, Herbalist." Displayed to the gaze of the passer-by were various assortments of lozenges and bunches of dried herbs, boxes of pills guaranteed to cure every ill, and a row of dirty glass bottles filled with yellow liquids, containing filthy-looking specimens of various repulsive objects. The glaring cards in the window advertised such desirable commodities as "Lowry's Wind Pills," "Lowry's Cough Tablets," and "Lowry's Herbal Ointment," while the window itself and the whole shop-front was dirt-encrusted, one pane being cracked across.

As I entered the dark little shop, a mere box of a place smelling strongly of camomile, sarsaparilla and such-like herbs, which hung in dried and dusty confusion all over the ceiling, there arose from a chair the queerest, oddest creature that one might ever meet, even in the diverse crowds of lower London. Morris Lowry, the herbalist, was a strange specimen of distorted humanity, hunch-backed, with an abnormally large, semi-bald head, a scrubby grey beard, and wearing large, old-fashioned, steel-rimmed spectacles, which imparted to him an appearance of learning and distinction. His legs were short and stumpy, his body rather stout, and his arms of inordinate length, while the whole appearance of his sickly, yellow, wizened face was such as might increase one's belief in the Darwinian theory. Indeed, it was impossible to look upon him without one's mind reverting to monkeys, for his high cheek bones and square jaws bore a striking resemblance to the facial expression of the ancestral gorilla.

Dressed in black cloak and conical hat he would have made an ideal stage wizard; but attired as he was in greasy black frock coat, and trousers that had long ago passed the glossy stage, he was certainly as curious-looking an individual as one could have found on the Surrey side of the Thames. He was no stranger to me, for on several occasions I had called there with Dick, and had chatted with him. Trade in herbs had dwindled almost to nothing. Nowadays, with all sorts and varieties of well-advertised medicines, the people of Newington, Walworth, and the New Kent Road did not patronise the old-fashioned herbal remedies, which, if truth be told, are perhaps more potent and wholesome than any of the quack nostrums flaunted in the daily papers and on the hoardings. Ten years ago the herbalists did a brisk trade in London, especially among lower class housewives who, having come up from the country, were glad enough to obtain the old-world decoctions; but nowadays the herbalists' only source of profit seems to be in the sale of skin soaps and worm tablets.

Old Morris, with his ugly, deformed figure and shining bald head, welcomed me warmly as I entered, and at once invited me into the little shop-parlour beyond, a mere dark cupboard which still retained the odour of the midday meal — Irish stew it must have been — and seemed infested with a myriad of flies. Possibly the fragrance of the herbs attracted them, or else they revelled among the succulent tablets exposed in the open boxes upon the narrow counter. These lozenges, together with his various bottled brews, tinctures of this and of that, the old man manufactured in a kind of dilapidated shed at the rear, which, be it said, often offended the olfactory nerves of the whole neighbourhood when certain herbs were in the process of stewing.

"Lily is out," croaked the weird old fellow, in response to my inquiry, "but I'll, of course, give her the message. She don't get much chance nowadays, poor child! When her mother was alive we used to manage to run down to Margit for a week or fortnight in the hot weather. But now — " and he shrugged his shoulders with quite a foreign air. "Well, there's only me to look after the shop," he added. "And things are not so brisk as they were a few years ago." He spoke with a slight accent, due, Cleugh had told me, to the fact that his mother was French, and he had lived in France a number of years. Few people, however, noticed it, for by many he was believed to be a Jew.

I nodded. I could see that the trade done there was infinitesimal and quite insufficient to pay the rent; besides, was not the fact that Lily had been compelled to go out and earn her own living proof in itself that the strange-looking old fellow was the reverse of prosperous? The herbal trade in London is nearly as dead as the manufacture of that once popular metal known as German silver.

"Lily has gone to see an aunt of hers over at Battersea," the old man explained. "But she'll be home at five. She's got her holidays now, and, poor girl, she's been sadly disappointed. She expected to go down to her married sister at Huntingdon, but couldn't go because her sister's laid up with rheumatic fever. So she has to stay at home this year. And this place isn't much of a change for her."

I glanced around at the dark, close little den, and at the strong-smelling shop beyond, and was fain to admit that he spoke the truth.

"I suppose your friend, Mr Cleugh, is busy as usual with his murders and his horrors?" he remarked, smiling. "He's a wonderful acute fellow. I always read the paper every day, and am generally interested in the results of the inquiries by the *Comet* man. Half London reads his interviews and latest details."

"Yes," I answered. "He's kept hard at work always. There seems to be a never-ceasing string of sensations nowadays. As soon as one mystery is elucidated another springs up somewhere else."

"Ah," he answered, his dark eyes gazing at me through his heavy-rimmed glasses, "it was always so. Never a day goes past without a mystery of some sort or another."

"I suppose," I said, "if the truth were told, more people are poisoned in London than ever the police or the public imagine." I knew that all herbalists were versed in toxicology more or less, and had a vague idea that I might learn something from him.

"Of course," he answered, "there are several poisons, the results of which bear such strong resemblance to symptoms of disease, that doctors are very frequently misled, and the verdict is 'Death from natural causes.' In dozens of cases every year the post-mortem proves disease, and thus the poisoner escapes."

"What causes you to think this?" I inquired eagerly, recollections of the tragedy in Kensington vividly in my mind.

"Well," he said, "I only make that allegation because every herbalist in London sells poisons in smaller or greater quantity. If he's an unwise man, he asks no questions. — If he's wise, he makes the usual inquiry."

"And then?"

"Well," the old man croaked with his small eyes twinkling in the semi-darkness, "the customer generally pays pretty dearly for the article."

"Which means that an entry is made in the poison-register which is not altogether the truth — eh?"

He smiled and nodded.

"When poisons are sold at a high price," the old herbalist answered, "the vendor has no desire to know for what purpose the drug is to be used. It is generally supposed that it is to kill vermin — you understand."

"And human beings are more often the victims?" I hazarded.

He raised his grey, shaggy brows with an expression of affected ignorance, answering —

"Who can tell? The herbs or drugs are sold unlabelled, and wrapped in blank paper. As far as the herbalist is concerned, his liability is at an end, just as a cutler sells razors, or a gun-maker revolvers."

"And do you really believe that there is much secret poisoning in London at this moment?" I inquired, greatly interested.

"Believe it?" he echoed. "Why, there's no doubt of it. Why do people buy certain herbs which can be used for no other purpose than the destruction of human life?"

"Do they actually buy poisons openly?" I exclaimed in surprise.

"Well, no, not exactly openly," he responded. "They are most of them very wary how they approach the subject, and all are prepared to pay heavily."

I looked at the odd, ugly figure before me. For the first time I had learned the secret of this trade. Perhaps even he retailed poisons to those who wanted such undesirable commodities, charging exorbitant prices for them, and entering fictitious sales in the poison-book which, by law, he was compelled to keep.

"Have you actually ever had dealings with any poisoners?" I inquired. "Remember," I added laughing, "that I'm not interviewing you, that we are friends, and that I don't intend to publish this conversation in the newspapers."

"That's rather a difficult question," he responded, with a look of mystery upon his face. "Perhaps I'd best reply that I've before now sold poisons to people who could want them for no other purpose than the removal of superfluous friends."

"But do they actually ask openly for this herb or that?"

"Certainly — with excuses for its use, of course," and he went on to remark how lucidly the science of poisoning was explained in a certain book which might be purchased anywhere for seven-and-sixpence, a work which had undoubtedly cost thousands of human lives. Then instantly I recollected. It was a copy of this same book that Dick had noticed in the morning-room at Riverdene.

"In this very room," the old fellow went on, "I've had some queer inquiries made by all sorts and conditions of people. Only the other day a young girl called to consult me, having heard, she said, that I sold for a consideration a certain deadly herb. By her voice she was evidently a lady."

His final observation increased my interest in this remarkable conversation.

"What was she like?" I inquired with eagerness, for since the affair at Phillimore Place I took the keenest interest in anything appertaining to poisons.

"She was rather tall and slim, dressed in black. But my eyes are not so good as they used to be, and, in the dark here, I couldn't see much of her face through her veil. She was pretty, I think."

"And did you actually sell her what she wanted?"

He hesitated a moment.

"Certainly, and at my own price," he answered at last in his thin, rasping voice. "The stuff, one of the most dangerous and little-known compounds, not obtainable through any ordinary channel, is most difficult to handle. But I saw that it was not the first time she'd had azotics in her possession," and he smiled grimly, rendering his face the more hideous. "From her attitude and conversation I should imagine her to be a very ingenious, but not altogether desirable acquaintance," he added.

"And didn't you note anything by which you might recognise her again?" I inquired. "Surely young girls are not in the habit of buying poison in that manner!"

"Well," croaked the distorted old fellow, with a grin, "I did notice one thing, certainly. She wore a brooch of rather uncommon pattern. It was a playing-card in gold and enamel — a tiny five of diamonds."

"A five of diamonds!" I gasped.

At that instant the truth became plain, although I hesitated to believe it. The brooch was Eva Glaslyn's; one that she had worn only three days before when I was last down at Riverdene, and while on the water with her I had remarked its quaintness.

Could it be possible that she had actually purchased a deadly drug of this hideous old man? Or were there other brooches of similar pattern and design? Thus were increased the shadows which seemed to envelop her. My soul seemed killed within me.

Chapter Thirteen
Dick Becomes Mysterious

The startling statement of Morris Lowry caused me very considerable uneasiness. On my return to Gray's Inn, however, I made no mention of our strange conversation to Dick, who returned that evening rather late after a heavy day of news-hunting. Old Lowry had evidently been in a confidential mood that afternoon, and I had no right to expose any secret of his extraordinary business. Therefore I kept my own counsel, pondering deeply over his statement when Cleugh had gone forth to meet Lily, wondering whether it might have been some other woman who had worn the brooch with the five of diamonds.

I sat at the window gloomily watching the light fade from the leaden London sky. The evening was stifling, for no fresh air penetrated to that small open space, surrounded as it was by miles and miles of smoke-blackened streets, and as night crept on the heavens became a dull red with the reflection of the myriad lights of the city.

Heedless of all, I strove to find some solution of the enigma. Inquiries made by Boyd, one of the shrewdest detectives in London, had failed utterly. He was now relying solely upon me. There was but one clue, that given by the landlord of the house, and this I had followed with the result that the circumstances had only grown more and more bewildering. As far as could be discerned there was no motive whatever in taking the lives of either the man or the woman, while the escape of Eva was an astounding fact of which I longed for an explanation from her own lips.

I loved her. Yes, the more I reflected as I sat there gazing aimlessly across the square, regardless of the fleeting time, the more I became convinced that she was all the world to me. I recollected her daintiness and her grace, the sweetness of her smile and the music of her voice, telling myself that she alone was my idol, that my love for Mary had after all been a mere boyish fancy, and that this affection was a true, honest, deep-rooted one, the outcome of a great and boundless love.

Was there, however, not a great and terrible suspicion upon her? By a mere chance, that chance which Fate sends so often to thwart the murderer's plans or give him up to justice, I had learnt that she — or some one answering exactly to her description — had actually purchased some poisonous compound. I had believed her to have been a victim on that fatal night, but now it seemed that, on the other hand, she was herself given to the study of poisons; a strange subject, indeed, for a woman to take up. Then calmly I asked myself if it were possible to cast all memory of her aside, and after reflection discovered that such a course was utterly unfeasible. To entertain no further thought of her was entirely out of all question, for I loved her with a fierce and intense affection, and thought of nought else but her strange connexion with this mystery which, if made public, would send a thrill through London.

There were some very ugly facts hidden somewhere, yet try how I would I could form no distinct straightforward theory. Eva was naïve and sincere, frank and open, undesigning and entirely inartificial, nevertheless beneath her candour she seemed to be concealing some dread secret.

The latter I was determined to discover, and while night drew on and shadowy figures crossed and recrossed the square, I still sat plunged in thought, pondering deeply to find some means whereby to approach her.

I love her — a woman upon whom the gravest suspicion rested of having purchased a deadly drug for some nefarious purpose. Truly in the fitful fever of life the decree of Fate is oft-times strange. Men have loved murderesses, and women have, before now, given their hearts, nay, even their lives, to shield cowards and assassins.

Suddenly a movement behind me brought me back to a sense of my surroundings, and I saw that Dick had returned.

"Why, you're back very early," I said. "Have you been down to the Crystal Palace?"

"Yes, of course," he answered gaily. "What have you been doing, you lazy beggar? It's past half-past eleven."

"Nothing," I answered, surprised that it was so late. "I tried to write, but it's too beastly hot to work."

"Quite fresh down at the Palace," he answered. "Big crowd on the Terrace, and the fireworks not at all bad."

"Lil all right?"

"Yes. Sends her regards, and all that sort of thing. But — " and he hesitated, at the same time tossing his hat across upon a chair, and seating himself on the edge of the table in that careless, devil-may-care style habitual to him.

"But what?" I inquired.

He sighed, and a grave expression crossed his face.

"Fact is, old chap," he said in an unusually earnest tone, "I fear I'm getting a bit tired of her. She wasn't the least bit interesting to-night."

"Sorry to hear that, old man," I said. "Perhaps she wasn't very well — or you may be out of sorts — liver, or something. A woman isn't always in the same mood, you know, just as a man is liable to attacks of blues."

"Yes, yes, I know all that," he exclaimed impatiently. "But I've been thinking over it a long time, and, to tell the truth, I'm no longer in love with her. It's no good making a fool of the girl any longer."

"But she loves you," I observed, knowing well in what affection she held my erratic friend.

"That's the devil of it!" he snapped. "To tell the truth, it has worried me a lot lately."

"You've neglected her very much," I observed, "but surely she's good-looking, a charming companion, and has a very even temper. You've told me so lots of times. Why have you so suddenly grown tired?"

"I really don't know," he answered, smiling, at the same time slowly filling his pipe. "Perhaps it's my nature. I was always a wanderer, you know."

I looked at him steadily for some moments, then said bluntly —

"Look here, Dick, you needn't conceal the truth from me, old fellow. Mary Blain has attracted you, and you are throwing Lil over on her account."

"Rubbish!" he laughed. "Mary's a nice girl, but as for loving her — " and he shrugged his shoulders without concluding his sentence.

Notwithstanding this protest, however, I felt convinced that I had guessed aright, and regretted, because I knew how well Lily loved him, and what a blow it would be to her. She and I had been good friends always, and I liked her, for she was demure, modest, and withal dignified, even though she were but a shop assistant.

"Well, is it really fair to Lily?" I suggested, after a rather painful pause.

"You surely wouldn't advise me to tie myself to a girl I don't love?" he protested, rather hastily. "You are a fellow with lots of common sense, Frank, and your advice I'd follow before that of any chap I know, but here you're a bit wide of the mark, I think."

"Thanks for the compliment, old fellow," I responded. "Of course it isn't for me to interfere in your private affairs, but all I advise in this matter is a little hesitation before decision."

"It's useless," he said. "I've already decided."

"To give up Lily?"

"I have given her up. I told her to-night that I shouldn't see her again."

"You did!" I exclaimed, looking at him in surprise. I could not understand this sudden change of his. A few hours before he had been full of Lil's praises, telling me how charming she could be in conversation, and declaring that he loved her very dearly. It was more than remarkable.

"Yes," he said. "You know that I can't bear to beat about the bush, so I resolved to tell her the truth. She'd have to know it some day, and better at once than later on."

"Well, all I can say is that you're a confounded brute," I exclaimed plainly.

"I know I am," he admitted. "That's the worst of it. I'm too deuced outspoken. Any other chap would have simply left her and ended it by letter. I, however, put the matter to her philosophically."

"And how did she take it?"

His lips compressed for an instant as his eyes met mine.

"Badly," he answered in a low voice. "Tears, protestations of love, and quite a scene. Fortunately we were alone together in the train. I got out with her at the *Elephant and Castle*, and took her home."

"Did you see her father?"

"No. And don't want to. He's no good — the ugly old sinner."

"Why?" I inquired quickly, wondering how much he knew.

But he evaded my question, answering —

"I mean he's a sanguinary old idiot."

"He idolises Lily."

"I know that." Then, after a brief pause he added, "I may appear a brute, a silly fool and all the rest, but I tell you, Frank, I've acted for the best."

"I can't see it."

"No, I don't suppose you can, old chap," he answered. "But you will entirely agree with my course of action some day ere long."

His words puzzled me, for they seemed to contain some hidden meaning.

"Are you absolutely certain that you've no further love for Lil?" I inquired.

"Absolutely."

"And you are likewise equally certain that it is not the personal charms of Mary Blain which have led you to take this step?"

"I'm quite certain of it," he answered. "You once loved Mary, remember, but broke it off. Surely we are all of us at liberty to choose our own helpmate in life?"

"Of course," I responded. "It was not, however, my fault that we parted. Mary was infatuated with another."

"That just bears out my argument," he went on. "She didn't love you, and therefore considered herself perfectly justified in her attachment with your rival. I don't love Lil."

"But it seems that you have parted from her in a really cruel and heartless manner. This isn't like you, Dick," I added reproachfully.

"Why are you her champion?" he asked, laughing. "Are you in love with her?"

"Not at all," I assured him with a smile. "Only I don't like to see a girl badly treated by any friend of mine."

"Oh, that's good!" he laughed. "You've treated girls badly in your time, I suppose. Have a peg, old fellow, and let's close the debate." Then he added, in the language of Parliament, where he so often reported the speeches of the Irish ranters, "I move that this House do now adjourn."

"But I don't consider that you've acted with your usual tact in this affair," I protested, heedless of his words. "You could, of course, have broken if off in a much more honourable way if you had chosen."

"I've been quite honourable," he declared, in a tone of annoyance. "I told her plainly that my love had cooled. Hark!" The clock on the inn hall was striking midnight. "There's no suspension of the twelve o'clock rule. Shut up, Frank, and be damned to you."

He crossed to the sideboard, mixed a couple of whisky-and-sodas, and handed me one, saying

"Thirsty weather this. My mouth's as dry as a kipper."

I willingly admitted that the summer dust of London was conducive to the wholesale consumption of liquid, but was nevertheless reflecting upon his remarkable change of manner towards Lily. Something, I believed, had occurred of which he had not told me.

He stretched himself in the armchair, placed his glass at his elbow, and began to blow a suffocating cloud from his most cherished briar.

“I wish you’d spend sixpence on a new pipe,” I said, coughing.

“This one cost fourpence halfpenny in Fleet Street nearly two years ago,” he answered, without removing it from his lips. “Don’t you like it?”

“My dear fellow, it’s awful.”

“Ah! So they said at the office the other day. Don’t notice it myself.”

“But others do. I’ll make you a present of a new one to-morrow.”

“Don’t want it, old chap. Have a drink yourself with the money. This one’s quite good enough for me. Besides, it’ll keep the moths out of our drawing-room furniture,” and he gazed around the shabby apartment, where, from the leather-covered chairs, the mysterious stuffing was in many places peeping forth upon the world.

We smoked on. Although I had been considerably annoyed by what he had told me regarding Lily, his imperturbable good humour caused me to laugh outright, whereat he observed —

“You’re really a very funny beggar, Frank. I like you exceedingly, except when you try and dwell upon themes you don’t understand. Those who do that are apt to wallow out of their depth. You don’t know my reasons for throwing Lil over; therefore it’s impossible for you to regale me with any good advice. You understand?”

“But what are your reasons?” I inquired.

“You shall know them before long,” he assured me. “At present I don’t intend to say anything.”

“This is the first time, Dick, we’ve had secrets from each other,” I observed gravely.

“No,” he answered. “You love the mysterious Eva, and have never told me so. That’s a secret, isn’t it?”

I was surprised that he had detected my love for her, and rather alarmed, because if he had noticed it others had doubtless remarked it also. Therefore I questioned him, but he only laughed, saying —

“Why, anybody who saw you together down at Riverdene couldn’t fail to guess the truth. People have sharp eyes, you know.”

I was silent. If this were actually true, then I feared that I had made a hopeless fool of myself, besides wrecking any chance of eliciting those facts which I had set my mind upon revealing at any hazard.

Presently he rose, crossing to his writing-table to scribble a letter, while I, lighting a cigarette, sat silent, still thinking seriously upon the words he had just uttered.

Through the veil of tobacco smoke I seemed to see that fair, smiling face gazing at me, ever the same open countenance, the same clear eyes of childlike blue, the same half-parted mouth that I had first seen on that fatal night in Phillimore Place. In my dream I thought that she beckoned me to her, that she invited me to speak with her, and saw in her eyes a calm, sweet expression — the expression of true womanly love. It was but the chimera of an instant, a vision produced by my wildly-disordered brain, yet so vivid it seemed that when it faded I glanced across to my companion’s bent figure, half fearing that he, too, had witnessed it.

There are times when our imagination plays us such tricks — times when the constant concentration of the mind reaches its climax and is reflected down the aimless vista of our vision, causing us to see the person upon whom our thoughts are centred. Such a moment was this. It aroused within me an instant and intense longing to walk again at her side, to speak to her, to hear her sweet, well-modulated voice — nay, to tell her the deepest secret of my heart.

Thus it was that without invitation, or without previous introduction to Lady Glaslyn, I called at the Hollies on the following afternoon. A neat maid showed me into a cosy, rather small sitting-room, and for a few moments I remained there in expectancy. Although the house was not a large one it bore no stamp of the *nouveau riche*. It was exceedingly well-furnished, and surrounded by spacious grounds, wherein were a number of old yews and beeches. Old-fashioned, queer in its bygone taste, it had stood there on the broad highway from historic Hampton to London for probably a century and a half, being built in the days when the villadom of Fulwell had not yet arisen, and Twickenham was still a quiet village with its historic ferry, and where the stage-coaches changed horses at that low-built old hostelry, the *King's Head*. The place stood back from the dusty-high road, half-hidden from the curious gaze, yet, surrounded as it now was by smaller houses, some of them mere cottages, while a few cheap shops had also sprung up in the vicinity, the place was not really a desirable place of abode. The district had apparently sadly degenerated, like all places in the immediate vicinity of the Metropolis.

Before long the door opened, and Eva, looking cool and sweet in a washing dress of white drill, and wearing a straw hat with black band, entered and greeted me cordially.

"Mother is out," she said. "I'm so awfully sorry, as I wanted to introduce you. She's gone over to Riverdene, and I, too, was just about to follow her. If you'd been five minutes later I should have left."

"I'm lucky then to have just caught you," I remarked. "But if you're going to Riverdene, may I not accompany you?"

"Most certainly," she answered. "Of course I shall be delighted," and the light in her clear blue eyes told me that she was not averse to my company. She ordered a glass of port for me, and then said, "It's a whole week since you've been down there. Mary has several times mentioned you, and wondered whether you'd grown sick of boating."

"I've been rather busy," I said apologetically.

"Busy with murders and all sorts of horribles, I suppose," she observed with a smile.

"Yes," I answered, regarding her closely. "Of late there have been one or two sensational mysteries brought to light!"

"Mysteries!" she exclaimed, starting slightly. "Oh, do tell me about them. I'm always interested in mysteries."

"The facts are in the papers," I answered, disinclined to repeat stories which had already grown stale. "The mysteries to which I referred were very ordinary ones, containing no features of particular interest."

"I'm always interested in those kind of things," she said. "You may think me awfully foolish, but I always read them. Mother grows so annoyed."

"It's only natural!" I answered. "We who are engaged on newspapers, however, soon cease to be interested in the facts we print, but of course, if they didn't interest the public our papers wouldn't have any circulation."

She glanced at me, and a vague thought possessed me, for the look in her eyes was one of suspicion.

When she had drawn on her gloves we together went forth through the garden and down to the road. Suddenly it occurred to me that we might go by train to Shepperton, and thence take a boat and row up to Riverdene. This I suggested, and she gladly welcomed the proposal, declaring that it would be much more pleasant than driving along the dusty, shadowless road from Shepperton to Laleham.

Half an hour later we were afloat at Shepperton, and although the afternoon sun was blazing hot, it was nevertheless delightful on the water. With her lilac sunshade open she lolled lazily in the stern, laughing and chatting as I pulled regularly against the stream. Her conversation was always charming, and her countenance, I thought, fresher and more beautiful at that hour than I had ever before seen. About her manner was an air of irresponsibility, and when she laughed it was so gay a laugh that one would not dream that she had a single care in all the world. She was dainty from the crown of her hat to the tip of her white *suède* shoe, and as I sat in the boat before her, I felt constrained to take her in my arms and imprint a fervent kiss of love upon those sweet lips, arched and well-formed as a child's.

My position, however, was, to say the least, an exceedingly strange one. I was actually loving a woman whom I suspected to be guilty of some unknown but dastardly crime. Dozens of times had I tried to impress upon myself the utter folly of it, but my mind refused to be convinced or set at rest. I loved her; that was sufficient. Nothing against her had been proved, and until that had been done, ought not I, in human justice, to consider her innocent?

Indeed, it was impossible to believe that this bright-eyed, pure-faced girl before me, light-hearted, and graceful in every movement, had actually secretly visited that dark little den in the Walworth Road and purchased a drug for the purpose of taking the life of one of her fellow-creatures. Yet she wore at her throat the small enamelled brooch with its five of diamonds, the ornament described by old Lowry, the ornament which she had told me she had purchased as a souvenir at one of the fashionable jewellers in the Montagne de la Cour in Brussels.

We had passed both locks, and were heading up to Laleham, when we suddenly glided into the cool shade of some willows, the boughs of which overhung the stream. The shadow was welcome after the sun glare, and resting upon the oars I removed my hat.

"Yes," she said, noticing my actions, "we've come up unusually quick. Let's stay here a little time, it is so pleasant. The breeze seems quite cool."

Let it be punt, canoe or skiff, what more delightful than to moor oneself snugly in the leafy shade, and with a pleasant companion "laze" away the hours until the time comes to take up the sculls and gently pull against the placid stream. Everything was so peaceful, so quiet, the ripple of the sculls alone breaking the stillness. Yet, after all, what a change has come over the river in recent years! Good "pitches" for anglers and quiet nooks for the lazy were, ten years ago, to be discovered in every reach. Now they must be diligently sought for, and when found a note must be made of them. Warning boards notifying that landing or mooring alongside is prohibited were almost unknown, now they greet one in every direction. It is a pity; nevertheless there are still many real joys in river life.

So we remained there beneath the willows, where the water was white with lilies and the bank with its brambles was covered with wild flowers, and as I "lazed" I looked into those clear blue eyes wherein my gaze became lost, for she held me in fascination. I loved her with all my soul.

Chapter Fourteen
This Hapless World

How it came about I can really scarcely tell. I remember uttering mere commonplaces, stammering at first as the bashful schoolboy stammers, then growing more bold, until at length I threw all ceremony and reserve to the winds, and grasping her tiny hand raised it to my lips.

"No," she said, somewhat coldly, drawing it away with more force than I should have suspected. "This is extremely foolish, Mr Urwin. It is, of course, my fault. I've been wrong in acting as I have done."

"How?" I inquired, her harsh, cruel words instantly bringing me to my senses.

"You have flirted with me on several occasions, and perhaps I have even foolishly encouraged you. If I have done so, then I am alone to blame. Every woman is flattered by attention," she answered, gazing straight into my eyes, and sighing slightly.

"But I love you!" I cried. "You surely must have seen, Eva, that from the first day we were introduced I have been irrevocably yours. I have not, I assure you, uttered these words without weighty consideration, nor without calmly putting the question to myself. Can you give me absolutely no hope?"

She shook her head. There was a sorrowful expression upon her face, as though she pitied me.

"None," she answered, and her great blue eyes were downcast.

"Ah, no!" I cried in quick protest. "Don't say that. I love you with a fierce, ardent affection such as few men have within their hearts. If you will but reciprocate that love, then I swear that the remainder of my life shall be devoted to you."

"It is impossible," she responded in a harsh, despairing voice, quite unlike her usual self. Her head was bowed, as though she dare not again look into my face.

Once more I caught her hand, holding it within my grasp. It seemed to have grown cold, and in an instant its touch brought back to me the recollection of that fatal night in Kensington. Would that I might lay bare all that I knew, and ask her for an explanation. But to do so would be to show that I doubted her; therefore I was compelled to remain silent.

"Why impossible?" I inquired persuasively. "The many times we have met since our first introduction have only served to increase my love for you. Surely you will not withhold from me every hope?"

"Alas!" she faltered, with a downward sweep of her lashes, her hand trembling in mine, "I am compelled."

"Compelled?" I echoed. "I don't understand. You are not engaged to Langdale?"

"No."

"Then why are you forced to give me this negative answer?" I asked in deep earnestness, for until then I had not known the true strength of my love for her.

The seriousness of her beautiful countenance relaxed slightly, still her breast slowly heaved and fell, plainly showing the agitation within her.

"Because it is absolutely imperative that I should do so," she replied.

Suddenly a thought flashed through my mind.

"Perhaps," I said, "perhaps I've been too precipitate. If so — if I have spoken too plainly and frankly — forgive me, Eva. It is only because I can no longer repress the great love I bear you. I think of you always — always. My every thought is of you; my every hope is of happiness at your side; my very life depends upon your favour and your love."

"No, no!" she cried, with a quick movement of her hand as if to stay my words. "Don't say that. You may remain my friend if you like — but you may never be my lover — never!"

"Never your lover!" I gasped, starting back as though she had dealt me a blow. I felt at that moment as though all I appreciated in life was slipping from me. I had staked all, everything, and lost. "Ah, do not give me this hasty answer," I urged. "I have been too eager; I am a fool. Yet I love you with a stronger, fiercer passion than any man can ever love you with, Eva.

You are my very life," and notwithstanding her effort to snatch her hand away, I again raised it reverently to my lips.

"No, no. This is a mere summer dream, Mr Urwin," she said, with a cool firmness well assumed, although she avoided my gaze. "I have flirted with you, it is true, and we have spent many pleasant hours together, but I have never taken you seriously. You were always so merry and careless, you know."

"You did not believe, then, that I really loved you?" I observed, divining her thoughts.

"Exactly," she answered, still very grave. "If I had thought so, I should never have allowed our acquaintance to ripen as it has done."

"Are you annoyed that I should have declared only what is but the absolute truth?" I asked.

"Not at all," she responded quickly, with something of her old self in her low, sweet voice. "How can I be annoyed?"

"And you will forgive my hasty declaration?" I urged.

"There is nothing to forgive," she replied, smiling. "I only regret that you have misconstrued my friendship into love."

I was silent. These last words of hers crushed all hope from my soul. She sat with her hand trailing listlessly in the water, apparently intent upon the long rushes waving in the green depths below.

"Then," I said in a disappointed voice, half-choked with emotion, "then you cannot love me, Eva, after all?"

"I did not say so," she answered slowly, almost mechanically.

"What?" I cried joyously, again bending forward towards her. "Will you then try and love me — will you defer your answer until we know one another better? Say that you will."

Again she shook her head with sorrowful air. She looked at me with a kind of mingled grief and joy, bliss embittered by despair.

"Why should I deceive you?" she asked. "Why, indeed, should you deceive yourself?"

"I do not deceive myself," I protested, "I only know that I adore you; that you are the sole light of my life, and that I love you devotedly."

"Ah! And in a month, perhaps, you will tell a similar story to some other woman," she observed doubtingly. "Men are too often fickle."

"I swear that I'll never do that," I declared. "My affairs of the heart have been few."

"But Mary?" she suggested, and I knew from her tone that she had been thinking deeply of her.

"Ours was a mere boy and girl liking," I hastened to assure her. "Ask her, and she will tell you the same. We never really loved."

She smiled, rather dubiously I thought.

"But surely you are aware that she loves you even now," Eva answered.

"Loves me!" I echoed in surprise. "That's absolutely ridiculous. Since we parted not a single word of affection has ever been uttered between us."

"And you actually do not love her?" she asked in deep earnestness, looking straight into my eyes. "Are you really certain?"

"I do not," I answered. "I swear I don't."

The boat was drifting, and with a swift stroke of the oars I ran her bows into the bank. Overhead the larks were singing their joyous songs and the hot air seemed to throb with the humming of a myriad insects. The afternoon was gloriously sunny, and away in the meadow on the opposite bank a picnic party were busy preparing their tea amid peals of feminine laughter.

"Well," she sighed, "I can only regret that you have spoken as you have to-day. I regret it the more because I esteem your friendship highly, Mr Urwin. We might have been friends — but lovers we may never be!"

"Why never?" I inquired, acutely disappointed.

"There are circumstances which entirely prevent such a course," she answered. "Unfortunately, it is impossible for me to be more explicit."

"So you are prevented by some utterly inexplicable circumstances from loving me?" I observed, greatly puzzled.

"Yes," she responded, toying with the tassel of her sunshade.

"But tell me, Eva," I asked hoarsely, again grasping her chilly, nervous hand, "can you never love me? Are you actually convinced that in your own heart you have no spark of affection for me?"

She paused, then glanced at me. I fancied I saw in her blue eyes the light of unshed tears.

"Your question is a rather difficult one," she faltered. "Even if I reciprocated your love our positions would not be altered. We should still be alienated as we now are."

"Why?"

"Because — because we may not love each other," she answered, in a low, strained voice — the voice of a woman terribly agitated. "Let us part to-day and never again meet. It will be best for both of us — far the best."

"No," I cried, intensely in earnest. "I cannot leave you, Eva, because I love you far too dearly. If you cannot love me now, then bear with me a little, and you will later learn to love me."

"In one year, nay, in ten, my answer must, of necessity, be the same as it is to-day," she responded. "A negative one."

"As vague as it is cruel," I observed.

"Its vagueness is imperative," she said. "You are loved by another, and I have therefore no right to a place in your heart."

"You are cruel, Eva!" I cried reproachfully. "My love for Mary Blain has been dead these three years. By mutual consent we gave each other freedom, and since that hour all has been over between us."

"But what if Mary still loves you?" she suggested. "You were once her affianced husband."

"True," I said. "But even if she again loves me she has no further claim whatever upon me, for we mutually agreed to separate and have both long been free."

"And if she thought that I loved you?" Eva asked.

In an instant I guessed the reason of her disinclination to listen to my avowal. She feared the jealousy of her friend!

"She would only congratulate us," I answered. "Surely you have no cause for uneasiness in that direction?"

"Cause for uneasiness!" she repeated, starting, while at that same instant the colour died from her sweet face. Next second, however, she recovered herself, and with a forced smile said, "Of course I have no cause. Other circumstances, however, prevent us being more than friends."

"And may I not be made aware of them?" I inquired in vague wonder.

"No," she said quickly. "Not now. It is quite impossible."

"But all my future depends upon your decision," I urged. "Do not answer lightly, Eva. You must surely have seen that I love you?"

"Yes," she answered, sighing. "I confess to having seen it. Every woman knows instinctively when she is loved and when despised. The knowledge has caused me deep, poignant regret."

"Why?"

"Because," and she hesitated. "Because I have dreaded this day. I feared to tell you the truth."

"You haven't told me the truth," I said, looking her straight in the face.

"I have," she protested.

"The truth is, then, that you would love me, only you dare not," I said clearly. "Is that so?"

She nodded, her eyes again downcast, and I saw that hot tears were in them — tears she was unable longer to repress.

When the heart is fullest of love, and the mouth purest with truth, there seems a cruel destiny in things which often renders our words worst chosen and surest to defeat the ends they seek.

"Then whom do you fear?" I asked, after a pause.

She shook her head. Only a low sob escaped her.

"May we not love in secret," I suggested, "if it is really impossible to love openly?"

"No, no!" she said, lifting her white hand in protest. "We must not love. I tell you that it is all a dream impossible of realisation. To-day we must part. Leave me, and we will both forget this meeting."

"But surely you will not deliberately wreck both our lives, Eva?" I cried, dismayed. "Your very words have betrayed that you really entertain some affection for me, although you deny it for reasons that are inexplicable. Why not be quite plain and straightforward, as I am?"

"I have been quite clear," she answered. "I tell you that we can never love one another."

"Why?"

"For a reason which some day ere long will be made plain to you," she answered in a low voice, her pure countenance at that moment drawn and ashen pale. "In that day you will hate my very name, and yet will think kindly of my memory, because I have to-day refused to listen to you and have given you your freedom."

"And yet you actually love me!" I exclaimed, bewildered at this strange allegation. "It is most extraordinary."

"It may seem extraordinary," she said in a voice that appeared to sound soft and afar, "but the truth is oft-times strange, especially when one is draining the cup of life to its very dregs."

"And may I not know this secret of yours, Eva?" I asked sympathetically, for I saw by her manner how she was suffering a torture of the soul.

"My secret!" she cried, glaring at me suddenly as one brought to bay, a strange, hunted look in those clear blue eyes. "My secret! Why" — and she laughed a hollow, artificial laugh, as one hysterical — "why, how absurd you are, Mr Urwin! Whatever made you suspect me of having secrets?"

Chapter Fifteen
The Near Beyond

The remainder of our pull to Riverdene was accomplished in comparative silence. Crushed, hopeless and despairing, I bent to the oars mechanically, with the feeling that in all else my interest was dead, save in the woman I so dearly loved, who, lounging back among her cushions, sighed now and then, her face very grave and agitated.

I spoke at last, urging her to reconsider her decision, but she only responded with a single word, a word which destroyed all my fondest hopes —

"Impossible."

In that bright hour when the broad bosom of the Thames sent back the reflection of the summer sun, when the sky was clear as that in Italy, when all the world seemed rejoicing, and the gay laughter wafted over the water from the launches, boats and punts gliding past us, we alone had heavy hearts. Overwhelmed by this bitter disappointment and sorrow, the laughter jarred upon my ears. I tried to shut it out, and with my teeth set rowed with all my might against the stream until, skirting the shady wood, we rounded the bend of the stream and suddenly drew up at the landing-steps of Riverdene.

"Why, here's Eva!" cried Mary, running down to the water's edge, her tennis-racquet in her hand. "And Frank, too!" Then, turning to Eva as we stood together on the lawn a moment later, she asked, "Where's your mother? We've expected her all the afternoon."

"Isn't she here?" asked Eva, in surprise.

"No."

"Well, she started to come here immediately after luncheon. She must have missed the train or something."

"She must, for it's now past five. I really hope nothing has happened."

"Nothing ever happens to mother," observed Eva, with a light laugh. "She'll turn up presently." Then she explained how I had called at The Hollies and she had brought me along. On reaching Riverdene she had instantly concealed her agitation and reassumed her old buoyant spirits in order that none should suspect. She was an adept at the art of disguising her feelings, for none would now believe that twenty minutes before her face had been blanched, almost deathlike in agitation.

Together we walked up the lawn, being warmly welcomed by Mrs Blain and introduced to several friends who, seated beneath a tree, were idling over afternoon tea, a pleasant function in which we were, of course, compelled to join.

Seated next to Mrs Blain I gossiped for a long time with her, learning that her husband was still in Paris, detained upon his company business. He was often there, for he was one of the greatest shippers of champagne, and much of his business was with firms in the French capital.

"I don't expect him back for at least a fortnight," she said. "The other day, when writing, I mentioned that you had visited us again and he sent his good wishes to you."

"Thanks," I answered. Truth to tell, I rather liked him. He was a typical City man, elderly, spruce, smartly dressed, always showing a large expanse of elaborate shirt-front, fastened by diamond studs, and a heavy gold albert, a fashion which seems to alone belong to wealthy merchants and to that financial tribe who attend and speak at meetings at Winchester House or the *Cannon Street Hotel*.

From time to time when I glanced at Eva I was surprised to see how happily she smiled, and to hear how light and careless was her laughter. Had she already forgotten my words and the great overwhelming sorrow her response had brought upon me?

To Mrs Blain's irresponsible chatter I answered quite mechanically, for all my thoughts were of that woman whom I loved. Deeply I reflected upon all she had said, remembering how intensely agitated she had become when I had implied that she was in possession of some secret. The vehemence with which she had denied my imputation was quite sufficient to show that I had unconsciously referred to the one object uppermost in her mind. I was undecided in opinion whether her refusal to accept my love was actually in consequence of her fear of Mary's jealousy. If so, then Mary was in possession of this secret of hers. There was no doubt in my mind that she really loved me, and that, if she were fearless, she would hasten to reciprocate my affection. Apparently hers was a guilty secret, held over her as menace by Mary Blain, and knowing this she had been compelled to respond in the negative. This theory took possession of me, and during the hours I spent at Riverdene that evening, dining and boating with several of my fellow-visitors, I reflected upon it, viewing it in its every phase, and finding it to be well founded.

Indeed, as I sat opposite the two girls at dinner, I watched the actions of both furtively behind the great silver épergne of roses and ferns, and although they chatted merrily, laughing and joking with their male companions, I nevertheless fancied that I could detect a slight expression of concealed annoyance — or was it of hatred? — upon Eva's face whenever Mary addressed her. Ever so slight, merely the quivering or slight contraction of the eyebrows, it passed unnoticed by the merry party, yet with my eyes on the alert for any sign it was to me a proof sufficient that the theory I had formed was correct, and that the woman I loved went in deadly fear of Mary Blain.

If this were really so, did it not add additional colour to the other vague theories that had been aroused in my mind through various inexplicable circumstances? Did it not, indeed, point to the fact that upon Eva, although she might have been a victim of that bewildering tragedy in Phillimore Place, there rested a terrible guilt?

I recollected how she had gone to St. James's Park to keep the appointment which the unknown assassin's accomplice had made, and the remarkable allegation of old Lowry, the herbalist — two facts which, viewed in the light of other discoveries, were circumstances in themselves sufficient evidence of her guilt. Besides, had she not, with her own lips, told me that one day ere long I should hate her very name, and thank her for refusing to accept my love?

Was not this sufficient proof of the correctness of my theory?

As evening wore on and darkness deepened into night, the strings of Chinese lanterns at the bottom of the lawn were lit, imparting to the place a very gay, almost fairylike, aspect. There were many remarks regarding the non-appearance of Lady Glaslyn. Mrs Blain seemed extremely anxious, yet Eva betrayed no anxiety, merely saying —

"She may have felt unwell and returned. I shall no doubt find her at home with one of her bad headaches."

Thus all were reassured. Nevertheless, the incident struck me as curious, for Eva's calm unconcern showed that her mother must be a woman of somewhat eccentric habits.

Simpson drove us both to Shepperton Station in the motor-car, and we caught the ten-thirty train, from which she alighted at Hampton while I continued my journey up to Waterloo. During the fifteen minutes or so we were alone together in the train our conversation was mainly of our fellow-visitors. Of a sudden I asked —

"Have you seen Mr Langdale lately?"

"Yes. I often see him. He lives quite near us," she answered frankly.

"You told me this afternoon, Eva, that you were not engaged. Are you confident there is not likely to be a match between you?"

"A match between us!" she exclaimed with an expression of surprise. "What, are you joking, or do you actually suspect that I love him?"

"I have thought so."

"Never!" she answered decisively. "I may be friendly, but to love a man of that stamp — a man who thinks more of his dress than a woman — never!"

I smiled at this denunciation of his foppishness. He was certainly a howling cad, for ever dusting his patent leather boots with his handkerchief, shooting forth his cuffs, and settling his tie. He parted his hair in the middle, and patronised women because he believed himself to be a lady-killer. Truly he was a typical specimen of the City "bounder," who might some day develop into a bucket-shop keeper, a company promoter, or perhaps a money-lender.

At the moment when we were speaking the train entered the station of Hampton, and she rose.

"Tell me, Eva," I said with deep earnestness as I took her hand to say farewell, "is what you told me this afternoon the absolute truth? Can you never — never reciprocate my love?"

Her lips quivered for an instant as her great blue eyes met mine. Even though she wore a veil, I saw that there were tears in them.

"Yes," she answered in a hoarse tone, "I have told you the truth, Mr Urwin. We may never love — never."

The train was already at a standstill, and she was compelled to descend hurriedly.

"Good-night," she said hoarsely as I released her hand. Then, without waiting for my response, she hurried away and was a moment later lost in the darkness of the road beyond the barrier.

The carriage door was slammed, the train moved on, and as it did so I flung myself back into a corner, plunged in gloom and abject despair. She was the only woman I had ever truly loved, yet she was held apart from me. It was the first passionate agony of my life. I suffered now as those do without hope.

I found Dick at home smoking furiously, and busily writing in duplicate for the morning papers a strange story he had that evening picked up out at Gipsy Hill concerning a romantic elopement, which would cause considerable sensation in those little tea-and-tennis circles which call themselves suburban society. He briefly related it to me without pausing in his work, writing on oiled tissue paper and taking six copies, one for each of the great dailies. My friend's position in the journalistic world was by no means an uncommon one, for many men holding good berths on newspapers add to their incomes by doing what in press parlance is termed "lineage" — that is contributing to other newspapers for the payment of a penny, or perhaps three-halfpence, a line.

I told him that I'd been down to Riverdene, but so engrossed was he in his work that he hazarded no remark, and when he had finished and placed the copies in separate envelopes, already addressed, he put on his hat and went forth to the Boy-Messenger Office in Chancery Lane, whence they would be distributed to the sub-editors about Fleet Street.

I lit a cigarette and stretched myself in the armchair, gloomily pondering. Of late we had spoken but little of the mystery in Phillimore Place, for other inquiries had occupied Dick's attention, and on my part, loving Eva as I did, I preferred to continue my investigation alone.

Perhaps I had been sitting there a quarter of an hour or so, when suddenly a strange dizziness crept over me. It might, I thought, be due to my cigarette, therefore I tossed it out of the window and sat quiet. But the feeling of nausea, accompanied by a giddiness such as I had never before experienced, increased rather than diminished, and in order to light against it I rose and attempted to cross the room. I must have walked very unsteadily, for in the attempt I upset a chair, the back of which was broken, beside sweeping Dick's terra-cotta tobacco-pot from the table and smashing it to fragments. I clutched at the table in order to steady myself, but found myself reeling and swaying as though I were intoxicated. My legs seemed unable to support me, and the thought crossed my mind that this seizure might be one of paralysis. The idea was horrible.

At length, after some difficulty, I managed to again crawl back to the chair, and sinking down, closed my eyes. By doing so my brain seemed more evenly balanced, yet it seemed as though inside my skull was all on fire, and I wondered if exposure to the sun while rowing had caused these remarkable symptoms. I recollected how blazing hot it had been from Shepperton up to the second lock, and how once Eva, ever solicitous for my welfare, had warned me to be careful of sunstroke.

Yes, I had been careless, and this was undoubtedly the result.

My hands were trembling as though palsied, just as my legs had done a few minutes before, yet strangely enough I felt compelled to clench my fingers into my palms. All my muscles seemed slowly to contract, until even my jaws worked with painful difficulty.

An appalling fear fell upon me. I was suffering from tetanus.

Resolved not to allow my jaws to close tightly, I opened and shut my mouth, knowing that if it became fixed I should die a slow, lingering death as so many thousands had done. If I could only keep my jaws working the seizure might, perhaps, pass.

I longed for Dick's return. At that hour there was no one I could summon to call a doctor. I glanced at the clock. He had been already gone nearly half an hour. Would he never come back?

The sickening dizziness increased, and seemed to develop into an excruciating pain in my throbbing temples. I placed my hand to my head and felt that the veins were standing out hard and knotted, just as though I were exerting every muscle in some feat of strength. Then almost at that very instant I was gripped by a fearful pain in the stomach, as though it were being torn by a thousand needles. A cold sweat stood upon my brow until it rolled down my cheeks in great beads. I tried to shout for help, but my tongue clave to the roof of my mouth, and my voice was thin and weak as a child's. My throat seemed to have contracted. I was altogether helpless.

My agony was excruciating, yet I could only await Dick's return. Perhaps he had met a friend, and was lounging in some bar ignorant of my peril. The only doctor I knew in the vicinity was a hospital surgeon who lived a little way down Chancery Lane, over the Safe Deposit Company's vaults. I clenched my teeth to endure the racking, frightful pains by which my body was tortured, and in patience awaited my friend's home-coming.

My eyes were closed, for the gas-light was too strong for them. Perhaps I lost consciousness. At any rate I was awakened from a kind of heavy stupor by Dick's tardy entry.

"Good God, Urwin!" he gasped. "Why, what's the matter? What's occurred? You're as white as a sheet, man!"

"I'm ill," I managed to gasp with extreme difficulty. "Go and get Tweedie — at once!"

He stood for a moment looking at me with a frightened expression, then turned and dashed away down the stairs.

I remember raising myself, after he had gone, in an endeavour to reach a cupboard where there was some brandy in a bottle, but as I made a step forward all strength let me. I became paralysed, clutched at the table, missed it, and fell headlong to the floor. Then all consciousness became blotted out. I knew no more.

How long I remained insensible I have only a very vague idea. It must have been many hours. When, however, I slowly became aware of things about me, I found myself lying upon my own bed partly dressed. I tried to move, but my limbs seemed icy cold and rigid; I tried to think, but my thoughts were at first only a confused jumble of reminiscences. There was a tearing pain across my stomach, and across my brow — a pain that was excruciating. It seemed as though my waist was bound tightly with a belt of wire, while my brain throbbed as if my skull must burst.

I opened my eyes, but the bright light of day caused me to close them quickly again.

Noises sounded about me, strange and distorted. I distinguished voices, and I knew that I was not alone. Again I opened my eyes.

"Thank Heaven! my dear old fellow, you are saved!" cried Dick, whose coat was off, as he bent down eagerly to me, looking with keenest anxiety into my face.

"Saved!" I echoed. "What has happened?" for at that moment I recollected little of the past.

Then I saw, standing beside Dick, my friend, Dr Tweedie, of the Royal Free Hospital in Gray's Inn Road, a mild-mannered old gentleman whom I had many times met during my inquiries at that institution.

"What's happened?" the latter repeated. "That's what we want to ask you?"

"I don't know," I answered, "except that I was suddenly taken frightfully queer."

"Taken queer! I should rather think you were," he said, bending down to get a better look at my countenance, at the same time feeling my pulse. "You're better now, much better. But it's been a very narrow squeak for you, I can tell you."

"What's been the matter with me?" I inquired mystified.

"You've been eating something that hasn't quite agreed with you," he answered with a mysterious smile.

"But that couldn't have brought on a seizure like this," I argued weakly.

"Well," the doctor said, "of course you can tell better what you've been eating than I can. Only one fact is clear to me."

"And what's that?" I asked.

"Why, that you've been within an ace of death, young man," he answered. "You'll want the most careful treatment, too, if we are to get you round again, for the truth is you've been poisoned!"

"Poisoned?" I gasped.

"Yes," he responded, handing me some medicine. "And this seizure of yours is a very mysterious one indeed. I've never seen such symptoms before. That you've been poisoned is quite plain, but how the accident has occurred remains for us to discover later."

Chapter Sixteen
In the City

Through several days I remained in bed, my limbs rigid, my senses bewildered.

Although we said nothing to Tweedie, Cleugh entirely shared my suspicion that if an attempt had actually been made upon my life it had been made at Riverdene. The doctor ran in several times each day, and Dick, assisted by old Mrs Joad, was as attentive to my wants as any trained nurse, snatching all the time he could spare from his duties to sit by me and gossip of men and things in Fleet Street, and the latest "scoop" of the *Comet*.

Tweedie was puzzled. Each time he saw me he remarked upon my curious symptoms, carefully noting them and expressing wonder as to the exact nature of the deleterious substance. He pronounced the opinion that it was some alkaloid, for such it was shown by the reagents he had used in his analysis, but of what nature he was utterly at a loss to determine. Many were the questions he put to me as to what I had eaten on that day, and I explained how I had lunched at one of the restaurants in Fleet Street, and afterwards dined with friends at Laleham.

"You ate no sandwiches, or anything of that kind at station refreshment bars?" he asked, when he visited me one morning, in the vague idea, I suppose, that the poison might, after all, be a ptomaine.

"None," I answered. "With the exception of what I told you, I had a glass of wine at the house of a friend at Hampton before rowing up to Laleham."

"A glass of wine," he repeated slowly, as if reflecting. "You noticed no peculiar taste in it? What was it — port?"

"Yes," I replied. "An excellent wine it was, without any taste unusual."

For the first time the recollection of that glass of wine given me by Eva at The Hollies came back to me. Surely she could not have deliberately given me a fatal draught?

"Often," he said, "a substance which is poison to one person is harmless to another. If we could only discover what it really was which affected you, we might treat you for it and cure you much more rapidly. As matters rest, however, you must grow strong again by degrees, and thank Providence that you're still alive. I confess when I first saw you, I thought you'd only a few minutes to live."

"Was I so very bad?"

"As ill as you could be. You were cold and rigid, and looked as though you were already dead. In fact, any one but a doctor would, I believe, have pronounced life extinct. Your breath on a mirror alone showed respiration, although the heart's movement was so weak as to be practically imperceptible. But don't trouble further over it, you'll be about soon," and shortly afterwards he shook my hand and went on his way to the hospital, already late on my account.

I longed to tell him all the curious events of the past, but saw that such a course would be unwise. If I did so, Eva — the woman I adored — must be prematurely judged, first because of old Lowry's revelations, and now secondly because of the suspicious fact of my illness after partaking of the wine she offered.

The idea that the attempt had been made upon me at Riverdene seemed very improbable, because I had dined in common with the other guests; the tea I had taken was poured from the same Queen Anne pot from which the cups of others were filled, and in the whisky-and-soda I had had before leaving I was joined by three other men who had rowed up from a house-boat about a quarter of a mile lower down.

As I lay there restless in my bed, trying vainly to read, I spent hours in recalling every event of that day, but could discover no suspicious circumstance other than that incident of the wine at The Hollies. I recollected how Eva after ringing for the servant and ordering it, had herself gone out into the dining-room, and had been absent a couple of minutes or so. Possibly she might only have gone there in order to unlock the cellarette, yet there were likewise, of course, other graver possibilities.

This thought which fastened upon my mind so tenaciously allowed me but little rest. I tried to rid myself of it, tried to scorn such an idea, tried to reason with myself how plain it was that she actually held me in some esteem, and if so she would certainly not seek to take my life in that cowardly, dastardly manner. Sometimes I felt that I misjudged her; at others grave suspicions haunted me. Yet withal my love for her never once wavered. She was my idol. Through those long, weary hours of prostration and convalescence I thought always of her — always.

I had written her a short note, saying that I was unwell and unable to go down to Riverdene, not, however, mentioning the cause of my illness, and in response there came in return a charmingly-worded little letter, expressing profound regret and hoping we should meet again very soon. A hundred times I read that note.

Was the thin, delicate hand that penned it the same that had endeavoured to take my life?

That was the sole question uppermost in my mind; a problem which racked my brain day by day, nay, hour by hour. But there was no solution. Thus was I compelled to exist in torturing suspicion, anxiety and uncertainty.

One hot afternoon I had risen for the first time, and was sitting among pillows in the armchair reading some magazines which Dick had thoughtfully brought me during the luncheon hour, when a timid knock sounded at the door. The Hag had left me to attend upon her other "young gentlemen" in the Temple, and I was alone. Therefore I rose and answered the summons, finding to my surprise that my visitor was Lily Lowry.

At once, at my invitation, she entered, a slim figure dressed in neat, if cheap, black, without any attempt at being fashionable, but with that primness and severity expected of lady's-maids and shop-assistants. Her gloves were neat, her hat suited her well, and beneath her veil I saw a pretty face, pale, interesting and anxious-looking.

"I didn't expect to find any one in, except Mrs Joad," she said apologetically, as she took the chair I offered. Then, noticing my pillows, and perhaps the paleness of my countenance, she asked. "What? You are surely not ill, Mr Urwin?"

"Yes," I answered. "I've been rather queer for a week past. The heat, or something of that sort, I suppose. Nothing at all serious."

"I'm so glad of that," she said. "I only called because I was passing. I've been matching some silk at the wholesale houses in the City, and as I wanted to give Mr Cleugh a message I thought I'd leave it with Mrs Joad."

"A message?" I repeated. "Can I give it?"

She hesitated, and I saw that a slight blush suffused her cheeks.

"No," she faltered. "You're very kind, but perhaps, after all, it would be better to write to him."

"As you like," I said, smiling. "You don't, of course, care to trust your secrets in my keeping — eh?"

She looked at me seriously for a moment, her lips quivered, and she drew a long breath.

"You've always been extremely kind," she said in a low voice, half-choked with emotion. "And now that I find you alone, I feel impelled to confide in you and seek your advice."

"I'm quite ready to offer any advice I can," I answered, quickly interested. "If I can render you any assistance I will certainly do so with pleasure."

"Ah!" she exclaimed, sighing again, "I knew you would. I am in trouble — in such terrible trouble."

"What has happened?" I inquired quickly, for I saw how white and wan she was, and of course attributed it to Dick's action in renouncing his pledge.

"You, of course, know that Mr Cleugh and I have parted," she said, looking up at me quickly.

"He has told me so," I responded gravely. "I regret very much to hear it. What is the reason?"

"Has he not told you?" she asked, her eyes filled with tears.

"No," I answered. "He gave no reason."

"Well," she explained, "he has judged me wrongly. I am entirely innocent, I assure you. In a place of business like ours we are compelled to be on friendly terms with the male assistants, and the other evening, as I was leaving the shop to go to the house where we girls live, at the other end of Rye Lane, one of the men — an insufferable young fellow in the hosiery department — chanced to be going the same way and walked with me.

"On the way, Dick — Mr Cleugh, I mean — passed us, and now he declares that I've been in the habit of flirting with these men. It is not pleasant for any girl to walk alone along Rye Lane at ten o'clock at night, therefore this young fellow was only escorting me out of politeness. Yet I cannot make Dick believe otherwise than that he is my lover."

"He's jealous of you," I said. "Is not jealousy an index of true love?"

"But if he loved me truly," she protested, bursting into tears, "he surely would not treat me so cruelly as this. I've done nothing to warrant this denunciation as a worthless flirt — indeed, I haven't."

"And you love him?" I asked with deep sympathy, for I saw how intense was her suffering.

"He knows that I do," she answered. "He could see but little of me because his work prevented him, yet I was supremely happy in the knowledge of his love. Yet now he has forsaken me," she added, sobbing. "I'm but a poor girl, and I suppose if the truth were known he admires some one else better educated and more attractive than I am."

"No, I think not," I said, although at heart I felt that she spoke the truth. "This is merely a lover's quarrel, and you'll quickly make it up again. Look at the brighter side of things — come."

But she shook her head gloomily, saying —

"Never. I feel confident that Dick will never come back to me, although — although I shall love him always," and she raised her veil to wipe the hot tears from her cheeks.

"No, no," I exclaimed, endeavouring to comfort her, "don't meet trouble half-way. That's one of the secrets of happiness. We all of us have our little spasms of grief and despair sometimes, you know."

"Ah! yes, of course," she cried quickly. "But this sorrow has, alas! not come alone. Still another misfortune has fallen upon me."

"What's that?" I inquired, surprised.

"My father!" she exclaimed huskily.

"And what of him?" I asked. "I called upon him a short time ago. Surely nothing has happened to him?"

"Well," she replied, "it occurred like this. I got permission this day week to leave business at five o'clock, and, as usual, went home. When, however, I arrived at the shop I found it shut, and to my amazement a bailiff was in possession."

"For debt?" I inquired.

"Yes. He showed me some papers, and said it would cost about four hundred pounds to settle both bill and costs of the court."

"And your father? What was his explanation?" I asked, greatly interested and surprised.

"He wasn't there," she responded. "That's the curious part about the whole affair. I made inquiries, and discovered that he had suddenly shut up the shop about noon three days before, and had gone off with a heavy trunk placed on a four-wheeled cab."

"Does no one know where he's gone?"

"Nobody," she answered excitedly. "It's so strange that he has not written me a single line in explanation. I can't understand it."

I paused for a few moments, deeply puzzled.

"From the fact that the bailiff was in possession it would appear that he had preferred flight to facing his creditors," I said slowly. "Were you aware that he was in debt?"

"Not in the least," she answered. "He has some property abroad, you know."

"Where?"

"In France, I think. He never spoke of it to any one, although I knew that the rent was remitted regularly by a draft on the Crédit Lyonnais in Pall Mall. I used to go there with him to receive the money. It was quite a pile of banknotes each quarter."

"Then he could not really have been so badly off as he appeared?" I observed.

"No. He was eccentric, and very miserly, and although he always had enough and to spare he used constantly to deplore our poverty. I took a situation merely to satisfy him, as he had so often expressed regret that I should be idling at home. There was, however, absolutely no real necessity."

"But surely," I said, "he has not intentionally left you alone in the world? He will write very soon. Perhaps just now he does not write for fear his whereabouts should become known. He's evidently escaped his creditors. Has he been speculating, do you think?"

"Not that I am aware of."

"Can't you think of any reason why he should have fled so precipitately?" I asked, at the same time reflecting that it might be due to the fact that he had aroused the suspicions of the police by the illegal sale of drugs.

"No," she answered. "None whatever, beyond what I've already explained. His flight is an entire mystery, and it was to seek the advice of Dick, as my closest friend, that I called here. How had I best act, do you think?"

"I really don't know," I replied, after some reflection. "His disappearance is certainly remarkable, but if he is in hiding, it is not at all strange that he should omit to write to you. He knows your address, therefore, when he deems it safe in his own interests to communicate with you and explain, he will do so, no doubt."

"Then I'm to wait in patience and see our home sold up?" she asked, tears again welling in her dark, luminous eyes.

"You can do nothing else," I said. "He evidently means that it should be sold, for he has made no attempt to rescue it."

"There are so many of my poor mother's things there. I should so like to keep them — her little trinkets and such trifles. It seems very hard that they should be sold to a second-hand dealer."

"That's so, but you have no means of rescuing them," I pointed out. "It is certainly very hard indeed for you to be left alone and friendless like this, but without doubt your father has some reason in acting thus."

"He's fled like some common thief," she cried, with a choking sob. "And now I haven't a single friend."

"I am your friend," I said, echoing her sigh. "You have my sympathy, Lily, and if I can render you any service I shall always be ready to do so."

She thanked me warmly in a voice choked by sobs, for the two great sorrows had fallen upon her, and she was overwhelmed and broken.

I promised I would speak to Dick, and if possible arrange a meeting between them, in order to try and effect a reconciliation. Inwardly, however, I knew that this was quite impossible, for he had really grown tired of her, and had more than once in the past few days openly congratulated himself upon his freedom. She remained a short time longer, and before she left had become more composed and was in better spirits.

Then, when she shook my hand to go forth, she said —

"I thank you so much for all your kind words, Mr Urwin. I have at least to-day found a real friend."

"I hope so," I laughed. "Good-bye."

"Good-bye; I hope you'll soon be about again."

Then the door closed and I was again alone.

I was heartily sorry for her, poor girl. The sudden flight of the old herbalist was, to say the least suspicious. That he had money and could pay the debt was certain. Without doubt he had disappeared on account of a too close attention from the police. Morris Lowry was, I knew, not very remarkable for paternal affection, therefore I feared that he had, as Lily suspected, left her at the mercy of the world.

A week later I was able to go down to my office again, and about six o'clock on the second day I had resumed my duties I accidentally met Boyd at the bottom of Fleet Street.

As merry as usual, we drank together at the *Bodega* beneath the railway arch in Ludgate Hill, but in reply to my eager questions he told me that absolutely nothing fresh had transpired regarding the curious affair at Kensington. I explained that I was still a frequent visitor at Riverdene, but up to the present had discovered nothing. I, of course, did not tell him all my suspicions, preferring to keep my own counsel and allow him to prosecute his inquiries after his own method. From his conversation, however, I saw that he had many other matters in hand, and from his attitude it seemed as though he had given up hope of obtaining a clue to the mystery.

On finishing our wine we rose from the barrel on which we had been sitting, and he having announced his intention to walk along to the bookstall in Ludgate Hill Station to buy a magazine for his wife — for he was just off home by motor-bus to Hammersmith — we strolled together through that short arcade leading to the station, at that hour crowded by hungry City men eager to get back to their suburban homes.

Into every door they surged, springing up the two staircases to the platform above as though they had not a further moment to live, while every few seconds the deep voices of the ticket-collectors cried the names of the stations from the City to Blackheath or Victoria, or from Herne Hill down to Dover. Amid this black-coated, silk-hatted, perspiring crowd a man suddenly brushed past me, rushing up the stairs two steps at a time, slipping through the barrier just as the door was slammed, and disappearing on to the platform.

"Hulloa!" cried Boyd, pressing my arm quickly. "See! Look at that man — the one with the bag, running up the steps. Do you see him?"

"Yes," I answered, myself confounded.

"Well, that's the fellow I saw in St. James's Park, and who got away so neatly from Ebury Street — you remember?"

"That man!" I gasped, utterly amazed.

"Yes. We mustn't lose sight of him this time. He can tell us something if he likes," and without further word he dashed away after the man who had hurried to catch his train, leaving me standing alone in amazement.

That man who had brushed past I had instantly recognised as none other than Henry Blain, who for so many weeks was supposed to have been in Paris.

This fresh development was certainly both startling and mysterious.

Chapter Seventeen
A Visit from Boyd

Without a second's hesitation I rushed up the steps after Boyd, but on gaining the platform found that a train had just gone out, and was at that moment disappearing across the bridge over the Thames. The detective, known to the ticket-collector as a police-officer, had been allowed to pass the barrier, and had evidently caught the same train as Blain.

There was certainly an element of deepest mystery in the fact that the unknown man who had kept the appointment in St. James's Park, and had afterwards taken such elaborate precautions against being followed, should be revealed to be none other than the once purse-proud proprietor of Shenley. Quite apparent it was, too, that the object of Eva's visit to the park was to meet him clandestinely, for what reason was a profound enigma. The more I revolved the strange events within my mind, the more absolutely bewildering they become.

True, I had made certain discoveries — discoveries which, rather than tending to throw light on the real author of the crime or its motive, only, however, increased the enigma and enveloped the woman whom I had grown to love so fondly in an impenetrable veil of suspicion.

Thoughts such as these filled my mind as, turning from the station in despair, I went back into the dust and turmoil of Fleet Street, crowded at that hour by tired thousands hurrying homeward. I loved Eva. Even though every proof I had obtained pointed to her complicity in the dastardly affair, she was still my idol. I thought daily, hourly, only of her, refusing always to suspect her, and endeavouring to convince myself that the truths I had elicited had no foundation in fact.

Love is blind. When a man loves a woman as I loved Eva Glaslyn at that moment, nothing can turn aside his passion. I verily believe that if at that hour I had stood by and seen her in the dock at the Old Bailey, condemned as a murderess, my affection for her would have been none the less. I lived for her alone. She was all that was dearest in the world to me. Mary Blain had, no doubt, noticed my infatuation, yet she had said nothing, she herself being, I believed, in love with Dick. At least I could congratulate myself that we had mutually agreed to allow the past to fade from our remembrance.

Nevertheless, when I thought of Eva, and told myself how passionate was my affection and how ardent my feelings towards her, the ogre of suspicion would sometimes arise and cause me to pause in my ecstatic dreamings. Had she not stiffened strangely, and refused to reciprocate my love? Had she not point-blank told me that we could never be more than friends? Had she not, indeed, herself hinted at her own guilt in that strange sentence which had fallen from her lips?

As I passed up Fleet Street that evening, jostling with the crowd, I thought of these things, and was plunged into gloom and uncertainty. The statement of old Lowry was one of which I felt in duty bound to obtain proof. Yet how? He had declared that a woman exactly resembling her had purchased a certain drug which could be required for one purpose alone, while a secret attempt had been made to take my life — by whom I knew not. Sometimes, in moments of despair, I entertained deep suspicions of her, but always I found my love in the ascendancy, and ended by refusing to believe the evidence which I had so diligently and patiently collected.

For months Scotland Yard had had the matter in hand, but discovering nothing, had allowed it to drop. Of course, in face of the statement made by the landlord of the house in Phillimore Place, Boyd was ever anxious to question Mrs Blain, but had wisely left this to me. And how had I succeeded? Only in making discoveries which, although startling in themselves, increased the mystery rather than solved it.

Even at that moment the identity of the victims remained still unknown. They were lying in nameless graves in Abney Park Cemetery, having been buried by the parish. The Blains alone could give us information as to who they were and who was the unnamed scientist whose discovery was now creating such a stir throughout Europe. Curious it was that he did not come forward and claim the discovery as his own, for he must have read accounts of it in the papers. My own theory in this matter was that he was unable to communicate with the Royal Institution for one simple reason, namely, that he was dead — that he was the man whom we found lying lifeless with that strange mascot, the penny wrapped in paper, in his pocket.

I walked along to Wellington Street, where I called in to see my friend Crutchley, one of the sub-editors of the *Morning Post*, who had just come on duty and was preparing for his night's work. In the offices of the morning papers activity begins when tired London takes her ease, for their night is as day, until at dawn the staff, weary after hours of work by electric light in stifling rooms, go forth chilled and jaded to their homes to sleep while the world works. For half an hour I sat in his den, where the table was already piled with telegrams and flimsy, while he, with coat off, shirt-cuffs turned up, and a cigarette in his mouth, sighed, sharpened his big blue pencil, and, as he chatted, commenced to "slaughter" wordy descriptions by too eloquent reporters. The world wants news, not "gas," is the motto of every working sub-editor. The public prefer facts without "padding," and to cut out the latter is the duty of the man who, from the sub-editorial chair, decides upon what shall appear and what shall be omitted, a duty which requires the greatest care and judgment. When I left him I recollected that Dick had gone to some place down in Essex for the *Comet*, and would not return to eat the diurnal steak in company. Therefore I wandered aimlessly along the Strand, and turned into a restaurant, afterwards spending the evening at the theatre.

Nearly three weeks went by and I heard nothing of Boyd, although I had written to him. At nearly ten o'clock one night, however, when I had returned to Gray's Inn alone, I found the detective standing in the half-light against the mantelpiece.

"Bad luck the other night," he said, after we had exchanged greetings.

"What, didn't you follow him?" I cried, surprised.

"No, that's the devil of it," he exclaimed in a tone of bitter disappointment, sinking into a chair. "You'll remember that that platform at Ludgate Hill is an island one, and just as I got through the barrier a train on the other side was moving off to Snow Hill and Moorgate Street, while one to Blackheath was just on the point of starting in the opposite direction. I, of course, jumped into the latter, feeling sure he'd be going out of town."

"And you found out your mistake too late?"

"I examined all the carriages at Loughborough Junction, but there was no sign of him. He evidently took the other train."

"Unfortunate," I answered, then sat for a few moments in calm reflection.

"Unfortunate!" he echoed. "It's more than that. We seem foredoomed to failure in this affair. I've had three men on the job ever since, but with no result. Even the 'narks' know nothing. But," he added, "when I pointed him out you seemed to know him. Am I right?"

I hesitated, wondering whether to tell him all the facts as I knew them and obtain his assistance in my further inquiries. It struck me that he, a professional investigator of crime, shrewd, clear-headed and acquainted with all the methods and subterfuges of evil-doers, might suggest some other means which had not occurred to me. I had hitherto been deterred from making any explanation of my discoveries and suspicions on account of my strong love for Eva, but now the idea took possession of me that if I explained the whole to Boyd and told him of my deep affection for her, we might work together, and perhaps at length obtain some solution of this most intricate of problems. I was sick with the giddiness of one who falls from some great height. I had lost my hold upon the dreams and hopes of life.

"You're quite right, Boyd," I said, handing him the cigarettes. "I know that man."

"Who is he? He looks rather gentlemanly. That shabby get-up of his was a fake, I'm sure."

"Yes," I responded. "He's a man pretty well-to-do. His name is Blain, and he is the husband of Mrs Blain, whom, you recollect, is supposed to have taken the house in Phillimore Place."

The detective gave vent to an unwritable exclamation.

"Blain!" he echoed, his face betraying a look of amazement, and pausing with a lighted vesta in his hand. "Well, that's indeed a facer!" Then he added: "He must, in that case, know something of the matter as well as his wife."

At that moment there was a tap at the door of the sitting-room, and old Mrs Joad entered with a letter which, she said, had come by the last post and she had forgotten to give it to me.

By the writing I saw it was from Eva, and eagerly read it. It was a brief note to say that her mother had been called away to her brother in Inverness, who was seriously ill, that The Hollies was closed, and that she had accepted an invitation to remain the guest of the Blains until Lady Glaslyn's return.

I handed the note to the detective without comment.

"Well," he exclaimed, looking up at me when he had read it, "there's nothing very fishy about that, is there?"

Then I recollected that he was in ignorance of my suspicions. Yet I loved Eva with all my soul and held back from placing any facts in the hands of this man who, with ruthless disregard for my affection or my feelings, would perhaps arrest her for complicity in the crime. And yet as I sat before him, watching his face through the blue haze of cigarette smoke, I felt impelled to seek his aid, for this tangled chain of recent events had utterly bewildered and unnerved me. I was not yet strong again after the strange seizure which had so puzzled the doctor, and a sense of gloom and despair had since overwhelmed me, arising perhaps from the constant suspicion that a secret attempt had been made upon my life.

To remain longer in that state of uncertainty was impossible. I felt I should go mad if I did not make some further determined effort to ascertain the truth. Some one, whom I knew not, had attempted to kill me. And why? There could be but one reason. Because I had succeeded in placing myself upon the actual track of the assassin. An attempt, cowardly and dastardly, had been made upon me, therefore I had every right to seek the aid of the police to discover its author.

This argument decided me, and casting my cigarette into the grate, I asked Boyd to give me his attention while I related to him all that I had discovered.

In an instant his free-and-easy manner changed, and as I spoke he sat leaning towards me, attentively listening to every word, but hazarding no remark. Without attempting to conceal anything, I explained to him first of all my great love for the woman who was under such terrible suspicion, and then as I narrated our conversation when alone on the river, and repeated her curious response to my declaration of love, he knit his dark brows seriously and gave vent to a grunt indicative of doubt. He was no blunderer, this detective. Unlike the majority he was well-educated, speaking French and Italian fluently, an adept in the art of disguise, a man who formed very careful theories, and whose appearance was never that of an agent of police. One would rather have taken him for a well-to-do Jew, or perhaps some prosperous City man of foreign extraction, for his dark complexion and aquiline features gave him an un-English appearance, and his invariable spruceness in dress accounted for his success in following criminals, who never dreamed that the smart, well-dressed gentleman of perfect manner was actually an emissary from Scotland Yard. His knowledge of foreign languages had caused him to be entrusted with numbers of very important inquiries political and criminal, and in tracking the guilty he had paid flying visits to nearly all the Continental capitals.

In his sharp eyes there was a strange glitter, I thought, as without interruption I told him what I knew. I advanced no theories whatever, but merely laid before him the plain unvarnished truth. Then, when I had finished, I said —

"Now, first of all, recollect that whatever may be the result of our inquiries I will do no harm whatever to the woman I love. Understand that entirely."

"I quite understand," he said gravely, speaking for the first time. "That's only natural. But the difficulties in our way appear almost insurmountable."

"Well?" I asked anxiously, "what is your opinion, now that I have told you everything?"

He shook his head, puffed thoughtfully at the fresh cigarette he had just lit, and then contemplated it thoughtfully.

"I have no opinion at present," he responded. "One might form half a dozen theories upon these facts, all equally wide of the mark."

"Then how are we to act?" I asked in dismay.

He raised his dark eyebrow's in gesture of bewilderment. Then he gazed gravely in my face.

"Look here, Boyd," I continued, "I love Eva Glaslyn, and to you I make no secret of it whatsoever. But at all hazards I mean to ascertain the truth."

"Even at the risk of convicting her?" he inquired, looking across at me quickly.

"Convicting her!" I echoed. "Then you really entertain the same suspicion as myself?"

"We may have suspicions without forming any theories," he responded calmly. Then he added, in a tone of regret, "It's certainly a thousand pities that you love her."

"Why?"

"Upon your own showing she appears to have very little regard for you."

"How?"

"Well," he answered slowly, "there's no doubt that the other day an attempt was made upon your life."

"And you suspect her?"

"We can suspect no one else," he answered.

"According to that old herbalist's statement she had purchased a certain drug of him. What could an innocent young lady require with this unnamed drug if not to administer it to some one she wanted to get rid of?"

"But she has no object in ridding herself of me," I urged.

"Of that I'm not quite so sure, my dear fellow," he observed, after a brief pause. "Recollect that on the morning when she went to St. James's Park in order to meet, for some mysterious purpose, the man whom we now know was old Mr Blain, she met you face to face. We have no idea what her actions were previously, but she may have believed that you had been spying upon her; therefore, on recognising you when you were formally introduced at Riverdene, she conceived a plan for getting you out of the way. It was with that object very possibly that she made the secret purchase at the herbalist's."

"No, Boyd, I can't believe it of her," I said quickly. "I won't believe it!"

"Very well," he said in the same calm tone as before. "But there's still another fact extremely puzzling, and that is why this man Lowry should have left in such a hurry. I must inquire at the Carter Street Police-Station, the district wherein he lived, and see whether there was anything against him. By the way," he added, "does your friend Cleugh know the whole of these facts you've explained to me?"

"No, not the whole — only some."

"Does he know that you've declared your love to Lady Glaslyn's daughter and been refused?"

"No."

"Then don't tell him," said the detective.

"I believe that the reason of his sudden weariness of Lily Lowry's society is due to the fact that he loves Mary Blain."

"All the more reason, then, why he should in future remain in entire ignorance of whatever facts we may elicit."

Then he paused, furiously consuming his cigarette and taking a long draught of the whisky-and-soda I had mixed and placed at his elbow.

"This is really a most remarkable mystery, Urwin," he exclaimed at length, twisting the plain gold ring upon his finger, a habit of his when pondering deeply. "There seem a thousand complications. It's absolutely the most astounding case that I've ever had in hand. Even Shaw, our superintendent at the Yard, a man whose deep-rooted conviction is that we never need fail if we really take an interest in an inquiry, acknowledged to me the other day that he could see no way to a clue. Of course, we might question Mrs Blain, or even arrest Blain himself on suspicion if we could find him again. But whoever is guilty has taken such careful precautions to obliterate every trace of a clue that both the superintendent and myself are agreed that the interrogation of either of the Blains would only result in defeating our ends." That was exactly my own opinion. I had many times wondered why the police had not made inquiries of Mrs

Blain on account of the statement by the landlord at Kensington, but it was now plain that the Director of Criminal Investigations, the greyheaded, loud-voiced, old gentleman whom I knew quite well at Scotland Yard, had decided otherwise.

"But why are you so anxious that my friend Cleugh should remain in ignorance of our movements?" I inquired.

"You say that he loves Mary Blain," answered Boyd. "He might in that case drop some unintentional hint to her of the direction of our inquiries. This matter, to be successful, must be entirely a secret between ourselves — you understand? To-day we've made a discovery — the identity of the man who threw some object into the lake — and it puts a rather fresh complexion upon the affair, even though it further complicates it considerably. You said that his wife has all along told you that her husband was in Paris — I think?"

"Yes," I responded. "She said he was there in connexion with some company which he was trying to promote."

"And all along he has been in London — in hiding."

"He may have just returned from Paris," I suggested. "Recollect that I've not been to Riverdene for some little time."

"No, my dear fellow," Boyd said. "His ingenuity in eluding us in Ebury Street showed that he had already prepared a snug hiding-place for himself before that tragedy at Phillimore Place. Besides, the other evening his clothes showed an attempt at disguise — didn't they?"

"Certainly. He's very smartly dressed always; indeed, rather a fop in his way."

"Depend upon it that he's never dared to set foot outside London all this time. He knows well enough that the Metropolis is the safest place in the whole world in which a criminal may conceal himself. Only a bungler attempts to get away abroad."

Silence again fell between us. The quiet was unbroken save for the slow ticking of the clock upon the mantelshelf. Of a sudden, with a rather curious glance, he bent forward to me, eagerly saying —

"Now in this affair we must be perfectly candid with each other. You must conceal nothing from me."

"I have concealed nothing," I protested, surprised at his curious attitude, as though he held me in some suspicion.

"I don't allege that you have," he answered. "But I want you to answer truthfully a question which is of highest importance. I want you to tell me whether, on the afternoon of the day you were called by Patterson to Kensington, your friend Cleugh was here, at home."

"No, he certainly wasn't. I arrived home first, and he came in perhaps ten minutes or a quarter of an hour later than usual," I answered, wondering what connexion this could have with the inquiry.

"And after you made the discovery you did not telegraph or communicate with him in any way? I take it that you were surprised to meet him in that house."

"Certainly I was," I responded. "But he had an appointment with Lily Lowry, and finding that she could not keep it, he came along to Kensington to ascertain the nature of the event about which Patterson had wired to me."

The detective's features relaxed into a strange smile.

"Would you be surprised then to know that your friend never called at the Police-Station on that evening, but went straight to Phillimore Place and there joined me while you were absent inquiring of the neighbours? That very evening I inquired of the constable on duty at the door of the station, and of others, all of whom told me that no one had called to inquire for Patterson except yourself."

"That's certainly extraordinary," I said in wonderment.

"Yes," he observed mechanically. "It's a very curious fact; one which appears to prove that he knew something more of the mysterious occurrence than he has admitted — in fact, that he was aware of it long before we were."

"What!" I gasped, gazing at my companion in alarm. "Surely you don't mean that you suspect Dick of having had any hand in the affair?"

Then, at that instant, I recollected how, when I had received the telegram on that memorable evening, his face had suddenly changed, and his hand had trembled.

Chapter Eighteen
"You will never Know — Never!"

Dick returned about eleven, and shortly afterwards Boyd swallowed another whisky-and-soda and left.

I thought my friend started slightly at finding the detective with me, but he betrayed not the slightest annoyance. Indeed, he himself started the discussion regarding the mystery, appearing in no way loth to discuss it in all its phases.

The detective's suspicion was certainly a startling one, and of course accounted for his anxiety that Dick should in future remain in utter ignorance of our actions. When Boyd had gone he at once commenced to question me upon what theories he had expressed, and in what direction he was prosecuting inquiries. Although I would not allow myself to suspect my best friend, I nevertheless preserved the silence which Boyd had imposed upon me, evading giving him direct answers, preserving the secret of the identity of the man seen in St. James's Park, and managing to put aside his questions by a declaration that personally I was sick of the whole matter, for I felt that it would now ever remain a mystery.

That night, however, I remained awake many hours thinking fondly of Eva, and calmly revolving in my mind all that had fallen from the lips of Boyd. He, one of the most skilful officers in London, had formed no theory. He only entertained certain suspicions, vague perhaps, yet by no means groundless. I had not seen Eva since that day when the strange, incomprehensible attempt had been made to take my life, and a strong desire again possessed me to stroll at her side, to hear her voice, to hold her hand. Was it, I wondered time after time, that hand, so soft, slim and delicate, that had actually attempted to secretly take my life?

The detective had calmly reviewed all the facts I had explained, and, as a professional investigator of crime, had openly expressed a suspicion in the affirmative.

Often had I wondered what kind of woman was Eva's mother, whom I had never met. That she was somewhat eccentric was evident from her daughter's words on the last occasion I had visited Riverdene. I lay there thinking of Eva, scouting every suspicion which the detective's words had aroused within me, until with the first streak of dawn I fell asleep and dreamed of her.

Next afternoon, without mentioning anything to Dick save the sending of a telegram to say I should not dine at home, I left my office half an hour earlier, and full of conflicting thoughts travelled down to Riverdene.

Having been informed by the servant that Mrs Blain and Miss Mary were absent in London shopping, but that Miss Glaslyn was at home, I was shown into the long, pleasant drawing-room which opened upon the wide lawn sloping to the river's brink. The great bowls of cut flowers diffused a pleasant odour, and the books and papers lying in the cosy-corner, with its soft cushions of pale-blue silk, betrayed signs of recent occupation.

It was a low-ceilinged, comfortable apartment, cool and restful after the dust and glare of the white road outside.

In a few moments the door opened and Eva entered, fresh and charming in a cool dress of cream flannel, her sweet face illumined by a smile of glad welcome.

"This is quite an unexpected pleasure, Mr Urwin!" she exclaimed, rushing towards me gladly with outstretched hand. "I had no idea that you'd come down to-day. The Blains are up in town, you know. I should have gone, only I had a rather bad headache. We went up to Windsor yesterday with the Thurleys on their launch, and I suppose the sun upset me. It was unbearably hot."

"Why do you persist in calling me Mr Urwin?" I asked in a rather reproachful tone, still retaining possession of her hand. "Cannot you call me Frank?"

She blushed slightly, and drew her hand forcibly away. Then motioning me to a seat she cast herself into a low armchair near me, stretching forth her tiny foot, neat in its silk stocking and patent leather shoe. She made no response to my suggestion, so I repeated it.

"Why should I call you by your Christian name?" she asked.

"Because I call you by yours, Eva," I answered earnestly. "I really can't bear this persistent formality."

She smiled, a rather curious smile it was, I thought.

"So you're staying as guest here?" I went on, after a moment's pause.

"Yes," she explained. "My Uncle Henry, in Inverness, is very ill and not expected to live; therefore they summoned mother by telegraph, with other members of the family. As the servants have had no holiday this year, she sent them away for a fortnight and closed the house, Mrs Blain having invited me here."

"Have you heard from your mother?"

"Yes, I had a wire yesterday to say that she had arrived, safely," she answered, not, however, without a second's hesitation, as though she were debating whether or no to tell me the truth.

"And Mr Blain has not returned from Paris yet?" I asked.

"No," she responded. "The Blains are talking of joining him next week, or perhaps the week after, and have invited me to accompany them. I should be delighted, for I love Paris."

"You find the shops interesting?" I laughed.

"Yes," she answered. "All women do, I suppose. At least I've met very few who, having been in Paris, haven't hunted for bargains at the Louvre, the Printemps, or the Bon Marché. Paris is worth visiting if only for one's hats, for you can often buy a hat for twenty francs exactly the same style and of better material than that for which you pay three or four guineas in Regent Street."

"I'm not much of an expert in such things," I laughed, nevertheless recollecting how curious it was that Blain remained still in London. Might not his wife and daughter have gone up that day to visit him in his hiding-place?

"But you've been awfully queer, I hear," she said concernedly. "You really don't look quite yourself even now. What has been the matter? We were all so concerned when we heard about it."

Our eyes met. In hers there was a deep, earnest look as though she were really solicitous of my welfare, yet I fancied somehow that those clear blue eyes wavered beneath my steady, searching glance. She watched me, reading me as easily as she would have read black letters on a white page.

"I was taken suddenly ill — the heat perhaps," I answered with affected carelessness. "I had run down, the doctor said. It was nothing very serious." She gave vent to a perceptible sigh of relief, then smiling sweetly as she ever did, said: "Well, it is indeed a pleasure to welcome you here again to-day." She still wore that brooch, the quaint little playing-card which had betrayed her visit to Morris Lowry. Its sight sent a strange thrill through me, for I remembered the object of her visit to that dark, dirty, obscure herbalist's.

"The pleasure is mutual, believe me, Eva," I answered, putting away from me instantly the gruesome thought oppressing me. "Through this whole month I have thought only of you."

She sighed, in an instant serious. Then glancing back to assure herself that there were no eavesdroppers, she said, "It would be far better, Mr Urwin — Frank — if you could leave me and forget."

"But I can't," I said, rising quickly and again taking her soft white hand. "You know, Eva, how deeply, how sincerely, how devotedly I love you; how I am entirely yours for ever."

I spoke simply and directly what I felt; I was calmer than I had been when I rowed her beneath the willows' shade.

"Ah, no!" she cried in a pained voice, rising to her feet with sudden resolution. "You really must not say this. I will not let you sacrifice yourself. I will not allow you to thus — "

"It is no sacrifice," I protested, quickly interrupting. "I love you, Eva, with all my soul. One woman alone in all the world holds me beneath the spell of her grace, her charm and her sweetness. It is yourself. Every hour I think only of you; ever before me your face rises in my day-dreams, and in those moments when I see your sweet smiles I tell myself that no other woman can ever have a place in my heart. Ah! you cannot know how fondly I love you," I said, raising the hand tenderly to my lips and imprinting a kiss upon it. "If you could only know you would never treat me with this cold, calm indifference."

Her bosom rose and fell slowly, and she was silent. I fancied that she shuddered slightly.

At that moment my position struck me as an extremely strange one, declaring love to one whom an expert detective suspected of having made a cowardly attempt upon my life. Was it just? I asked myself. Yes, in this I was justified, for I loved her, even though I had more than once been inclined to agree with Boyd in his misgivings.

"I was not aware of any indifference," she faltered at last, raising her great eyes, so clear and earnest, for an instant to mine. "I had merely urged you to reflect."

"Reflection is unnecessary," I answered quickly. "I know that I love you truly. That surely is sufficient."

"It might be if I were free," she responded in a low, hoarse voice. "But I tell you to-day, Frank, as I told you before, this love dream of ours is impossible of realisation."

"Then you do reciprocate my love?" I cried, in joyous eagerness. "Come, tell me. Do not keep me longer in suspense."

"I have already told you," she answered in a low, intense voice. "Of what use is it to continue this painful discussion?"

"Of every use," I cried in desperation. "Give me one word of hope, Eva. Tell me that some day you will try and love me better than you do now; that some day in the future you will become my wife. Tell me — "

"No! no!" she cried, snatching her hand away and receding from me. "No, Frank, I cannot — I will not lie to you."

"Then can you never love me — never?" I cried despairingly.

"Never," she answered hoarsely, and her answer struck deep into my heart. "I have sinned — sinned before God and before man — and love no longer knows a place in my heart," and her fine head was bowed before me.

"Sinned!" I gasped. "What do you mean?"

"I am as a social leper," she panted, raising her head and looking at me with wild, unnatural gaze. "If you knew the dark and awful truth you would shun me rather than kiss my hand. Yet you say you love me — you! who would have so great a cause to hate me if you knew the ghastly truth!"

"But," I cried, wondering at these strange words, and with my suspicions again aroused, "I do love you, nevertheless, Eva. I shall always love you, I swear it, for my very life is yours."

"Your life!" she echoed in a weird, harsh voice, as she stood, pale-faced, swaying before me, her hands clasped to her breast, her lips cold and white. "Yes," she said, in a strange, half-hysterical tone. "Yes, it is true, too true, alas! that your future is in my hands. Only by a miracle have you come back to life, a grim shadow of a crime to taunt, to defy, to denounce. Ah! Frank, you do not know the terrible truth; you will never know — never!"

I was bewildered. Horror possessed me. The darkness of an irreversible fact spread over her and made her terrible to me. All must be given up. Conscience pronounced this dread decree and multiplied the pain a thousand times.

Destiny had once more taken me by the elbow.

Chapter Nineteen
Eva Makes a Confession

"Why may I not know the truth?" I asked the blanched and agitated woman before me. Her involuntary declaration that I had only returned to life by little short of a miracle was in itself clear proof that she was aware of the attempt made to assassinate me. I therefore determined to question her further and ascertain whether Boyd's grave suspicion had any absolute foundation. "You know, Eva," I went on, standing before her with my hand upon her shoulder in deep earnestness, "you know how strong is my affection; you know that you are all the world to me."

Often during my many visits to that riverside house, so cool and peaceful after the busy turmoil in which fate compelled me to earn my bread, I had spoken of my love for her, and now in my desperation I told her that I could not leave the woman whom I had so long worshipped in the ideal, whom I had instantly recognised as being the embodiment of that ideal, of whose presence I could not endure to be deprived even in thought.

She stood silent, with her back to the table, looking into my eyes while I told her these things. A ray of sunlight tipped her auburn hair with gold. Sometimes she would seem to yield to a kind of bliss as she listened to my avowal; to forget all else than ourselves and my words. At others a look of anguish would suddenly cloud her features, and once she shuddered, pressing her hands to her eyes, saying —

"Frank, you must not! Spare me this. I cannot bear it! Indeed I can't."

Sometimes, in the days that had passed, when I had spoken of my love, joy and pain would succeed each other on her face; indeed, often they would be present at the same moment. From the look of complete abandonment to happiness that sometimes, though never for long, shone on her features when we had idled up that shady, picturesque backwater, where the kingfishers nested, I felt that she loved me, and that eventually that love would gain the victory. Thus, continually, I tried to elicit an expression of her feelings in words. Sweet to me as was the confession of her looks, I sought also a confession of speech.

Alas! however, she seemed determined to give me no single word of encouragement.

"But why," I asked, as she stood there with bent head, her hand toying nervously with her rings, "why is it that when I speak of what most occupies my heart you become silent or sorrowful?"

She smiled, a strange, artificial smile, and for an instant her clear blue eyes — those eyes which spoke of an absolute purity of soul — met mine, as she replied —

"Can a woman explain her caprice any more than a man can understand it?"

Without heeding this evasion I went on —

"Is it that you are already pledged to marry some other man?"

"No," she answered, quickly and earnestly.

"Then it is because you do not wish me to love you," I observed reproachfully.

Her look startled me, for it contained besides a world of grief and pity, something of self-reproach. She regarded me strangely, first as if my words were a welcome truth, then, while her brow darkened, a mental anguish forced itself into her expression.

"You were mad to come here to me," she said, with a quick, apprehensive look. "If you knew the truth you would never again cross the threshold of this house."

"Why?" I demanded, in an instant alert.

"For a reason that is secret," she responded with a shade of sadness.

That ring of earnestness in her voice it seemed impossible to counterfeit. Puzzled, I gazed at her, striving to read her countenance. Her head was bent, her colour changing; do what she would she could not keep the blood quite steady in her cheek.

"But may I not know, Eva?" I implored. "Surely you will not refuse to warn or guide one who is so entirely devoted to you as I am?"

"I cannot warn you, except to say that treachery may be sweetly concealed, and danger lurk where you may least suspect its presence."

"You wish to place a gulf between us," I cried impatiently. "But that's impossible. I cannot rest without you; I am drawn to you as though by some power of magic. I am yours in life, in death."

"Ah, no!" she cried suddenly, putting up her hands to her face. "Speak not of death. You are making vows that must ere long be broken," and she sighed deeply.

Was not her attitude, standing there pale and trembling, the attitude of a guilty woman who feared the revelation of her crime? I looked again at her, and becoming convinced that it was, I regarded her with inexpressible scorn and love, horror and adoration. She seemed to have changed of late. She pondered over my words, weighing them without any idle misleadings of fancy. Did she never dream as she had done when we first met?

"Why must my vows be broken when my love for you is so fervent, Eva?" I demanded, in a voice a trifle hard, I think.

She shuddered and gave a gesture of despair as if there were, indeed, no defence for her. A great darkness was over my mind like the plague of an unending night.

"I have warned you," she responded, in a strange low tone. "If you really love me as you say you do, remain away from this house."

"Why are you so anxious that I should not visit you?" I demanded, puzzled. Then I added: "Of course in order to gain your love I am prepared to accept any conditions you may propose. If I do not again come here, will you meet me in London?"

"I can say nothing of the future," she answered slowly. "For your own sake — indeed, for mine also — do not come here again. Promise me, I beg of you."

This request was the more curious in the light of recent events. Was it that she could not bear me to kiss the hand that had attempted to slay me?

"All this is very strange, Eva," I said with a sudden seriousness. "I cannot understand your attitude in the least. Why not be more explicit?"

The heart of man is an open page to women. Love, though greatest of all selfish ecstasies, must yet have self-forgetfulness. She had none. She glanced at me and seemed to divine my thoughts. She cast a furtive look across the room to the lawn beyond, and I read on her face the birth of some new design.

"I have been quite explicit," she laughed, with a strenuous attempt to preserve her self-control. "I merely give you advice to keep away from this house."

"Yes, but you give me no reason. You do not speak plainly and openly," I protested.

"One cannot speak ill of those of whose hospitality one is partaking," she answered with a calm smile. "Is it not sufficient for the present that you are warned?"

"But why?" I demanded. "I am always a welcome guest here."

Again she smiled, with a strange curl of the lip, I thought.

"I do not deny that," she answered. "Have I not, however, already pointed out that treachery may be marvellously well concealed?"

Did she really warn me of the danger of associating with these intimate friends of hers merely because in her heart she really loved me? or had she some ulterior motive in getting me out of the way? She was hand-in-glove with this suspected family, therefore the latter seemed the theory most feasible.

Yes, she was undoubtedly playing me false.

A new thought suddenly arose within me, and with my eyes fixed upon her I said, in a voice hard and determined —

"Eva, just now you gave utterance to a remark which is to me full of meaning. You said that I had escaped death by little short of a miracle. True, I have." Then I paused. "Yet, if the truth were told, have you not also escaped a swift and sudden end by means almost as miraculous?"

Her face blanched instantly, her mouth, half-opened, seemed fixed. She was unable to articulate, and I saw what an effect this speech of mine had upon her. She tottered to the table and laid her hand upon it in order to steady herself. Her eyes glared upon me for an instant, like those of some animal brought to bay.

Yet, with a marvellous self-control, her white face a moment later relaxed into a smile, and she replied — "I really don't know to what you refer. In the course of our lives we have many hairbreadth escapes from death, for dangers are around us on every side." By this I saw what a consummate actress she was, and was filled with regret that I had thus referred to the tragedy at Kensington, fearing lest this revelation of my knowledge should hamper Boyd in his inquiries. Through all she kept a calm and steady judgment that was remarkable.

"Reflect at leisure," I responded, "and perhaps you will not find my words quite so puzzling as your own veiled references."

"A few minutes ago," she exclaimed reproachfully, "you declared that you loved me. Now, however, you appear to entertain a desire to taunt me."

"With what?"

She hesitated, for she saw how nearly she had been entrapped. Every woman is a born diplomatist, so she answered —

"With having endeavoured to mislead you."

"I only know that I love you, Eva," I said in softer tones, again tenderly taking her hand. "I only know that I think of no other woman in all the world besides yourself. I only know that I cannot live without your love."

Her bosom heaved and fell painfully, and from her large blue eyes tears sprang — quick, salt, bitter drops that burned her as they fell.

"Ah, no?" she cried protestingly. "Do not let us talk of that. Do not let us dream of the impossible."

"Then you really love me?" I cried in quick earnestness, bending over her, my arm about her slim waist.

But she shuddered within my grasp. Her frame was shaken by a convulsive sob, and gazing upon me with serious eyes she, in a low whisper, gave her answer.

"Alas! I cannot — I — I dare not!"

I drew back crushed and hopeless. Once again the strange thought possessed me that Mary Blain held her within her power; that although she actually loved me she feared the relentless vengeance of that woman who posed as her most intimate friend, who smiled upon us both, although in her heart was a fierce and jealous hatred.

Eva's was a strange character. She seemed a brilliant antithesis — a compound of contradictions — of all that I most detested, of all that I most admired. Her whole character seemed a triumph of the external over the innate; even though she presented at first view a splendid and perplexing anomaly, there was yet deep meaning and wondrous skill in the enigma when I came to analyse and decipher it. What was most astonishing in Eva's character was its antithetical construction, its consistent inconsistency, which rendered it quite impossible to reduce it to any elementary principles. The impression she gave was that of perpetual and irreconcilable contrast.

In those months I had known her she had enchanted me. Her mental accomplishments, her unequalled grace, her woman's wit and woman's wiles, her irresistible allurements, her starts of hauteur, her vivacity of imagination, her petulant caprice, her fickleness and her falsehood, her tenderness and her truth, all had dazzled my faculties and bewitched my fancy. She held absolute dominion over me.

My reference to that fatal night when I had discovered her apparently dead in that weird house in Kensington had utterly unnerved her. I had apparently, by those words, given her proof of the strong suspicion which she had entertained, and now she held aloof from me as from an enemy. Again and again Boyd's forcible words recurred to me. Try how I would I could not place from me the increasing belief that she had actually given me that fatal draught on the last occasion when we met.

Yet, after all, she had my welfare at heart to some extent, or she would not utter this strange inexplicable warning; she would not have so pointedly told me that the family whose guests she was were my actual enemies. The latest passion of my love had long ago kindled into a quenchless flame, and again, after this declaration of fear which she had uttered, I repeated my inquiry as to its cause.

But she shook her head, and remained silent to all my entreaty, even though her panting breast plainly showed her agitation. Had she, I wondered, really perpetrated a deed of horror? Was she, although so pure-looking and so beautiful, one of those women with inexorable determination of purpose, an actual impersonation of the evil powers?

At her invitation we strolled together across the lawn to a shady spot at the river's brink, where we sat in long wicker chairs, tea being brought to us by the smart man-servant. Again and again I sought to discover some truth from her, but she was ever wary not to betray either herself or those under whose roof she was now living. As I lounged there by her, gazing upon her neat-girdled figure, so graceful and striking in every form, I could not help reflecting that, in a mind not utterly depraved and hardened by the habit of crime, conscience must awake at some time or other, and bring with it a remorse closed by despair, and despair by death.

Had her conscience been awakened that afternoon? To me it seemed very much as though it had.

"How strangely you talk, Eva," I said, when we had been conversing together a long time beneath the trees, and the sun was already sinking. "You seem somehow to entertain an extraordinary antipathy towards me."

"Antipathy!" she echoed. "Oh, no, you are really mistaken. You ask me to love you, and I express myself unfortunately unable."

"But why unable?"

She sighed, but was silent. Her eyes were fixed far away down the tranquil river which ran with liquid gold in the sunset.

From my lips there poured swift, eager, breathless, unconsidered words in all their unreason, all their wisdom, their nobility, their ignorance, their folly, their sublimity. Yet I meant to their very uttermost every syllable I uttered.

"Tell me now," I urged. "You wish me to leave you without a single word of hope. You give me a negative reply without reason or explanation."

"I have a reason," she answered in a low, mechanical tone, a voice quite unusual to her.

"What is it?"

"I am a stern fatalist in principle and in action," she responded.

"And is it that which prevents you from reciprocating my affection?"

"No," she answered, shaking her head sadly, and glancing at her rings. "I know that happiness can never more come to me. To love would only be to increase my burden of remorse."

"Remorse?" I cried, in a moment recollecting all the mysterious past.

"Yes," she answered in a hard tone of melancholy and despair. "A remorse that arises from the pang of a wounded conscience, the recoil of the violated feelings of my nature, a horror of the ghastly past, a torture of self-condemnation strong as my soul, deep as my guilt, fatal as my resolve, and terrible as my crime."

"Your crime!" I gasped.

She had at last confessed. I sat gazing at her absolutely dumbfounded. My brain seemed dead in me.

"Yes, my crime," she responded, her face white and hard set, her clenched hands perceptibly trembling. "Now at least you are aware of the reason that I will not accept your love. I, the woman whom you love, am unworthy, degraded and perverted, a woman who would have suffered a thousand deaths of torture rather than have betrayed myself, but who is now without pity or fear, unconscious, helpless, despair-stricken, although still linked with my sex and with humanity. Death alone would be welcome to me as bridegroom." Then panting, she added, rising to leave me: "No, Frank, this must all end to-day. I can never love you. It is utterly impossible. You cannot know — you will never know — how I suffer."

She had gone from me. She was to me a thing terrible, and almost loathsome. Yet she was dear to me. I was ready to give my life to ransom hers.

She stretched out her hand and musingly touched mine. I shrank as if the contact burned me.
She saw my involuntary gesture of aversion. It set her heart harder on the thing she meant to do.

Chapter Twenty
A Night Adventure

In the silent evening hour, as the dusk darkened and twilight slowly faded into night, I was conscious of a kind of fascination against which my moral sense rebelled, but from which there was no escape. We talked on, I striving ever to learn the truth, she careful to conceal it from me. I saw how unexpected but natural were her transitions of temper and feeling, noted the contest of various passions, the wild hurricane of resentment melting into tears, faintness and languishment, and endeavoured time after time, but always in vain, to obtain a further confession from her lips.

That she existed in deadly fear of some dread secret being revealed was vividly apparent, just as it was also clear that my ill-timed observation regarding her mysterious presence in that house of mystery at Kensington had placed her upon her guard, and proved to her a fact of which before she had no confirmation. Her airy caprice and provoking petulance, which had so attracted me when we had been first introduced, had been now succeeded by a mixture of tenderness with artifice, and fear with submissive blandishment. She quailed before me when I rebuked her tenderly for her lack of confidence in me, partly because of her female subtlety, partly owing to natural feeling.

Nevertheless, when I reviewed the situation, and calmly and deliberately reflected upon her attitude, I saw plainly that she regarded me as something more than a mere acquaintance, even though her character was so complicated that no one sentiment could exist pure and unvarying in such a mind.

Therefore, sadly, with a heavy feeling of non-achievement, I took a long and lingering leave of her, and was driven back to Shepperton Station by Simpson, my mind overflowing with puzzling thoughts. Great as was my hesitation to believe that her conscience was a guilty one, nevertheless her own words were now sufficient proof that my suspicions were not unfounded. Yet I loved her. I still adored her with all my soul, even though I had kissed the slim white hand that had sought to send me to the grave.

These and a thousand similar thoughts whirled through my bewildered brain as I sat back alone in the ill-lit railway carriage. Puzzled and baffled, I sat plunged in deepest melancholy and despair, when, on the train drawing up at the quiet, lethargic station of Hampton, the door of the compartment was suddenly flung open, and a well-known cheery voice cried —

"Hullo, Urwin! Get out here. I want to speak to you."

I roused myself instantly, recognising Boyd standing on the platform in the semi-darkness. With an expression of surprise at such a meeting I jumped out and joined him, he explaining that he had come down from Waterloo with the object of finding me, and had waited at Shepperton Station for my arrival there. He, however, had not spoken to me, lest the man Simpson should chance to mention the fact at Riverdene.

"But why are you down here?" I inquired surprised.

"Well," he answered in a low voice, "we've got a piece of most secret investigation before us to-night. I've waited for your assistance. We are going to search The Hollies."

"Search the Hollies?" I echoed.

"Yes," he answered. "You'll remember Miss Glaslyn's letter to you, stating that the house was closed and the servants are away on holiday. Therefore, now's our time. We must, however, act so that Lady Glaslyn and her daughter have no suspicion that the place has been overhauled. I obtained a search-warrant from Sir John Gibbons, the chief of the local bench, this morning, and now we'll just satisfy our curiosity."

"But the place is locked up, isn't it?" I suggested, amazed at this sudden resolve.

"Of course. We must get in how we can, only being careful not to attract the attention of any neighbours, and to leave no trace behind that intruders have entered."

"Then we are to go to work like burglars?" I observed, smiling.

"Exactly," he answered.

We had now left the station, and were walking along an ill-lit path which skirted the railway until we gained the high road leading into Old Hampton. He explained the precautions he had taken, namely, to tell the constable on the beat of our intentions, and imposing upon him secrecy, and also to arrange for the local plain-clothes officer to be on duty in the vicinity. His proposal seemed to possess all the elements of adventure, therefore, notwithstanding my hesitation to commit any act which might further implicate the woman I loved, I expressed myself eager and ready to accompany him.

Nine o'clock chimed from the square old tower of Hampton Church, that landmark so well-known to those who frequent the river, and Boyd declared that it was too early to commence operations. People were about, and we might be observed. Therefore we entered that old-fashioned inn where the ancient sign is still suspended from a beam across the road, a hostelry much patronised by boating-parties, who there replenish their hampers, and entering the billiard-room we whiled away the time, playing and gossiping with a couple of tradesmen, who, judging from their pronouncements, were local notabilities, perhaps District Councillors.

We remained until the landlord called "Time, gentlemen, please!" then lighting our cigars went forth, strolling through the quaint old-world village, and skirting the long, high wall of Bushey Park towards Lady Glaslyn's. The night was dark and overcast, a gusty wind had sprung up precursor of rain, and in our ears sounded the hum of the telegraph wires. The weather favoured us. For such an excursion Boyd did not care for a perfectly still night.

At length, when we had been walking perhaps a quarter of an hour along the dark, deserted road, a man, bearded and rather shabby-looking, suddenly emerged from the shadow of the wall and greeted Boyd with the policeman's password —

"All right, sir."

"Are the things there?" Boyd inquired.

"Yes, sir. I've put the lamp, the jemmy and the keys under a laurel bush on the left of the back door."

"Well," said my friend, "I think you'd better come with us. We may have some difficulty in getting in."

"Very well, sir," the man answered, and continued to walk by our side. He was smoking a pipe, and as we neared the house he knocked out the ashes and placed it in his pocket.

"No dogs there, I hope?" Boyd said, addressing him.

"No, sir. None."

I confess to feeling a thrill of excitement, for the business of "breaking and entering a dwelling-house" was entirely new to me. The Hampton Road is ill-lit, and after ten at night utterly deserted, therefore in our walk we met no one except the solitary policeman, who stood beneath a lamp and greeted Boyd with a low "All right, sir," as we passed on towards The Hollies.

All was in darkness. Not a soul was about save ourselves and the policeman standing watchful and motionless beneath the street-lamp fifty yards away. The well-kept garden with its laurels, its monkey-trees and its old yews was shut off from the road by a high wall, in which was a pair of heavy iron gates giving entrance to the gravelled drive. These gates were locked and secured by a chain and formidable padlock, a fact which showed that to enter we must climb them. The houses on either side were of rather meaner order than The Hollies, and in one of them a light still showed in an upper window.

In order not to attract the occupiers of these houses we conversed in low whispers, and in obedience to the local detective's suggestion climbed the gates one after another and carefully descended within the garden. On either side of the house extended walls some ten feet in height, with doors in them giving access to the rear of the premises, and again, guided by the plain-clothes man, we scaled this wall, a somewhat perilous process, it being spiked on the top. As it was, indeed, I made a serious rent in an almost new pair of trousers, much to Boyd's amusement.

At last, when we were in the rear garden, our guide began foraging beneath a laurel bush and brought forth a dark lantern, a short, serviceable-looking jemmy, and a big bunch of skeleton keys.

"I examined the place this afternoon," he explained. "This door is the only one locked from the outside, therefore if we can pick the lock we shall be able to enter and get away without leaving a trace."

"Very well," Boyd said impatiently. "Let's get to work," and taking the keys he went to the garden entrance and commenced work upon the lock, while his assistant lit and held the lantern.

Every effort, however, to open the lock proved a failure.

"It's a Chubb, a Bramah, or one of those lever locks," said Boyd, in a low tone, giving it up after he had tried all the keys in vain. "It won't do to force the door, for that'll betray us."

"Why not try a window?" I suggested.

"No, sir," said the plain-clothes man. "They're all barred, I'm afraid."

"But those on the first floor," I suggested, looking up at one, evidently a landing window, over the door.

"We might try if we could only reach it," Boyd said, laying down the keys upon the doorstep. "If we forced the catch we could screw it down again before we left."

In order to discover something by which we might gain access to the window we all three crept carefully across the lawn and down the long old-fashioned garden to an outhouse, where, after some search, we found an old and rotten ladder, half the rungs of which seemed missing. This we carried back, and a few moments later Boyd, mounting, with a strong clasp-knife which he had taken from his pocket, began slowly working back the catch, until at last he was able to throw up the window and crawl in. Without a sound I followed, the local detective clambering in after me.

We found ourselves on the first floor landing, therefore, descending the stairs to the main hall, we lit the candles provided by the plain-clothes man, and after taking the precaution to let down the blinds of the front windows, commenced an active search of the drawing-room, that spacious old-fashioned apartment into which I had been shown when I had called. Our search, directed by Boyd, was careful and methodical; neither nook nor corner escaped him, although we replaced everything just as we found it. So large were the rooms that we found the lights we carried were not sufficient to give us proper illumination, therefore we sought the gas-meter, and after turning on the gas, lit jets in the various rooms. Fortunately all the windows were furnished with Venetian blinds, therefore we let them down and closed them, so that no light should be noticed outside.

An air of desolation hung about the place, and every sound we made echoed weirdly, for at dead of night all noise becomes exaggerated. The drawing-room yielded practically nothing, therefore we passed into a well-furnished morning-room, and thence to the dining-room, which we likewise thoroughly overhauled. None of these rooms bore any trace of the struggle with poverty which the innkeeper's wife had alleged. Indeed, in the drawing-room was a fine grand piano of one of the best-known makers, together with several rare works of art. All the rooms bore signs of being the abode of a rich and cultured family, the old oak in the dining-room being, I noted, genuine, evidently antique, Italian, while the upholstery and carpets were of the first quality. On the walls of those ground-floor rooms were many examples of old as well as modern masters, one portrait hanging in the dining-room representing Eva herself, a half-length picture, undoubtedly from recent sittings, signed by an artist extremely well-known in London. In this room also were antique high-backed oak chairs, lined with old tapestry, the back and arms bearing armorial bearings embroidered in coloured silks, evidently the arms of the Glaslyns, for a similar device was upon the plate.

On ascending to the first floor we found the house to be of far larger proportions than we had imagined, for off a long, well-carpeted corridor opened quite a number of bed and other rooms, each of which we proceeded to inspect.

"We haven't found a single thing below," Boyd observed to me, as we entered the first of these rooms, evidently one of the spare bedrooms, for the place was very dirty and neglected in comparison with the other apartments. "Let's hope we may come across something here."

Nothing was locked, and five minutes sufficed to show us that no attempt had been made to conceal anything in any of the two chests of drawers, or in the wardrobe. So thoroughly did Boyd search that in each room he went around the wainscoting, tapping it with the jemmy and examining any part which appeared to be loose or movable. The next room, apparently Lady Glaslyn's room, with a small dressing-room adjoining, we searched with redoubled energy, but beyond establishing the fact that her ladyship was not in want of money by the finding of three five-pound notes placed carelessly in an unlocked drawer, there was nothing to arouse our curiosity.

"Three five-pound notes placed carelessly in an unlocked drawer."

Adjoining the dressing-room, with its window overlooking the road, was a small but elegant apartment upholstered in pale-blue, quite a luxurious little room with a piano; evidently a boudoir. The carpet was so thick and rich that our feet fell noiselessly, while near the window was a handsome Louis XV escritoire inlaid with various woods and heavy mountings of chased ormolu. A pretty cosy-corner occupied the angle beside the tiled hearth, while the little bamboo table with its small shelves spoke mutely of cosy five-o'clock tea often served there.

"I wonder what's in this?" Boyd said, advancing to the escritoire while his assistant lit the gas.

Finding it locked, my friend bent, examined the keyhole carefully, and then commenced to ply the various skeleton keys. For some time he was unsuccessful, but at length the lock yielded and he opened it. Then, while the local officer took the dark lantern and went along the corridor to explore what further rooms there were, and their character, Boyd and I proceeded to carefully examine every paper, letter or document the escritoire contained. Some letters were addressed to Lady Glaslyn, others to Eva, but most of them were ordinary correspondence between relatives and friends, while the folded documents were receipted bills, together with a file of papers relating to some action at law regarding property near Aberdeen.

Behind the receptacle in which we found these letters was a panel which Boyd at once declared concealed some secret drawers, and being well versed in all the contrivances of cabinet-making, he very soon discovered the means by which the panel could be released. As he had predicted, its removal disclosed three small drawers.

To the first I gave my attention, while he took out the contents of the second. The letters, of which there were seven or eight, secured by an elastic band, I took out and read, being puzzled greatly thereby. They were all type-written and bore the post-mark "London, S.E." The first had been received about three months before, the last as recently as a fortnight ago. They were very friendly, commencing "Dear Eva," and although the writer was apparently extremely intimate, there was, however, not a word of love, a fact which gave me some satisfaction. They all, without exception, contained a most mysterious reference to "the Silence," in terms extremely guarded and curious, one urging the utmost caution and declaring that a grave peril had unexpectedly arisen which must, at all hazards, be removed. The writer did not appear to be a very educated person, for in many places there were mistakes in spelling, while all were devoid of both address or signature, bearing only the single initial "Z."

I passed them over to Boyd, asking his opinion, and as he sat at the writing flap reading them we were both suddenly startled by hearing a plaintive cry near us. It was a poor lean cat, who had accidentally been shut up there and was undoubtedly starving.

"These letters are very strange," Boyd observed, looking up at me. "I wonder to what the silence refers?"

"I don't know," I said. "There's evidently some very good reason that they've been concealed here."

As I was speaking I took from beneath some letters, still remaining in the secret drawer Boyd had opened, a wooden pill-box, from which I removed the lid, there being disclosed a small quantity of a peculiar greyish-blue powder.

"Hulloa!" Boyd exclaimed, with a quick glance at it. "What's that, I wonder? No label on the box. It looks suspicious!"

"Yes," I agreed. "I wonder what it is, that it should be so carefully concealed?"

"Leave it aside for a moment," he said.

Then taking up a large envelope which, while I had been reading the letters, he had been carefully examining, he drew from it two photographs.

"Do you recognise the originals of these?" he inquired with a grave smile.

"Great Heavens!" I gasped. "Why, they are the man and the woman whom we found at Phillimore Place!"

"Exactly," he said, in a voice of satisfaction, just as his assistant re-entered.

Then, before I could recover from my bewilderment, he took up the little wooden box, exclaiming —

"This powder here is a very suspicious circumstance, but we'll test it at once."

Turning to the local officer he said —

"I saw you eating something when you met us and you put part of it in your pocket. What was it?"

"A sandwich. My wife always makes me one when I go out on night-duty," the man explained.

"Have you any of it left?"

For answer he drew from his pocket a portion of an uneaten sandwich and placed it upon the table. Boyd, with his pocket-knife, cut off a piece of the meat, upon it sprinkled a grain or so of the mysterious powder, and threw it down to the hungry cat, which was mewing loudly, and purring round our legs.

The thin creature, ravenously hungry, devoured it, but ere ten seconds had passed, and while we all three were watching attentively, it staggered, with a faint cry, and almost without a struggle rolled over, dead.

"As I suspected," Boyd observed, turning to me. "This is the powder from the herbalist's."

"So far," continued Boyd, thoughtfully, pushing his hat to the back of his head, "we've proved one thing — that this stuff is poison."

"Yes," I said. "But these photographs? Is it not extraordinary that we find them here among Eva's possessions?"

"It's all extraordinary," he answered. "The letters more strange than anything," and he unlocked the third drawer expectantly, only, however, to find it contained something small wrapped in a piece of dirty wash-leather. He placed it before him, carefully opening it and disclosing something which caused us both to give vent to exclamations of surprise.

Inside was a most commonplace object, yet to us it had a meaning peculiarly tragic — a single penny.

Both of us recollected vividly the finding of a similar coin carefully wrapped in paper upon the body of the man at Phillimore Place, and there must, we decided, be some mysterious connexion between our two discoveries.

"These letters," observed Boyd, putting aside the coin and its wrapping and taking up the correspondence he had been examining when I had found the box of mysterious powder, "they are all addressed to Miss Glaslyn, and in one only, as far as I can see, is her mother mentioned. They evidently refer to some deep secret."

"Do you think the silence can refer to the affair at Kensington?" I suggested, holding one of the letters in my hand.

"It's impossible to tell," he answered. "We have now the clearest proof that these letters were preserved in secret by Eva Glaslyn, together with some unknown but fatal drug, and the photographs of the victim. Therefore, if circumstantial evidence may be trusted, I should be inclined to believe that these letters refer to the matter which we are investigating. Perhaps, indeed, the peril mentioned in one of the letters refers to your own endeavours to fathom the mystery."

"The whole thing is utterly bewildering," I said, re-reading the letter in my hand, a communication which certainly was of a most veiled character, evidently being type-written to disguise the writer's identity.

"There is no object whatever to be gained by adopting your suggestion," it ran. "The only absolutely safe course is to continue as in the past. The silence is effectual, and for the present is enough. All your fears are quite groundless. Show a bold front and be cautious always. If you wish to write, send your letter to the old address."

Each of the others were similarly unintelligible, except perhaps the later one, in which the writer said: "You are right. I, too, have discovered cause for apprehension. A peril threatens, but if the secret is preserved it cannot harm us."

With the mass of papers and correspondence spread before us we all three examined these suspicious letters very carefully. In the drawer which Boyd had opened was, among other things, a few girlish trinkets and souvenirs of the past, and a note signed "Mary Blain," and dated from Riverdene a couple of months before.

In the face of recent events it was a somewhat noteworthy missive, for beginning "Dearest Eva," it gave her an invitation for tennis on the following day, Tuesday. "I have also your admirer," she went on, "and he will no doubt come. Perhaps I shall be compelled to go to town to-morrow afternoon on business, the urgent nature of which you may guess. If I do I will convey your message to the quarter for which it is intended. Be careful how you act, and what you say to F," (meaning, I suppose, myself), "for I have no great faith in him. His friend is, of course, entirely well-disposed towards us."

I passed it to Boyd, and when he had read it, asked —

"What's your opinion of that? Is the person mentioned myself? and is the friend actually Dick?"

"It really seems so," he responded, with knit brows. "In that case they must have long ago suspected you of being aware of their secret. This would, of course, account for the cowardly attempt to take your life."

"By means of this unknown drug here — eh?" I suggested bitterly, pointing to the small box which I had a moment before closed.

"Certainly," said the detective. "There can now be no further doubt of Miss Glaslyn's complicity in the affair."

"I wonder who is the author of these type-written letters?" I said. "If we knew that, it would let a flood of light into the whole matter."

"We shall, I hope, discover that in due course," he answered. "Let's finish these investigations before discussing our next move," and he continued, carefully placing back the letters in the secret drawers, now and then pausing to re-read one which chanced to attract his attention.

"Look at this," he said, passing one over to me after he had glanced at it.

It was written on pale green paper in a fine fashionable woman's hand, a few brief lines, which ran: —

"My dear Eva, — I could not come to-day, but shall be there this evening. Everything is complete. When the truth becomes known the discovery will, I anticipate, startle the world. It must, for reasons you know, remain a strict secret. Do not breathe a word to a soul. — Yours ever.

"Anna."

"That may refer to the invention we found in the laboratory; a scientific discovery which no one has come forward to claim. But who, I wonder, is Anna?"

"She might be the dead woman," Boyd suggested.

"True," I agreed. "So she might."

During fully half an hour we still remained in that small cosy boudoir, which seemed to be Eva's own room, examining everything carefully and taking the utmost precaution to replace everything exactly as we found it. In this Boyd displayed real genius. Whatever was moved he rearranged it with an exactness little short of astounding. His astuteness was remarkable. Nothing escaped him, now that he was on the trail.

Yet, as I wandered about, examining things here and there, I could not repress a feeling of reproach, for had I not, after all, assisted in this secret search which had resulted so disastrously for the strange, mysterious woman I so dearly loved? She was now under the suspicion of the police. They would keep her under surveillance, for the evidence we had already obtained was sufficient to induce any magistrate to grant a warrant for her arrest. A sudden sense of a vast, immeasurable loss fell upon me.

The small box containing the greyish-blue powder had been replaced in the concealed drawer, and everything had been rearranged in the room, when the local officer said —

"At the end of the corridor there's another sitting-room."

"Very well," Boyd answered. "Let's see what it's like," and we all three, lights in hand, followed our guide until we entered a smaller sitting-room.

An easel stood in it and it was apparently used by Eva as a studio, for she, I knew, took lessons in painting. Upon the easel stood a canvas half finished, while near the window was a small writing-table, the one long drawer of which was locked. The lock was a common one and quickly yielded to Boyd's skeleton keys, but within we only found another collection of old letters, a quantity of pencil sketches, colours and other odds and ends connected with her art studies. Boyd was turning them over methodically, when suddenly an involuntary exclamation escaped him.

"Ah! What's this?" he ejaculated, at the same time drawing forth a card about the size of a lady's visiting card, and held it out to me.

Upon it was drawn in ink a circle. It was executed in exactly the same manner as that we had found concealed beneath the plates in the dining-room at Phillimore Place.

Again he turned the things over and drew out three or four other cards of similar size and style, each bearing a device, one having upon its face the straight line exactly like that we had found in Kensington.

"You recognise these devices?" he inquired.

"Of course," I responded in an awed voice, utterly bewildered. "What, I wonder, can they denote?"

He shrugged his shoulders, examined each card carefully beneath the rays of his lamp, felt it, and after carefully examining all the heterogeneous collection of things in the drawer, placed them back again, closed it, and relocked it.

"Those cards bear some very important part in the tragedy, I feel assured," he said when he had finished, and turned to me with a puzzled expression. "They look innocent enough, and the devices are in no way forbidding; nevertheless, it is strange that we find here, in her possession, exact duplicates not only of the cards, but also of that coin carried by the dead man."

"It's all utterly astounding," I declared. Then, with a touch of poignant regret and despair, I added: "All these discoveries would cause me the highest gratification if I did not love her as fondly as I do."

"You surely could not make a murderess your wife, Urwin?" my friend said. "In this matter remember that we are striving to fathom a mystery which is one of the most profound and remarkable that has ever been reported at the Yard."

"I know," I answered, glancing around that small room wherein my well-beloved had spent her days in the study of art. "But what I cannot understand is how, being an actual victim of the tragedy, she is nevertheless at the same time implicated in the affair."

"That will be made plain later," he said with an air of confidence.

"One thing is quite clear, that she purchased certain poisons which are only known to those well versed in toxicology. We have that on old Lowry's own authority. If, then, she bought this drug it could only be for one purpose, namely, to commit murder. Well, she made an attempt upon you; therefore, why should you endeavour to shield her?"

"Because I love her," I answered, still unconvinced by his argument.

"Bah! Love is entirely out of the question in this matter, my dear fellow," he said, with a gesture of impatience. "She may have fascinated you because of her unusual beauty, but beyond that — well, in six months' time you'll thank Providence that you've not married her — mark my words."

That was exactly what she herself had said, I reflected. She had prophesied that one day, ere long, I would hate the very mention of her name.

From room to room we passed, examining everything, allowing nothing to escape us. There was assuredly no sign of poverty in that house, but really the reverse, a lavish display of costly objects, which showed that its owner was capricious, with money at her command. No expense seemed to have been spared to render that abode the acme of comfort and modern convenience.

In one of the bedrooms in that same corridor, a room which we decided was Eva's from various dresses and other things it contained, we found standing upon the table a large panel photograph of a kind-faced, middle-aged woman, which the local officer at once recognised as that of Lady Glaslyn.

Boyd, taking it up, examined it long and earnestly beneath the light of the bull's-eye.

"Devilish good-looking for a woman of her age," he remarked thoughtfully, as he slowly replaced it upon the table. "Do you know?" he added, turning to me, "I fancy I've met her somewhere — but where I can't for the life of me recollect. What do you know about the family?"

"Very little beyond what's in Burke, which only devotes three lines to them. The baronetcy was conferred in 1839, and Lady Glaslyn's husband, Sir Thomas, died six years ago. No mention is made of their country seat, so I presume they haven't one."

Boyd stroked his beard and gave vent to a low grunt of doubt.

"Well," he said, "I'm almost positive that I've met her before somewhere. I wonder where it was."

Quickly we rearranged the articles in the room which we had disturbed and passed on to the next, the door of which faced us, forming the end of the long corridor.

"Hulloa!" Boyd cried. "What does this mean?"

We both looked, and by the light of the lantern saw that the door was a double one and that right across it was a long bar of steel or iron painted and grained the colour of the wood so as not to be noticeable, and securing it strongly.

"This is decidedly funny," the detective continued, bending down to examine something. "Look! it's sealed!"

I bent eagerly beside him, and there saw that the great sliding bolt ran in three large hasps, and that one of the knobs of the bolt was secured by wire to the hasp, the two ends of the wire being secured together by a round seal of molten lead about the size of a shilling. By this the bolt was rendered immovable.

"Extraordinary!" I gasped, as we all stood wondering what might be therein concealed. "If we cut the wire then our presence here will be betrayed," I said.

But Boyd, who was still examining the seal with great care, exclaimed at last, pointing to it —

"Do you see two letters on the seal, 'R.' and 'M.'?"

"Yes," I answered. "What do you think they denote?"

"They tell us how this seal was impressed," the detective responded. "These initials stand for Rete Mediterranea, and the machine with which the seal has been impressed is one of those used at every Italian railway station to seal merchandise and passengers' baggage. It has certainly been placed upon the wire by one who knew how to handle the instrument with dexterity."

"There must be something in that room which her ladyship desires to keep secret," I remarked, both amazed and excited at this latest discovery.

"Yes," remarked Boyd. "At all hazards we must explore it."

"But how," I queried, "without tampering with the seal?"

His brow clouded for a few moments, then again he examined the seal and wire with the utmost care. He stood motionless, looking at it for fully a minute, then turning to the local officer, said —

"I'm going downstairs a moment. Don't touch it till I return."

We both sat upon an ottoman in the corridor for nearly a quarter of an hour, during which time we heard noises downstairs; until Boyd at last rejoined us with a look of satisfaction in his face, and bearing in his hands something which looked like a huge pair of rusty shears with wooden handles.

"I thought I'd find it," he observed, wiping the perspiration from his brow. His hands and face were blackened as though he had been groping in a cellar. "This is the seal," and opening his other hand he displayed an old discoloured pewter teaspoon, adding, "And here's a bit of lead — or what's as good."

I took the sealing machine from him and examined it carefully. It was red with dust, and had apparently been thrown aside and neglected for a long time.

"Now," said Boyd to his assistant, "I've lit a fire downstairs in the kitchen, and by the time we've done it'll be sufficiently fierce to melt the lead."

"Then you intend to break open the door?" I exclaimed.

He smiled, and for answer took from his pocket a champagne-knife, cutting the wire with a sharp click, untwisting it from the knob, and placing it with its seal in his pocket.

In breathless eagerness we watched him push back the bolt, and stood expectant; but when he tried the door he found it to be still locked. Again he went swiftly to work with his bunch of queer-looking keys, and at last he saw one of them gently turn, and he pushed wide open the door of the chamber of secrets.

Next second the bright light of Boyd's bull's-eye flashed into the interior, and all three of us fell back with exclamations of surprise and horror. Our discovery was truly astounding.

The horrible sight was most weird and terrifying. Upon the threshold I stood speechless, utterly unable to move, for the ghastly spectacle made my hair rise as my eyes became riveted upon the noisome interior of that long-closed chamber.

Our nostrils were filled with a foetid, nauseating smell of decay which burst upon us as the door was opened, and at the shock of witnessing the repulsive sight within, the candle I had held dropped from my trembling fingers and was extinguished. Slowly, however, I recovered it, taking a light from the one held by my friend's assistant, and then entered the place.

It was not a large room, but the shutters of the window had, we afterwards discovered, been secured by screws and strongly barred. In the centre was a square table, covered with dust, and several common wooden chairs stood around. In the empty rusted grate stood a kettle and a couple of cooking-pots, while upon a side table were a few plates and a couple of cups and saucers. Along one side stood an old camp bedstead, and lying upon it, half-covered with a dirty blanket, was a figure that had once been human but which was now a sight so gruesome and so horrible that even Boyd, used as he was to such things, drew away and held his handkerchief to his nose.

The features were beyond recognition, but by the shortness of the hair the body was evidently that of a man. One arm hung helpless, shrivelled and discoloured, while on the floor close by were the broken portions of a cup which had evidently fallen from the dead man's claw-like fingers.

"This is another facer!" Boyd exclaimed in a tone of absolute bewilderment. "I wonder who he was? It seems by the pots and plates that he was held a prisoner here — an invalid or imbecile, perhaps, unable to help himself. Evidently the servants knew nothing of him, for he cooked his food himself. Phew!" he added. "Let's get outside in the passage to breathe. This air is enough to poison one."

Half-choked, we went outside, all three of us, and discussed the startling situation while breathing the purer air. I offered both my companions cigarettes, which they lit eagerly with myself.

Then, after a few minutes, we returned and resumed our investigations. About the room were several books in French and German treating of political economy and other subjects, a couple of old newspapers, two or three novels, and a number of scientific books which showed their reader to be an educated man. The room had originally been a bathroom, we concluded, for there was a water-tap and a large pipe for waste, and this unfortunate man, whoever he was, had evidently not existed wholly in darkness, for on examining the shutters we found that one of the panels was movable, and at that spot the pane of glass was broken, thus admitting both light and air. Again, there was a small gas-stove ring, used so universally in London to boil kettles, and this was still connected by a flexible pipe to a gas bracket on the wall. Hence it was quite apparent that the room had been specially fitted for the occupation of the unknown man now dead.

Upon the dusty table were several pieces of writing-paper covered with some writing in German, a language which I unfortunately could not read, while beside them I picked up an object which held me amazed and astounded — a plain card similar to those we had found at Phillimore Place and among Eva's secret possessions.

Beyond those writings in German we found nothing else to give us a clue to whom the dead man might be, and even these writings were no proof as to his identity. We found no writing materials there, hence our doubt that the writing had been traced by his hand.

Into every hole and crevice we peered, disturbing the rats who had scampered here and there on our unexpected intrusion, but discovering nothing else of especial interest, we, after about half an hour, went forth, glad to escape from the poisonous atmosphere. I closed and locked the door, when Boyd, cutting out a piece of bell-wire from one of the bedrooms, re-secured the bolt, and after melting the pewter spoon below in the kitchen fire, replaced the seal in such a manner that none could tell it had ever been disturbed.

Truly our midnight search had been a fruitful one. What might next transpire I dreaded to think. All was so mysterious, so utterly astounding, that I had become entirely bewildered.

Chapter Twenty Two
In Defiance of the Law

The discovery of the horror concealed within that closed room opened out an entirely fresh development of the mystery. On discussing it with Boyd after we had stealthily left the house we were in complete agreement that the dead man must have either been in hiding there, or else, being an imbecile, had been kept under restraint. The fact of the door being barred on the outside strengthened Boyd's belief in the latter theory, while I made the suggestion that he might have been imprisoned and died of starvation.

"No," Boyd answered, "I don't agree with you there, for it is quite plain that Lady Glaslyn must have been aware of his presence, and perhaps, indeed, arranged the room. There is every evidence that he was supplied with food at intervals, and cooked it himself, which shows that, even if an invalid, he was sufficiently active. My idea is that he may have been some relation whose demented condition her ladyship wished to keep from her friends and other members of the family, and that having died suddenly she was compelled to lock and seal the door, dreading the publicity of a coroner's inquiry, when the truth must have been made public."

"True," I said. "That's, of course, a very feasible theory. But if she were in the secret, Eva, too, must have known."

"Of course," he said. "She can tell us everything if she chooses. It's a pity that the dead man's face is unrecognisable."

"Again, is it not strange that we should have found in there one of those same cards?"

"Yes, rather," responded my friend. "But at present it is useless to advance all kinds of wild theories. We must stick closely to facts if we would succeed. We have to-night made certain discoveries, startling enough in all conscience, and among them have elucidated the secret which Lady Glaslyn has hidden from every one. Now we must seek to discover the motive which caused her to apply that seal to the door, as well as ascertaining the reason her daughter has that mysterious drug among her possessions, together with the photographs of the two unknown victims."

"I wonder how long it is since the man died in that room," I said. "What a horrible existence he must have led shut up there, gaining all his light and air through a broken pane of glass. He was studious, at any rate, judging from the character of the books with which he had been supplied."

"And a linguist too," Boyd remarked, remembering that the books were in other languages besides English.

"Strange that the curiosity of the servants was not aroused," I said. "They would be certain to wonder what was in a room sealed up as that is."

"To satisfy them would be easy enough," the detective answered. "Her ladyship undoubtedly told them that certain family heirlooms, old furniture, or something, was stowed away there, and that the seal had been placed upon them by the trustees, or somebody. Trust a woman for an excuse," and he smiled grimly.

We walked on together for some time in complete silence. The young day grew wider and brighter and redder in the sky. We had passed through Twickenham, and now, in the dawn, were making our way towards Richmond, whence we could catch the early workmen's train to Waterloo.

"You must keep your friend Cleugh in entire ignorance of all this. Tell him you've been out to visit some friends, say at Ealing or Uxbridge, or somewhere, and that they compelled you to stay the night. If he were to know, the whole result of our investigations might be rendered abortive."

"Of course I'll do as you wish," I answered. "But I can't for the life of me see why you entertain any suspicion of Dick. He's been all along eager and ready to assist me to clear up the mystery. To publish the details of the curious affair seems his one object." Boyd smiled again with veiled sarcasm.

"And a very interesting story he'll have for publication, it appears to me," he said, laughing. Then he added after a second's pause, "One of the oddest facts in the whole affair is that the pair we found dead in Phillimore Place have never been missed by their friends."

"Or the dead man at The Hollies, for the matter of that," I added.

"Yes," he said in dubious tone. "There are yet some facts which we must learn ere we can piece the queer puzzle together and read the whole. Only then can we discover who was the man whom Lady Glaslyn has so carefully hidden. It's a devilish funny business, to say the least."

"Has it occurred to you that she may have left not intending to return?" I asked.

"Well, no," he responded. "I scarcely think she has flown, or her daughter would have secured the contents of her escritoire. She evidently believes her secret quite safe, and is therefore entirely fearless." The Richmond Road with its many trees was pleasant in that hour when the clear rose-flush of dawn was still in the sky, and as we walked the cool wind rose fragrant with the smell of the wet grass, refreshing after the foetid atmosphere of that closed room and its gruesome occupant.

We chatted on, discussing the startling discoveries we had made, he giving me certain instructions, until we got to the station and entered a compartment. The latter being crowded with workmen, further conversation on the subject was precluded.

Soon after six I returned to Gray's Inn, and making an excuse to Dick for my absence, snatched an hour's sleep before going down to my office. My heart was hard; my blood fire. Fate had been merciless.

"I began to think something had happened, old chap," Dick had said when I had entered his room and awakened him. He sat up in bed and looked at me rather strangely, I thought. Then he added: "You don't seem as though you've had much sleep, wherever you've been."

In my excitement I had quite forgotten that my clothes were dirty and torn, and my face unwashed, and I fancied that his pointed remark caused a slight flush to rise to my cheeks.

How I performed my duties that morning I scarcely knew, for my brain was in a whirl with the amazing discoveries of the past night, I loved Eva, yet the contents of those concealed drawers were sufficient in themselves to convince Boyd of her guilt. A fearful and perpetual dread seized me lest she should be arrested. Boyd's method of work was, I knew, always bold and decisive. A detective, to be successful, must act without hesitation. In this affair he had obtained evidence which, from every point of view, proved but one fact, and one alone — her guilt. Indeed, I now remembered with bitterness how she had to me openly declared herself guilty; how she had prophesied that one day I should hate all mention of her name. Did it not seem quite clear, too, that this very drug which I had found in the small wooden box, the drug which had been instantly fatal to the poor brute upon which we tried it, was the same which had been administered to me by her hand?

When I thought of that I felt glad that I had assisted my friend of Scotland Yard, and that with my own hands had unearthed evidence which must lead to her conviction. Her arrest was, I knew from my friend's remarks, only a matter of days, perhaps, indeed, of hours.

"You can't now seek to shield Miss Glaslyn," he had remarked when we had been waiting for the train on Richmond platform. "The proofs are far too strong. If we could only discover the author of those type-written letters we would be able to find out what the Silence refers to, and to move with much more certainty. As we can't, we must fix our theory firmly and act boldly upon it."

"Do you mean that you intend to apply for a warrant against her?" I inquired, dismayed.

"We shall obtain one against somebody, but who it may be of course depends entirely upon the result of our subsequent investigations. People don't keep bodies locked up in their houses without some very strong motive."

It now struck me as exceedingly strange why Eva should have been so anxious to prevent me revisiting Riverdene. She had hinted that the Blains were my enemies, yet was it not more likely that my presence reminded her too vividly of her sin, and she also feared the vengeance of Mary Blain? There was undoubtedly some deep motive underlying this effort to prevent me visiting the Blains, but as I reflected upon it I failed to decide what it might be. She had spoken of it as though it were for my benefit, and as if she had my welfare at heart, yet I could not fail to detect how hollow was the sham, for the Blains were my friends of long standing, and since my visit at Mary's request my welcome had always been a most cordial one.

Mary had certainly no cause for jealousy, for she and I had on several occasions, when alone on the river, spoken of the past. She had, indeed, ridiculed my boyish love for her, and observed that we were both older and more discreet nowadays. I had long been assured by her words and her attitude that her affection for me — if she had really ever entertained any — had entirely passed away.

No, I could not understand Eva's present attitude. It was entirely an enigma. She seemed filled with some nameless terror, the reason of which our discoveries seemed to prove up to the hilt.

Day followed day, each to me full of anxiety and bewilderment. On parting from Boyd he had told me to remain in patience until he communicated with me. I was not to return to Riverdene, neither was I to mention a single word to Dick regarding recent occurrences.

I wandered from end to end of London day after day, reporting the events which daily crop up in the Metropolis. It seemed to me as if those days would never end. I saw nothing but the face of Eva. The world which had seemed to me so beautiful had changed; Heaven was cruel. It created loveliness only to pollute and deform it afterwards. Out of my dreams I was brought face to face with facts that sickened me. The old landmarks of my faith were gone. Whatever happy hopefulness of nature I possessed was crushed. I was bewildered and sick at heart. Yet through it all I could not thrust away from me Eva's wondrous beauty. Her form, her gaze, her smile, her sigh — I could think of nothing else. Yet the mockery of it all stung me to despair, and despair is man's most frequent visitor.

A week thus passed. I saw her in the air, in the clouds, everywhere; her voice rang in my ears; she was so lovely — and yet she was so vile — a poisoner!

One afternoon I had returned to Gray's Inn unusually early, about three o'clock, put on my old lounge-coat, a river "blazer," and sat down to write up an interview for publication next day, when I heard a ring at the door, voices outside the room, and a few moments later Mrs Joad entered, saying — "'Ere's a lady wants to see you, sir."

"A lady?" I exclaimed, turning quickly in my chair. "Ask her in."

I rose, brushing down my hair with my hand, and next moment found myself face to face with Eva.

She advanced with her hand outstretched and a smile upon her face, that countenance that was ever before me in my day-dreams.

"How fortunate I am to find you in," she exclaimed, half breathless after the ascent of the stairs. "I've been to your office, and they told me that you were probably at home."

"It is I who am fortunate," I answered, laughing gaily, placing the armchair for her and drawing out a little oaken footstool, a relic from some bygone generation of men who had tenanted those grimy old rooms.

With a sigh she seated herself, and then for the first time I noticed the deathly pallor of her cheeks. Even her thick veil did not conceal it. She was in black, neat as usual, but her skirt was unbrushed and dusty, and her hair was just a trifle awry, as though she had been travelling about some hours.

"I have called upon you here for the first and for the last time," she said in a broken voice, looking seriously across to me, as the unwonted tears sprang into her eyes.

"The last time!" I echoed. "What do you mean?"

"I have come to wish you farewell," she said in a low, faltering voice. "I am leaving London. My mother and I are going abroad."

"Abroad? Where?" I cried, dismayed.

"My mother's health is not good, and the doctor has ordered her to the South immediately. He says that she must never return to this climate, because it will hasten her malady to a fatal termination. Therefore, in future we must be exiles." She was looking straight into my face as she spoke, and those great wondrous eyes of hers that I had believed to be so pure and honest never wavered. "I leave to-morrow and join her," she added.

"Then she has already gone!" I exclaimed, the truth at once flashing upon me that Lady Glaslyn had actually fled.

"Yes. The doctor has so frightened her that I could not induce her to stay and pack. I shall join her in Paris," she explained quite calmly. "There is no help for it. We must part."

"But surely," I said in desperation, "you will not leave me thus? You will return to England sometimes."

"I really don't know," she answered in a strained, hoarse voice.

"At least you will give me hope that some day you will be my wife, Eva," I said, tenderly grasping her hand, which seemed limp and trembling. "You know how fondly I love you, how — "

I started quickly and turned, puzzled at the unusual sound of voices, without finishing the sentence. One voice I recognised speaking in deep tones to Mrs Joad, and dropping the hand I held I rushed out, closing the door behind me.

As I did so, I came face to face with Boyd, accompanied by two plain-clothes officers.

"We've followed her here," he explained. "She means to get away abroad, therefore we must now execute the warrant. I regret it, for your sake."

A loud piercing shriek from within told me that she had overheard those fateful words.

"No," I cried. "By Heaven! you shan't arrest her!" and I resolutely barred his passage to the inner room. "As I love her you shall never enter there! She shall never be taken as a common criminal!"

Chapter Twenty Three
Her Ladyship

Boyd, seeing my fierce determination, held back, a look of undisguised annoyance upon his face.

"I have a duty to perform. I beg of you not to obstruct me, Mr Urwin," he said coldly. "It is quite as unpleasant to me as to you."

"Unpleasant!" I echoed. "I tell you that you shall not arrest her," and I stood firmly with my back to the door of my room.

"Come," he said, in a tone of persuasion. "This action of yours cannot benefit her in the least. She has made every preparation for flight. Her trunk is in the cloakroom at Charing Cross Station, and she means within an hour to get away to the Continent. Let me pass."

"I shall not," I roared.

"In that case I shall be compelled to use force, however much I regret it."

As he uttered these words the door was suddenly flung back, and I saw Eva's tragic, almost funereal, figure in the opening. She was white to the lips, her countenance terribly wan and haggard.

"Enough!" she cried hoarsely. "Let the police enter. I am ready," and she tottered back, clutching at the corner of my writing-table for support.

Her outward purity and innocence were a rare equipment for the committal of a crime. Who, indeed, would have suspected her of guile and intrigue? When Love is dead there is no God.

We were standing together in my sitting-room, Boyd being our only companion. A dozen times I had implored her to speak the truth, but without avail. She stood pale and trembling, yet still silent before us. Terror held her dumb.

"Those who turn King's evidence obtain free pardon," the detective gravely observed, speaking for the first time.

She laughed a little to herself.

"You might have striven for ever in vain to solve the mystery," she answered at last, apparently bracing herself up for an effort. "Those who aimed that terrible blow, so swift and so fatal, were not the kind of persons to be ever caught napping. They never made a false move, and always took such elaborate precautions that to solve the enigma would be impossible to any one unacquainted with previous events."

Her breast rose and fell quickly in her wild agitation. She was stirred by emotion to the depths of her being.

"I was weak and helpless," she faltered. "God knows how I have suffered; how deep has been my repentance. Hear me to the end," she urged, turning her fine eyes to mine. "Then, when I have told you my wretched if astounding story, Frank, judge me as you think fit — for I am yours."

"Speak!" I said anxiously. "My justice shall be tempered with mercy."

By that sentence she had acknowledged her love for me, but now I hesitated. She was accused of murder.

"Then I must begin at the very beginning, for it is a long and most complicated story, a story of a deep-laid intrigue and conspiracy, and of a duplicity extraordinary," she said, her thin, nerveless hand trembling in mine as I held her with my arm about her waist. "In the days when I had reached my sixteenth year I lived with my mother abroad, in Italy for the most part, because it was cheap, and further because my father, who had been guilty of certain shady transactions, had been compelled to fly from England. He had treated my mother shamefully, therefore they were separated, and mother and I lived economically in these cheap pensions in Florence and Rome which seem to exist as asylums for the well-bred needy. A few days after I was sixteen, while we were at an obscure pension in Siena, my mother took typhoid and died, leaving me absolutely alone in the world, and practically penniless. Nearly a year before we had received a letter from my father's solicitors in London stating that he had died in poverty in Buenos Aires, therefore I was utterly alone. The position of a friendless girl on the Continent is always serious," she said, with a catch in her voice. "Acting upon the advice of some English people in the pension I went to Florence and saw there the Consul-General, who not only gave me money from the British Relief Fund, which is supported by English residents in that city, but also interested himself actively upon my behalf and obtained for me a post as governess in a wealthy Italian family living near Bologna. In their service I remained nearly three years, until, by the death of the head of the house, the family became scattered, when I took a fresh engagement with a lady who advertised for an English companion. She was a Madame Damant, a good-looking woman of forty-five, whose father, I understood, had been Italian, and whose mother English. She spoke English quite as well as I did, and had a fine apartment in Florence, where she received a good deal, for she was well-known there. With the winter over we travelled first to Paris, where we stayed several months, and then to Switzerland. Our life was pleasant, as Madame had plenty of money and we always lived at the best hotels."

She paused and drew a long breath. There was a hardness about her mouth, and tears were in her eyes.

"It was in Zurich that I had my first misgivings, for there one day in late autumn we were joined by a strange old gentleman, Hartmann by name, whom I understood was Madame's brother, a curious old fellow, whose main object in life appeared to be the carrying out of certain scientific experiments. He remained with us in the same hotel for nearly a fortnight, during which time Madame, who was extremely well-educated, held frequent consultations with him upon scientific matters, until one day I was overjoyed when she announced that we were all three to go straight to London."

"Then the Lady Glaslyn at The Hollies was not your mother?" I gasped, profoundly amazed at this revelation.

"I am about to explain," she went on in a hard voice. "On the night before our departure from Zurich I chanced to pass the door of Madame's bedroom after everybody had retired to rest, and seeing a light issuing from the keyhole was prompted by natural curiosity to peep within. What I saw was certainly strange. In one hand she was holding an unopened bottle of Benedictine liqueur upside down, while with the other she took a hypodermic syringe filled with some liquid, and with the long thin needle pierced the cork, then slowly, and with infinite care, she injected the liquid from the tiny glass syringe. Afterwards she withdrew the hollow needle, glanced at the parchment capsule beneath the light, and having satisfied herself that the puncture made was quite unnoticeable, she shook the bottle so as to thoroughly mix the injected liquid with the liqueur. Then I saw her wrap the bottle carefully in a number of towels and place it in her trunk. Next day, when packing, I glanced at the bottle with some curiosity, examining the parchment covering the cork, but so tiny had been the puncture that I failed to discover the hole. The parchment had, I think, been touched with gum, which had caused the tiny hole to close."

"That liqueur was evidently poisoned," Boyd remarked, his brows knit in thought.

"Yes," she answered. "I have every reason to believe so, although the true state of affairs did not dawn upon me until long afterwards. When alone in our compartment in the *wagon-lit* between Basle and Calais, Madame, however, made a very extraordinary proposal to me. She confessed that her husband had been made the scapegoat of some financial fraud in England and was in hiding somewhere near Paris, therefore, in going back, she feared that if she went under her right name — Damant — that the police would begin to make active inquiries regarding monsieur. She wished, she said, to avoid this and set up a house in some pleasant suburb of London, so as to have a *pied-à-terre* in the country she so dearly loved. Now my mother was dead, and no friends in England knew her, so many years had she lived on the Continent, why should she not pass as Lady Glaslyn and I as her daughter? At first this proposal utterly staggered me, but when she pointed out how much more I would be respected as her daughter instead of her companion, and told me of the manner in which she intended to live — a manner befitting her assumed station — I at length gave my consent, for which she made me a present there and then of a very acceptable bank-note."

"Then that woman only posed as your mother!" I exclaimed. "She was not the real Lady Glaslyn?"

"Certainly not," answered my beloved frankly. "At first I was very indisposed to be a party to any such transaction, but she had shown me so many kindnesses, and had always been so generous, that I, a friendless girl, felt compelled to accede. Ah! if I had but known what lay behind all that outward show of good feeling and sympathy I would have cast her accursed money from me as I could cast the gold of Satan. I would rather have made matches for a starvation wage, or slaved at a shop-counter, than have remained one day longer beneath her roof. But she was full of cool ingenuity and marvellous cunning, and on my acceptance of this proposal instantly set to work to bind me further to secrecy. This was not difficult, alas! for I was entirely unsuspicious of treachery, and least of all of my generous friend and benefactor. After some search and many interviews with house-agents we found The Hollies, which she purchased, together with the furniture just as it stood, and ere long neighbours began to call upon us, and we soon entered local society. Many times in those dull winter days I pondered long and deeply upon what I had seen in Zurich, wondering for what reason she had so carefully prepared the bottle which had passed the customs at Charing Cross undiscovered, and still remained locked in the travelling-trunk, surrounded by the wrappings she had placed upon it."

"Was any of the liqueur given to any one?" asked Boyd grimly.

Ere she could respond the door was thrown open, and Dick entered with Lily Lowry. He had, it transpired, gone that day and besought her forgiveness.

In a single glance he realised what had occurred, and without a word he closed the door, and both stood in silence to listen to her statement.

How strange a thing is this life of ours! We are in hell one hour, and in heaven the next.

Chapter Twenty Four
The Truth Revealed

"Remain patient and I'll explain," Eva answered, glancing at the new-comers. "First, however, let me relate a very curious circumstance. Hartmann, who lived somewhere in London, we saw seldom, but very soon after taking possession of The Hollies, there one day called an old friend of Madame's, accompanied by her husband. They were the Blains. Mrs Blain afterwards came frequently to us at The Hollies, and we often spent the day at Riverdene, while so intimate did the two women become that Madame took the house next to that rented by Mrs Blain in Kensington."

"Next door?" I gasped, astounded. "In Upper Phillimore Place?"

"Yes, the house next to the one you entered on that fatal night was in the occupation of Madame," she explained. "We seldom went there, however, although I personally preferred the bright life in Kensington to that at Hampton. From the many private conversations, meaning looks and mysterious whisperings exchanged between Madame and Mrs Blain there was soon aroused within me a vague suspicion that something secret was in progress. I liked old Mr Blain exceedingly, and Mary became my best friend; nevertheless, my misgivings were strengthened, when one day Hartmann, unusually shabbily dressed and accompanied by the Blains, arrived at The Hollies and the trio were closeted for quite an hour with Madame. At length there also arrived a youngish good-looking man with a lady of about his own age, and they were at once admitted to the drawing-room, being enthusiastically welcomed. After half an hour or so we all dined together, but in the drawing-room before dinner I noticed two tumblers half-filled with dirty water, in one a tiny glass rod evidently used for mixing, as though Hartmann had been exhibiting some of his secret experiments. On entering the dining-room, Madame introduced her new guests to me as Mr and Mrs Coulter-Kerr, and sitting beside the husband I found him a most interesting and intelligent man, who literally adored his wife. In the course of conversation it transpired that the newly-arrived pair were from India, and had taken the Blains' town house for the season, and further, that Hartmann, who had apparently become one of their most intimate friends, had established his laboratory in one of the top rooms of that house."

She paused and glanced across to the detective, who was listening attentively with folded arms. As she related her story her great clear eyes became more luminous.

"A week later," she continued, "we went to London and there saw a good deal of our next-door neighbours. Madame was on terms of the closest intimacy with them, and frequently we would dine there, or they would dine with us, while one evening Hartmann — who did not live there, but only came to continue his scientific studies, assisted by Mr Kerr, who took the keenest interest in them — invited us up into his laboratory, and after showing us Mr Kerr's collection of pet Indian snakes, which I confess I did not appreciate, he exhibited to us an experiment which he told us had never been successfully accomplished by any other man except himself, namely, the liquefaction of hydrogen. To succeed in this, he told us, all his efforts had been directed for years, and now that he had successfully solved the problem he would one day launch it upon the scientific world as a bolt from the blue. Our friends gave excellent dinners, were evidently possessed of almost unlimited means, and were never so happy as when the Blains and ourselves were at their table or playing cards with them. Soon, however, another matter caused me deep reflection. One evening at The Hollies, after the Blains and Hartmann had been closely closeted with Madame, discussing, as they so often did, their private affairs, I found lying beneath a book upon the table, and apparently overlooked, several plain cards, and others with devices, lines and circles roughly-drawn in ink. Then two or three days later, when I chanced to call in at the Kerrs, I noticed, stuck behind a mirror over the mantelshelf, some cards exactly similar. I was alone, therefore my curiosity prompted me to examine them. Upon them I found exactly similar devices!"

"Ah! what connexion had those cards with the affair?" interrupted Dick.

"A very curious one," she responded, pale, yet now firm in her determination to tell us everything. "Their discovery caused me a good deal of thought, especially as the secret consultations with Mr Blain became more frequent when, after a fortnight or so in London, we returned to The Hollies. One day, however, a further incident happened, which was, to say the least, extraordinary. While alone in Madame's bedroom the cook entered, asking for some coppers to pay for some small article which had been brought. She wanted sevenpence. I had only sixpence in my purse, but remembering that in the little cabinet where Madame kept her jewels I had seen a penny on the previous day I unlocked it and took it out. Strangely enough, this penny was wrapped up in paper. I took it in my hand and turned it over to assure myself that it was not any rare foreign coin, and was about to hand it to the cook when Madame herself came in. 'What's that you have?' she cried, in an instant pale-faced in alarm. I told her that I had taken the penny from the cabinet, whereupon she betrayed the greatest apprehension, and snatched up a piece of paper in which she carefully re-wrapped it. Then, telling me on no account to again touch it or open it, she gave the cook a penny from her pocket and dismissed her. Almost next instant I felt an indescribable numbness in the hand that had held the forbidden coin. The fingers seemed paralysed, and I had a faint idea that I had felt a strange roughness about the face of the copper, as though it had been chipped. I complained to Madame of the curious feeling, whereupon she flew to her small travelling medicine-chest, which she always kept locked, and took therefrom a phial, from which she poured a few drops of a dark green liquid into a glass of water. 'There,' she said, betraying quite undue alarm, I thought, 'drink that. You'll be better very quickly.' I gulped it down. It tasted very bitter, but within a quarter of an hour I felt no further pain. My hand had in a few seconds commenced to swell, but the medicine at once arrested it. Until long afterwards it never occurred to me that upon that penny was one of those insidious but most deadly of poisons known to toxicologists, which, entering by an abrasion of the skin, would have quickly proved fatal had not my employer at once administered an antidote. Later, I succeeded in obtaining possession of that coin, and found upon it a series of almost infinitesimal steel points, a puncture or scratch from any one of which must result in death."

I recollected how we had discovered that coin in her escritoire. We might congratulate ourselves that neither of us had held it in our hands without its wrappings.

"For a long time I was greatly puzzled by these and other circumstances. Certain scraps of conversation which I overheard between Madame and Blain, and between my employer and Hartmann, increased my suspicions, and especially so when I found Madame carrying on a series of secret experiments in her own rooms, often boiling certain decoctions over the tiny spirit-lamp used to heat her curling-irons. Several of the liquids thus manufactured she placed in the tiny phials of her medicine-chest. All this time, while passing everywhere as my mother, Lady Glaslyn, she was extremely kind to me, until I even began to believe that my suspicions were unfounded. Only now do I know how subtle was her cunning, how ingenious and how daring she was. One day, in April, I, however, had my suspicions still more deeply strengthened by a strange request she made to me, namely, that if at any time I should chance to witness any uncommon scene in her house, that I would breathe no word to a single soul. This struck me as peculiar, and I demanded the reason, whereupon she smiled, giving me bluntly to understand that my own safety lay alone in my secrecy, and pointing out that by obtaining quantities of goods and jewellery on credit, as I had done at her request from firms in Regent Street and Oxford Street, in the name of Lady Glaslyn, I had placed myself in grave peril of being arrested for fraud. I saw instantly that this woman who had posed as my friend had most cleverly spread about me a web from which there was now no possible escape. She evidently desired my assistance in whatever nefarious purpose she had in view."

"What a position!" I exclaimed. "Then the woman had compelled you to obtain the goods by fraud in order to secure a certain hold over you?"

"Of course," she answered in a low, firm tone. "But that's not half the craft and cunning she displayed, as you will perceive later. I know I have acted wrongly, and should have long ago placed my suspicions before the police, but I feared to do so, lest I should be arrested for the fraud. From day to day I lived on in anxiety and breathless wonder, Mrs Blain or Blain himself being constant visitors to The Hollies, while now and then Hartmann would come down from London, as if called in for consultation. At length, one day in early June, we returned to the house in Upper Phillimore Place, Madame announcing her intention to remain there a month. Our neighbours, the Coulter-Kerrs, were delighted at our return, for they seemed to know hardly a soul in London. After we had been there about a week Mrs Blain and Mary called one afternoon, and while I chatted to the latter in the dining-room, Mrs Blain talked privately with Madame in the room beyond. The door was closed, as usual, and they were conversing only in low whispers, when suddenly their voices became raised in heated discussion. A quarrel had arisen, for I heard Mrs Blain exclaim quite distinctly: 'I tell you I have never dreamed of any such thing; and I'll never be a party to it. Such a suggestion is horrifying!' Then Madame spoke some low words, to which her companion responded: 'I tell you I will not! From this moment I retire from it. Such a thing is infamous! I never thought that it was intended to act in such a manner.' To this Madame made some muttered observation regarding 'absurd scruples' and the impossibility of detection, whereupon Mrs Blain flounced forth from the room in a high state of indignation, saying, 'Mary, it's time we should go, dear, or we shan't be home for dinner.' Then she made a cold adieu to the woman who had been her most intimate friend, and with her daughter departed." Eva's breath came and went rapidly in the intensity of her emotions, her thin nostrils slightly dilated, and as she paused her lips were firmly pressed together.

"Next morning, at about eleven, almost before Madame was ready to receive, Blain himself called," she went on. "He was grey-faced and very grave, but after a rather long interview he left in high spirits, wishing me farewell quite gaily. On the following day the Coulter-Kerrs were in great distress about their servants, for both were dishonest, and upon Madame's declaration that she could immediately find others they had been discharged at a moment's notice. About five o'clock that afternoon both husband and wife, with whom I was on the most friendly terms, came in to chat with Madame about the servants, and after we had conversed some time tea was brought, of which we all partook. Then Madame invited them in for whist after dinner, as was our habit, for we were all inveterate players. About six o'clock, while I accompanied Mr Kerr next door in order to prepare their makeshift meal, Mrs Kerr — Madame always called her Anna — remained behind to make some arrangements for one of our servants to go in temporarily. Suddenly, about twenty minutes later, while I was in the kitchen washing some salad, I became conscious of a strange, sharp pain which struck me across the eyes, followed almost instantly by a kind of paralysis of the limbs and a feeling of giddiness. I ascended to the hall, calling loudly for help, and from the drawing-room heard Mr Kerr's voice, hoarse and strange-toned, in response. With difficulty I struggled up the second flight of stairs, but on entering the room where the tiny red light burned — some curious Indian superstition of Mrs Kerr's — I saw in the dusk that Kerr had fallen prone on the floor and was motionless as one dead. Then, helpless, I tottered across to a chair, and sinking into it all consciousness left me."

Both Boyd and myself stood breathless at these startling revelations.

"When I came to myself," she continued, "I was back in Madame's house next door. She had forced some liquid between my lips, and was injecting some other fluid into my arms with a hypodermic syringe. I was amazed, too, to notice that she had changed her dress, assumed a grey wig, and wore a cap with bright ribbons, in most marvellous imitation of an old lady. While I thus remained on the couch in the back sitting-room, dazed and only half conscious, there came a loud ring at the door and I overheard a police-officer making inquiries of 'Mrs Luff' regarding the people next door. Then I knew that Kerr's body had been discovered, and that Madame was personating the previous occupier of that house. I was not, however, aware at that time of how Hartmann had called upon Madame and had carried Mrs Kerr through a small breach made in the fencing of the garden at the rear into her own house, or that I had been brought back by the same way into ours. Madame, when all was clear, went that night down to The Hollies, leaving me alone with the servants, who, having apparently been sent out upon errands during the events described, knew nothing. I therefore kept my own counsel, and recollecting having overheard Blain, when taking leave of Madame on his last visit, refer to an appointment he had with Hartmann in St. James's Park, I resolved also to keep it. I did, but instead of meeting him," she said, addressing me, "I met you."

"I recollect the meeting well," I answered. "Continue."

"Well, I returned to The Hollies, but it was evident from Madame's manner that she was in deadly fear. I was not, of course, aware of what had actually occurred, although I entertained the horrible suspicion that both my friends had fallen victims. She took me partly into her confidence later that day, for the police, she said, would discover an 'awkward accident' next door, and that she must not be seen and recognised as Mrs Luff. She told me that, in order to avoid any unpleasant inquiries, Hartmann had entered the place before the police, and had carried away every scrap of anything that could lead to their identity, and as I knew from Mr Kerr's previous conversation that all his letters were addressed to Drummond's Bank, it seemed improbable that the bodies would be identified. 'It's a very serious matter for us,' Madame said to me earnestly. 'Therefore say nothing, either to Mrs Blain or Mary.' By that, and other subsequent circumstances, I knew that both were in ignorance. They had no hand whatever in the ghastly affair, for after the quarrel they never again met Madame.

"Weeks went by," she continued, after a pause. "I still remained on friendly terms with Mrs Blain and her daughter, knowing them to be innocent. Madame never went out, but once or twice Hartmann visited her. Whenever he did so, high words usually arose, regarding money, it seemed, and once Blain, who by his family was supposed to be still in Paris, came late at night, ill-dressed and dirty. It was then that I first learnt the motive for the ingenious conspiracy. Blain seemed in abject fear that the police had somehow established the identity of the dead man. If so, he said, all had been futile. Hartmann, it appeared, had a daughter whom I had never seen, and it was through her that the activity of the police had been ascertained." Then, turning her eyes again to me with an undisguised love-look, Eva exclaimed, "The tortures of conscience which I suffered through those summer days when you declared your love are known to God alone. My position was a terrible one, for I saw that by preserving this secret I had been an accessory to a most foul and cowardly crime, and I held back from your embrace, knowing that one day ere long I should be arrested and brought to punishment. I lived on, my heart gripped by that awful sin in which I had been unwittingly implicated. Then one day you called at The Hollies and I gave you some wine from a fresh bottle which I opened myself. It was wine which Madame had specially ordered from the stores on my account because the doctor had prescribed port for me. That wine was poisoned, and you narrowly escaped death. The fatal draught was intended for me! Hartmann and Madame Damant had, indeed, brought poisoning to a fine art."

"Was poison never in your possession?" inquired Boyd gravely.

"Yes," she responded without a second's hesitation. "After the affair at Phillimore Place I discovered Hartmann's address, and from a paper in Madame's jewel-cabinet I copied some strange name — Latin, I think — which I knew related to one of the secret poisons. Then, in order to satisfy myself as to Hartmann's position, I went to him to obtain some. My idea was that the information I could thus obtain would be of use if I were arrested. I found that under the name of Morris Lowry he had for years kept a herbalist's shop near the *Elephant and Castle*. Fortunately, by reason of my veil, he did not recognise me, and after some haggling gave me some greyish powder in a small wooden box securely sealed. I discovered afterwards that his daughter was in love with your friend Mr Cleugh, therefore it must have been through the latter that the old man became aware of the movements of the police."

"Yes," said Lily simply, "it was." The revelation held her dumbfounded.

"Then Hartmann and Lowry were actually one and the same?" I observed, bewildered.

"Certainly," Eva answered, all her soul in her eyes. "But there was yet a further curious incident. A few days after you had taken that fatal draught from my hand, Madame, in sudden anger, discharged all three servants. Then, when they had gone, she had a small square hole about six inches wide cut in the wall of one of the rooms — a bathroom adjoining my bedroom

— close down to the floor, and before it was fitted a sliding panel in the wainscoting. Afterwards she had a strong iron bar placed upon the door, and the whole re-painted and grained. Then, having furnished the place roughly as a living-room, there came secretly late one night the wretched poisoner Hartmann, *alias* Professor Douglas Dawson, flying from the police for some previous offence, as I afterwards discovered. Some German police-agents had got wind of his whereabouts. He entered that room, and when he was inside Madame fetched an apparatus I had never seen before, a kind of punch, and with it placed a leaden seal upon the door. Fresh servants were at once engaged, and these were told that inside that room was a quantity of antique furniture belonging to a friend who had gone abroad. Meanwhile Madame herself supplied the fugitive with food, cooked and uncooked, drink and books, and for a fortnight or so he lived there in secret. I held him in loathing and in hatred, yet I dared not utter a word or even flee from that house of terror, knowing well that in such case I, too, would quickly fall a victim to the machinations of what seemed a widespread conspiracy. I was in possession of their secret, and might turn informer. That was the reason those half-dozen bottles of port wine had been so generously given to me by my ingenious employer. I dared scarcely to eat or drink, and often slipped out secretly and bought cooked meat and bread to satisfy my hunger. One day, when Madame had ventured up to London, I chanced to enter the bedroom I had previously occupied. The panel was cautiously pushed back, and the man within asked for something to drink. I answered that I only had some port, all the rest being locked up. 'Then give me that,' he said. I hesitated, then in sudden desperation I went to the cupboard where the wine was and handed him an unopened bottle. He gave a grunt of satisfaction, and the panel closed. That wine, Frank," she added, a deathlike pallor on her cheeks, "was the same as that of which you partook. Madame had prepared it with her little syringe as she had done the Benedictine."

She paused, placing her hand upon her panting breast.

"When she returned," she continued at last, for the nervousness which had agitated her at first gave place to strength and confidence, "her first question was of Hartmann. I told her of his request, and how I had acceded to it, giving him a bottle of the wine she had so generously ordered for me. She grew livid in an instant, and stood speechless, glaring at me as though she would strike me dead. Then rushing up to the room she drew back the panel and called him by name. There was no response. In an instant she knew the truth. Without uttering a single word to me, but ordering the servants to close the house as we were going away for a week or two, she made instant preparations for departure, and after seeing everything securely bolted and barred, she left with a trunk on a cab for Fulwell Station, while I, with my small trunk, took refuge with my friends the Blains, with whom I have since remained."

"But the motive of that secret assassination at Phillimore Place?" I asked, astounded at her story.

"Only within the past few days have I discovered it," she answered. "The crime was planned with extraordinary care and forethought. If it were not for this confession which you have wrung from me, the police would never, I believe, have elucidated the mystery. The reason briefly was this. Coulter-Kerr was an Englishman living in Calcutta, who had been left a great indigo estate in the North-West by his uncle, and had returned to England with a view of selling it to a company. The estate, one of the finest in the whole of India, realised a very handsome income, but both he and his wife preferred life in England. Blain, being a speculator and promoter of companies, besides an importer of wines, having been introduced to him, conceived a plan of obtaining this magnificent estate, and with that object had approached Hartmann who in his turn had enlisted the services of Madame Damant, both of them being very desperate characters. Hartmann lived in London, and was supposed to be the most expert toxicologist in the whole world, while Madame was a woman whose previous adventures had earned for her great renown in certain shady circles on the Continent.

"Blain, it appeared, had already been out to India to visit the estate, and on his return had paid a couple of thousand pounds deposit, agreeing to purchase it privately of Kerr for two hundred thousand pounds — the valuation made upon it by a valuer whom he had taken up with him from Bombay — and then to turn it into a company. A date was arranged when the money should be paid over at the house in Phillimore Place in exchange for the deeds duly executed, Hartmann, in whose experiments Kerr was so interested, to be present to witness any document necessary. In accordance with Blain's request the deeds were therefore prepared beforehand and executed, and all the papers relating to the transaction placed in order in the large deed-box in which they had been brought from India. In accordance with the cunningly-devised plan, Blain called upon the Kerrs on the afternoon arranged — the afternoon of the day of the tragedy — and found Kerr ready with all the legal papers and receipts duly executed. Blain, however, was profuse in his apologies, stating that, owing to some slight difficulty with his bank, he was unable to draw that day, but would do so on the day following, and would return at the same hour. The Kerrs, on their part, expressed regret that they could not ask him to remain to dinner, but explained that they had no servants."

Again she paused. Her story held us all speechless.

"I have already explained how the Kerrs afterwards visited me and took tea, and the terrible tragedy which followed. Hartmann was, without doubt, concealed in that house at the time, watching for the unfortunate man's end, and without delay secured the deed-box and all the receipts and papers, carrying them next door, searching the body of the man, and placing certain things in his pockets, namely, the forged banknotes and the penny wrapped in paper, which would puzzle the police, while Blain had caused that same evening to be posted from the *Grand Hotel* in Paris, a letter to the man now dead, addressed to Drummond's Bank, expressing satisfaction at the termination of the negotiations, and acknowledging the safe receipt of the deeds and transfers from the messenger he had sent. This was, of course, to carry out the fiction that for several weeks he had been in Paris on business connected with the floating of the company, and to enable him to prove an *alibi* if ever required. Blain, when in India, took good care that it should be widely known that he intended to purchase the estates, so that his sudden possession would not be considered strange. There was a man, it afterwards transpired, who was actually staying at the *Grand* in Paris in the name of Blain, and he had posted the letter, while I further discovered that this ingenious swindler had actually borrowed the sum of two hundred thousand pounds for three days to pass through his bank, so that he might show that he had paid for the property."

"Then Blain is in actual possession of the deeds, which only require the stamp of the courts in India for the property to become his?" Boyd observed.

"Yes," responded my beloved. "But the fear that you have discovered the dead man's identity has hitherto prevented him taking possession or raising money on the deeds. He has placed them somewhere in safety, I suppose, and is now most likely out of the country."

"Absolutely astounding!" I gasped. Then, on reflection, I inquired the meaning of the cards which had so puzzled us.

"Horrible though it may seem," she said, "they were used to cast lots as to who should actually administer the poison, being shuffled and dealt face downwards. There were fifty, only two of which were marked. It was, I have learnt, the mode in which the Anarchists of Zurich cast lots, the person receiving the one with the line to commit the crime, while whoever received the circle became the accomplice and protector. With grim disregard for consequences these very cards were afterwards used by the assassins and their victims to decide upon partners for whist, sometimes being placed beneath the plates at dinner when, on entering the room, the guests were allowed to choose their places, afterwards turning up their cards. This gave rise sometimes to great amusement. What would the unfortunate pair have thought could they have known the truth? Alas! I did not know it until too late, or I would have given them warning, regardless of the consequences."

Boyd briefly explained how he had seen Blain throw something into the lake in St. James's Park, whereupon Eva suggested that the object he thus got rid of was no doubt one of the poisoned coins with which Hartmann had supplied him at his request.

I referred to the incident of the telephone, and Eva explained how she had since discovered that Blain had made an inquiry by telephone, in full belief that it was Hartmann who had responded. When next day he discovered his mistake he saw how narrowly he had escaped the police. Mary's letter to me had, no doubt, been a coincidence, but her subsequent visit was at her mother's instigation, it having been discovered that I was aware of the terrible tragedy.

"You received some type-written letters?" Boyd observed. "Who wrote them?"

"Blain," she replied, surprised that he should be aware of this. "He knew that I had discovered the secret, and wrote urging me to take the utmost precautions to preserve what he guardedly referred to as the Silence."

"But you say that Madame herself took tea with her victims?" I said. "She did not suffer."

"Certainly not," responded my beloved. "In her expert hand these poisons, discovered by Hartmann, may be fatal to one person and perfectly harmless to another. She no doubt drank some prophylactic first, which at once counteracted any ill effect of poison taken afterwards. Hartmann seems to have re-discovered the secrets dead with the Borgias, for Madame can, I believe, secrete a swift and deadly poison within almost anything."

"Where is she now?" asked Boyd quickly. "We must take immediate steps for her arrest, as well as Blain's."

"Madame has flown to the Continent, but where I have no idea," she replied. "To-night I intended to go to Paris and try to obtain a situation as governess, for I feared to remain longer in England, knowing of the body of Hartmann lying in that closed room at the Hollies."

"You must remain," Boyd said quietly. "Your evidence will be required."

"Ah, no! I cannot," she declared, bursting into a torrent of tears. "After this confession I —" and her voice was choked by sobs as she covered her haggard face with her hands.

"After this confession, darling," I said tenderly, "I love you none the less."

Then, clasping her swaying figure to me in wild ecstasy, I felt the swell of her bosom against my breast, and I covered her cold, tear-stained cheeks with passionate kisses, while she, for the first time, raised her sweet full lips to mine in a fervid, passionate caress, and murmured that she loved me.

Ah! what joy was mine at that moment. A new life had been renewed within me, for I knew that by the sacred bond of an undying affection she was bound to me for ever.

Chapter Twenty Five
Conclusion

Upon events which occurred immediately afterwards there is little need to dwell, save to declare that the hours that followed were the most joyous of all our lives; and further, that the post and the telegraph that night carried over the seas a demand to the police for the search and arrest of Madame Damant and the unscrupulous schemer Henry Blain.

A little more than a year has now gone by since that well-remembered day of confession, and Eva and I are happily united man and wife, while Lily Lowry no longer toils at her counter but is married to Dick, against whom Boyd's suspicions were, of course, entirely unfounded. By the death of a maiden aunt, who never gave me sixpence while alive, I have fortunately found myself possessed of sufficient to live independently in a house embowered in trees on the banks of the Exe, in Devon, while Dick, who is still "the *Comet* man," lives in a neat villa out at Beckenham. Eva and I are frequent guests there, and on such occasions the conversation often turns to those breathless summer days up the Thames and that extraordinary mystery so intricate and puzzling — a mystery which never, after all, appeared in the *Comet*.

Of Mrs Blain and Mary we hear but very little. They left Riverdene broken and crushed, poor things, and went to live in a small house at Bournemouth upon the wreck of the fugitive's fortune. No word has since been heard of him, but as the deed-box containing many of the papers was found by the police in a garret in the Rue du Maure in Paris, from which the occupier — an Englishman answering to Blain's description — had mysteriously disappeared, it is almost beyond doubt that he had committed suicide rather than starve. Hartmann's unclaimed scientific discovery is still the wonder of the Royal Institution, and Patterson is still stationed at Kensington. As for Madame Damant, she was three months ago arrested in Venice, where, in the course of a sensational trial, it was proved that she had most ingeniously poisoned a wealthy German contractor whom she had inveigled into marriage, and to-day she is serving a life-term of imprisonment. The Italian Government does not give up its subjects for offences committed abroad, or she would otherwise have been brought to London for trial, and the readers of newspapers would have been startled by the details of this, one of the most skilful and extraordinary plots of secret assassination ever devised by the devilish ingenuity of man or woman.

The End.